***Drunk on Peace and Quiet*, a first novel by West Virginian Becky Hatcher Crabtree, is filled with action, suspense, and wry, mountain humor.**

Penelope Ann Davis leaves Atlanta, without a word to anyone, to escape an abusive, older brother. She ends up in a small town in southern West Virginia where she changes her name and lives an ordinary life, until her brother turns up at church one Sunday and shows every intention of staying. There follows a series of troubling events: money missing from the church, for which Stella (née Penelope Ann) is blamed; Civil War artifacts missing from the home of a widow; the murder of Stella's best friend; soliciting money for a kidney transplant for a new member of the church, and finally Stella finding herself in danger when the older brother discovers her identity.

Everything resolves quickly at the end with a surprising twist.

—Jim McBrayer, Facilitator, Appalachian Writers Series, Historic Rugby, TN

Drunk on Peace and Quiet

Becky Hatcher Crabtree

Best wishes,
Becky Crabtree

ISBN Trade Cloth 978-1-888215-53-3

ISBN Trade Paper 978-1-888215-54-0

Library of Congress Control Number: 2015949685

Cover photograph: Steve Boothe
Chapter photographs: Becky Hatcher Crabtree
Illustration conversions: Jeffrey Duckworth, Duck of All Trades
Book design: Connie Taylor, Fathom Publishing Company

Fathom Publishing Company
PO Box 200448
Anchorage, AK 99520
www.beckycrabtree.com

dedicated to

the spirit

of strong women

everywhere

who hunger for

the giddy warmth

of stress-free lives:

to simply be

drunk on peace and quiet

Table of Contents

Preface (or Why I Wrote This)

My childhood lacked late night TV and today's magical electronic entertainment. Instead, "Tell me a story." was our constant bedtime plea. Most nights my mom or dad or a brother would oblige. Tarzan, Bomba the Jungle Boy, Hopalong Cassidy, Biblical stories, Epaminonimous, and many more tales satisfied me.

Now, I read to feed the life-long hunger of needing words and characters outside of reality. Sometimes my bedtime stories were obviously made up as the story-teller went along. Like them, this book of Stella and her life was also made up as I wrote, sometimes from bits of experiences, often from rumor, and every now and then the stuff of daydreams. What fun it has been to add a story back into the cycle of stories to be told!

Acknowledgements

At an interview years ago, I told the employer that I "was born to do this." Indeed, it seemed that everything I had ever done prepared me for running an alternative high school and I got the job. I believe every moment in our lives depends on the past, the contacts, education, choices, and experiences we have had. This story is no different. It wafted its way out of my imagination using the realistic structure of actual places.

In addition, there are many who figured specifically in the book's creation. Writing seminars at the John C. Campbell Folk School and at Historic Rugby, Tennessee, both led by the incredibly generous and talented author of Appalachian mysteries, Vicki Lane, boosted my confidence and skills.

For information on the law, Sandro Jankovic, Chuck Coburn, Debra Dalton, and the ladies in the Monroe County Sheriff's Office answered my questions. Steve Boothe supplied wonderful photos of Peters Mountain. Reverend Brent Brown supplied the organizational schema of the United Methodist Church and some wonderful tales from church life. The hard-working congregation of our home church models only good behavior, not the made-up deceptions and implied rottenness in this story.

Peterstown's current eighth graders, someday the James Monroe High School Class of 2020 (the number makes me laugh and hope their vision will be perfect) was full of ideas for page number placement and book size. Adam Durham and Sidney Cozort brought drama to the promotional video, your acting was appreciated.

Connie Taylor, Fathom Publishing Company, again, is full of the latest ideas in the book-publishing world and offers them ever so kindly. No one works harder in getting a book ready or in attending to detail. Artist Jeff Duckworth, Duck of all Trades, created the lovely images in the book.

More generally, friends from the North Slope of Alaska, both Inupiat and non-Native, have influenced my life and writing forever. Earl Finkler and Bob Thomas, radio personalities at KBRW helped get the word out about this book.

My dear friend, Thelma Bradley Booth, told stories about mountain living that made me laugh and cry. Elizabeth Robertson and Trish Beasley are consummate WV school professionals who have a contagious sense of humor. It pops up often both in reality and my writing.

Merri Jackson Hess' knowledge of Atlanta helped give Stella an authentic place to grow up. Merri's support of this book (and my sometimes crazy life) is treasured.

Roger, my hubby for forty years, put up with more than I care to list. The plot suggestions he made strengthened the story. I think he loves Stella a little bit, too!

Jay St. Vincent encouraged me to keep writing (more than once) and contributed her editing expertise. Without her, this book would not have been written.

Becky Crabtree Hatcher
August 2015

Major Donors

Chris H. Hatcher
Nancy & Terry Kornegay
Aimee Romeijn & Gary Boen

Donors

Katie Adkins
Anonymous Friend
Lindsay Anderson
The Beasley Family
Tim, Deanna, Dillon, & Dalton Bradley
Wanda Buchanan
Sharon Feinblatt Dall
Rafael Chodos
Wendy & Tim Crabtree
Alicia Coulter
Earl, Chris, & Avu Finkler
Steve & Vanni Culbertson
Hess Family Book Club
Merri Hess
Karel Hull
Dinah & Sandro Jankovic
Angela Ne'Shay Kelly
Debra Kirby
Lynn & Chip Lacey
Carol L. Makar
Nancy Nicolos
Connie McCoy
N. McKenzie
Oneda Pack
Julie Peck
Elizabeth Robertson
Kathy Robertson
Garry & June Tipsword
Jay St, Vincent
Carol Wentz
Larry & Karen Widener

Chapter 1
May: Simply Hoping for Rain

I don't know what everybody else was praying for in church that Sunday, but I was sending up thoughts for a good soaking rain. My peas, planted two weeks ago, needed a drink. On the bright side, though, our regular preacher was back in the pulpit. Last week, the lay speaker had kept us extra late with eternal praying. I call it eternal since it went on forever. He prayed that we didn't forget the potluck dinner following church, for the people who were out of work, the children without food, then he prayed for the victims of mudslides in India. I was pretty sure he was going to name every person who got muddy before the tired congregation echoed his ending with a weak amen. It wasn't just that the Baptists got a head start on us to the Sunday lunch buffet at Hometown Restaurant, that prayer threw a wet blanket on any zest for life that we still had at the end of the service.

Today, from my regular pew on the front left of the sanctuary, four rows back to be exact, I peeked during the prayer and saw Anna Bradford on the second row of the other side struggling to stand. She was pulling herself up before the silent prayer ended and the pianist hit the first chord for the opening hymn. It seemed like she was trying to be upright before anyone else noticed how hard it was for her. My arms ached to help her up, but I was seated too far away. She wouldn't sit with me either, because her place for years had been in the second pew on the right, with Charles, her husband, and their two daughters. Charles was dead and the girls were grown and gone and Anna sat alone.

Tradition can go to the devil, I thought, not for the first time; *next week, I'll leave my unofficial pew and go sit with her.*

Chapter 1

The congregation of my little country church was dear to me, their traditions had become my traditions, well, mostly, but Anna was dearer. Thirty-five years ago, I was a timid twenty-two-year-old girl, tending to an elderly lady on Peters Mountain and Anna had befriended me, explained the unwritten rules of West Virginia living and took my part when I stepped in it unknowingly. She prepped me with church practices, too. I knew our group of Methodists generally expected ritual and order, but I also knew that most of them enjoyed a rare break from the routine.

Today we were having that break in the action. The Voices of Glory Gospel Singers were performing instead of the usual Sunday message. Some worshippers allowed themselves a glow of optimism. The chance of getting to Hometown Restaurant before the Baptists let out church was better than usual. Often, there was not a hope in heaven of Pastor Beauregard Booth hushing before long past high noon. This knowledge had not come from Anna, but from years of my own hungry observation.

When it was time for the sermon, there was an edgy silence and then three sturdy men in tailored suits came up the center aisle singing into their microphones. They turned with a flourish at the front and continued to sing. Our congregation began to sway and sing along with the familiar hymn, "Will the Circle Be Unbroken?" as the music blasted clear and crisp from large speakers on either side of the altar. The men were dressed more stylishly than any of the men in the audience, even though the buttons of the suit jackets were pulling snugly on the buttonholes. They wore vests and ties and brightly colored button-up shirts. Their pants had crisp creases ending at the toes of shiny pointed leather shoes. Little pointed silk hankies in their suit coat jackets matched each shirt, blue and green and yellow. I straightened my faded dress and tried to tuck wisps of my ever-frizzy hair back in place to rival their neat appearances. Yes, they were slick as a magazine and smelled good, too; woodsy aftershave fumes wafted halfway down the aisle.

I joined in the clapping and singing, and watched the fleshy men. The music was grand, and I enjoyed it. As I watched, my eye caught on the lead singer, the one wearing the blue shirt and the oldest of the three. As he placed his microphone on a stand and gestured with his arms, I caught a good whiff of cologne and the memory of long ago burst into my thoughts.

Mom had let us sleep late by mistake, and we were hurrying to get ready for school. My brother was a high school senior, and I must've been a tenth grader. I had gotten to the bathroom first, and Timmy Lee was pounding on the bathroom door. He always wanted more time to primp in front of the medicine cabinet mirror and slap on cologne. I put the metal bathroom door hook into the eye on the door facing to lock it. I thought I was safe for another few minutes, but suddenly there was a crash. He broke through the board, ripping out the hook-and-eye fastener and shoved me into the shower. He knocked me back into the shower corner and I slid into the floor. I tried to use my arms to cover my head, but he still kicked me in the ribs and face until the black and white tiles were tinged with red.

I massaged my neck with one hand and escaped from the memory as the hymn ended and vigorous applause filled our little sanctuary. Just remembering Timmy Lee had made me sick at my stomach, but I relaxed some when I looked over to check on Anna and saw her delicate hands raised up chin-high, clapping gently. The men's voices were lovely, deep and pure and fit their choice of old-fashioned hymns. There was something about that lead singer, though. When his eyes lit up and darted around the sanctuary, my mind paused, memories of

my brother's eyes flashed before me again, and I was slammed back into the past.

He was a little boy, maybe six years old and had taken a tiny kitten from our mama barn cat before it was ready to leave its mother. The poor thing was sucking the air, trying to eat anything. Timmy Lee offered it the twisted corner of a dishrag wet with terrible tasting stuff: lemon juice and turpentine. His eyes gleamed with satisfaction at the kitty's sour expressions.

I gripped the back of the pew before me and shook my head to end that awful memory. The singers were introducing each other to the congregation and explaining their mission. "We aim to use the gift of music God gave us to renew and inspire devotion to God."

"Amen," the other men murmured.

The man in the green shirt added, "And we are doing it across the back roads of America."

The congregation responded with hearty amens.

They seemed like nice enough men, but their smiles and laughs were a little forced. Something about their pudgy bodies bothered me, especially the lead singer. He wore the bright blue shirt and a couple of fancy rings. One of them was a black onyx ring that cut into his pinky finger. I tried to have a better attitude and turned my eyes towards fragile little Anna. She was leaning forward and nodding her head. I relaxed again when I saw her joy.

The lead singer had taken over the microphone and was working himself up to sound like an old-timey preacher. He kept a pounding beat of his words with a breathy repetition of the last consonant of each line. "I accepted the Lord when I was just a boy, praise Jesus-suh. And I have been blessed richly an-duh one of my greatest blessings is my son, Adam, singing tenor right here for God and for you today-yuh. The Lord continues to work wonders in my life-fuh, to bless me with this mission to win souls for him-muh. I give thanks for that and for-ruh my won-derful family who makes my work-kuh possible. Hallelelujah!"

He wiped spit from both corners of his mouth with a starched handkerchief and pressed lips against the microphone again, "Do you like our singing?"

The congregation "amen-ed" and "yes, Lord-ed."

"We gonna sing some more for you in a minute-tuh, but we want to share with you that our ministry is an expensive one, and a difficult one, an-duh, we need ever one of you out there, to make sacrifices to help this ministry, an-duh, spread God's word-duh."

It was all so phony. I was fighting the urge to scream and swallow down the bile rising in my throat. These guys were crooks, but I composed myself somewhat as he went on and on. The offering was taken, and I had to reach across empty seats for the offering plate. My arm seemed detached from my body, but I nodded thank you to my neighbor and smiled not because I was glad to get the plate but because to cheer myself I imagined how good it would feel to go over the finances of the Voices of Glory with my accounting software and catch these fakes.

Boy, you better believe I put nothing in that offering. After I handed it off, I bowed my head and tried to look like I was praying but I was trying to get a grip on my unChristian-like thoughts.

Then, the preacher requested a hymn that was unfamiliar to the singing group but they agreed to give it a try. It was popular in our area, but the singers needed to see the music and the words so the ushers scurried around gathering up three hymnals. The organist played the song through once and then the singers held the songbooks up high to see the words. I watched the jeweled rings on the lead singer's fingers.

My heart stopped. I thought I was going to faint, so I closed my eyes, but when I opened them it was still there. Or, rather, it wasn't there. The right middle finger of the lead singer, pressed against the navy blue hymnal, was missing a nail, shortened by one joint. Timmy Lee's middle finger had been shortened at the same joint, the result of a shop class accident.

It ***is*** *him. The nightmare of my life, the reason I ran away from home on graduation night, the monster that is my brother stands before me in the front of my own church.*

Chapter 2
May: The Past is Present

Although my world had shifted, I was still sitting in my usual polished oak pew at the Lindside United Methodist Church rubbing my neck and surrounded by fifty other members of the congregation. The service was winding down and I tried to act normally, just wasn't sure I could pull it off. I could feel stray hairs unfolding on my neck, my neat white bun coming undone and it occurred to me that my life was unraveling in about the same way.

Timothy Lee looks like he's about ready for market, his ole jowl flesh jiggling below his face. Thought I'd never have to see those smirking eyes again. He's still lying and my friends're buying. Out of money, too, those ritzy car salesman suits are frayed around the edges. Adam has grown up a good-looking man. Can't even tell he had pig eyes and a big head when he was born .... Wonder where Adam's mom is ... not on the bus with these boys for sure. Wonder if she's even still alive; hard living and drugs plus living with Timmy Lee's a fast track to the graveyard for sure .... Does he have any clue who I am? Do I dare test him to find out? Oh, Lordy, why in the world did he have to show up here?

The Voices of Glory boomed out the Doxology. I lifted eyes to the altar and felt better. Then I looked at Timmy Lee.

Let's see if he knows me – I'm gonna look him right in the eyes while he sings the amen. Nope, no recognition. Can I stop hatin' him enough to fake my way through the rest of the service? I have survival skills; it's not like this is a new problem, flipping hatred to positive vibes. I've got years of practice.

I focus on what I want to try to simplify this crisis. *In an ideal world what would I want? Him and his ilk out of my life, my quiet life, my life that values doing the right thing, that leaves me drunk on excessive peace and quiet. I want to enjoy my home, the trust I have earned in this new life with my precious friend Anna, my animals, and Jonas, the love of my life.*

Ever since I had left Atlanta I had known that I would have to deal with Timmy Lee again someday, but I had not yet come up with a plan. I was afraid, and, as decades had come and gone, that fear had lessened until I had been able to put a big pile of boulders on a tiny pulsing fear and felt at peace with my life. Once, when I watched a TV show about repressed memories, it had flashed through my head that I was doing some heavy repressing myself. Now Timmy Lee's explosion back into my life at church, the place I felt most at peace, amounted to a personal assault. I just didn't know what to do next, but, without a doubt, it was time for some kind of action.

I looked him dead in the face again as he walked out the main aisle with Preacher Booth. He and Adam went to stand beside the preacher at the back of the church and glad-handed each of the churchgoers as they exited. No way I was touching that evil, even to shake hands. My stomach rolled. As I scurried towards the side door, Anna told me she was going to get a ride with Sally Spencer, hugged me tight, and joined the ladies leaving out the main aisle. *I'm outa here; maybe I can get out the door before someone invites me to Hometown Restaurant for Sunday dinner. I need air, deep breaths of clean air, and a shower. I have to go home and shore up my crumbling life.*

Chapter 2

A drizzly rain must've moved in minutes before I arrived home from church. I sure didn't notice then but here I was, drenched and dripping in the living room, a pathway of water behind me through the kitchen. Although my earlier desire for water for my garden had been met, it was no longer my priority. My mind was set on bigger problems. Life sure is funny and mine had been interrupted in an ugly dang way and at church of all places, at my own church. The worn leather recliner gave me the come hither and I snuggled into it to think. It helped to come home to peace and quiet after that horrendous church service.

I pressed my face into the chair and caught the scent of old leather. It smelled like my grandpa's wallet and brought me back to that tender faraway moment my grandpa dug into his front pocket for his wallet.

The last time I saw Grandpa was high school graduation night, June something, 1970. He found me lined up in the hallway and offered me a handful of thin twenty-dollar bills spread out like a poker hand. Kids made fun of him because he carried his money in his front pocket unlike other men around town. His hip pocket had been picked when he was a honeymooner at the World's Fair in St. Louis and he'd had to work to buy a train ticket for Grandma and him to get home. He never carried money in his hip pocket again. His kind eyes were sad as he pushed the money towards me without a word. I wondered if he had noticed that my bruised face was plastered with Mom's makeup so I could get through the graduation ceremony. Right or wrong, I had grabbed the money and used it to get as far away as I could as fast as I could. Getting that diploma and getting outa town were all I could think about. Didn't go back when he died. Or when Grandma passed. Didn't want to chance any upsets. I figure they understood.

As I nestled deeper into the soft leather, I relived the details of my Class of '70 graduation night, thirty-seven years ago.

I had taken my green marbled Samsonite train case to the school in one hand and my white dress on a clothes hanger in the other. I told Mom that I needed something to carry hairspray and makeup but truth be told, I had stuffed everything I could in it: shirts and underwear and two pair of slacks, the $300 I had managed to save, and pictures of my dad. Even as I shut the lid and hooked the brass clasps, I started feeling freer.

There wasn't any point in making an appearance at the reception after the graduation; I knew Mom wouldn't be there, so I went back to the home economics room to change. While a few other girls were whooping it up and running around in their petticoats hugging each other, I wiggled into my black jeans, a sweatshirt and jeans jacket, pulled on bobby socks and tennis shoes, grabbed my Samsonite and silently slipped out the back door of the school. It didn't seem far to walk to the Greyhound bus station, but I had studied the city map and knew it was over a mile.

The bus left at ten o'clock that night with me on it, enjoying the sights and smells. To this day, when I smell a combination of diesel fumes and stale cigarette smoke I just breathe it in and remember that northbound bus. It smells like freedom.

After a few hours riding, I willed myself to go to sleep but new people and cool air poured in at every small town bus station and my eyes popped wide open at every stop, just watching. By the middle of the night, I had to go to the bathroom so I got off at Charlotte for a while, then got on the next bus heading away from Georgia. It stopped at a tiny station in Wytheville, Virginia. As I climbed back on yet another bus, the excitement was fading. I resolved to get off as soon as it was daylight, but the mountain roads really did a number on my stomach and by the time we pulled into Bluefield West Virginia, I was sick as a dog. I stumbled into the bathroom there, carried the train case into the stall and retched into the toilet.

I cleaned up and headed outside. It was still night, but the sun was just starting to peek out from behind the mountain and I needed to walk, so I headed uphill. I topped the hill and saw the downtown area before me. There was hardly any traffic but every car spooked me so I took a right off the main street. There was an alley with neon lights blinking in the dawn and, on the corner, the Bluefield Recreation Center still going strong, juke box music and the sound of billiard balls breaking – a buxom redheaded woman in a form fitting dress was standing in the door laughing and smoking a thin cigarette. She watched me, our eyes met and she raised her eyebrows and chin up at me as if in recognition. We both turned at a crash of breaking glass to see a man flying through a window across the alley from Vito's Bar onto the sidewalk in front of Aldo's Cafe. I scurried on, turned the corner and found a steep set of stone stairs, ducked into them, climbed up to the first landing and lay down under a tree.

I woke up cold and wet in the fog of morning to the screeching of trains in the train yard below. I found myself on a tier of a hillside lawn, shadowed by a huge white house. A sign in the yard dangled from a post "ROOMS FOR RENT." I trudged up the rest of the steps and tapped at the door. I tapped again and the inside wooden door squeaked open and the kindly face of Blanche Boswell appeared. She was breathing hard. "Can I hep you child?" Blanche held the storm door open wide enough to look me up and down.

"The sign says you got rooms to rent?" My voice sounded older than I felt. Fear hit me about then with the immediate worry was that I was going to get caught and sent home. I thought about running until she put a trembly hand on my shoulder.

"Don't fret. I got something. Mostly, I rent to N&W men. They sleep between runs on the train and share a kitchen and a bathroom." Her eyes swept me again.

"I got one room ain't spoken for. Reckon you can be quiet?" I nodded, was too weary for words. "C'mon then." She led me up the curving stairs slowly, leaning her massive body up with one foot and a cane and following with the other foot on each of the stair steps, then shuffled down a long hall to the back of the house. She stopped at a tiny room just beside the bathroom and pushed open the door. "$7.00 a night or $40 a week."

I didn't move. She added, "That includes breakfast and supper every day." I fumbled in my train case for two of Grandpa's twenties and reached them to her without a word. They disappeared into the folds of her apron. She took a few steps, then turned and called out over her shoulder, "We eat downstairs at 6 and 6." I heard the stairs creaking under her while I surveyed my new home: water stains on the ceiling, strips of wallpaper torn loose that had been painted over in an unsuccessful attempt to stick them back, an iron bed with a chenille bedspread and a beat up dresser, and a cracked, yellowed shade on a broken window. I closed the door and slid the big deadbolt into place. I raised the bedspread with one hand, crawled under it, curled on my side around my overnight case, and slept through that day and night in the sweetest, safest haven I had known since Daddy had died.

To this day I remember the peace I felt in that bleak little room, but now, I sat shivering and fearful, my wet clothes sticking to me. Either there were ghostly pockets of cold air moving into my living room or I was starting to chill.

The whine and scratch at the door was definitely of this world. I broke the silence chuckling at my own foolishness and peeked out the window to check. There was Sugar, my sweet red dog, under the overhang at the door, shaking wet fur. "Okay, okay, I'm coming." And I went to welcome Miss Sugar and get on with life, starting with a dry shirt.

I had options. It calmed me to realize that I had some control over my life and that action was usually more satisfying than inaction. What could I do? I couldn't confront Timmy Lee, wasn't ready for that yet. It had been decades since I had seen him in person but my hatred, so long quiet, burned with a white-hot flame.

What was he after? Money, always money, but there was no big money in Lindside, no wealth outside of land and livestock. And I would know because I kept the books for nearly a dozen clients. Monroe County farmers famously carried a roll of big bills in their overalls pocket for cash deals on hay, equipment, or animals but they were also notoriously frugal. The thriftiness of their Scottish heritage was evidenced in the income and expenses ledgers that I kept. I looked out the sliding doors through the trails of rain and gathered my scattered thoughts. The mountain view before me was worth a million dollars, but views were plentiful and free for the taking.

Timmy Lee wouldn't want anything beautiful or pure, he'd want to bully and cheat just to get his way. During my years of torment at his hand, he didn't want to take my possessions as much as he wanted to be *able* to take them, to have power over me. My stomach joined my churning mind and I sank back in the leather chair.

Seeing Timmy Lee at church had triggered the fear and disgust that I thought was tempered by over thirty years of absence. My heart had not grown fonder. The Christian expectation was to forgive him. That was another little difference I had with the doctrines of Christianity, as I was not inclined in that direction in this particular situation. It had been an unspoken prayer request of mine for years, to find the strength to forgive Timmy Lee. Didn't feel right to forgive and forget.

It felt better to get away and stay away. My life was testimony to my belief.

At one time I had believed that if I relived the cruelty enough, my mind would tire of it and I could let it go, become numb to the pain. That didn't work out but I rewound my mind one more time, settled back in the recliner, and played back a mental episode of my own personal "Days of Our Life."

The freshman lockers at Briercliff High were in a dead-end wing distant from the front office, beyond the art classrooms and the band practice room. Like the rest of the 14 year olds in my class, I didn't go there except to my locker. Timmy Lee arrived after school one day as I was exchanging books I didn't need for homework for those I did. He leaned against the locker nearest mine. "I need five bucks." At 75 cents an hour babysitting, I wasn't exactly rolling in money.

"So, get a job."

"I'm playing football, we practice every evening, no time for a job."

I snorted. "So that's your latest excuse?" I slammed the locker door and spun around to face Timmy but he pushed me so hard against the lockers that my shoulders made the same banging sound as the slamming door. I was as surprised by the motion as I was by his expression. He'd bugged me my entire life, but I had had my dad's protection until his death and then another year or two while Timmy Lee conquered Mom. In my junior high years, I had been in a different school and able to avoid him or smooth his tantrums away with compromises.

This time his jaw was set and his eyes were narrowed, a smirk plastered on his red face. Timmy Lee enjoyed his anger. He held me against the locker, rubbed his thumb back and forth over the other fingertips on that hand, especially the shortened finger, then made a circle with thumb and forefinger before pinching my neck hard in five places, one for each dollar, he said. That rubbing and AOK circle became his trademark move every time before he hurt me. By then I had quit screaming and wriggling. No one heard and I couldn't get free. He walked two fingers from my neck to my breast, twisted my nipple and laughed while I screamed and fought. Then he shoved me again and left.

Three days later the black bruises were starting to turn yellow and I was getting a lot of unwanted attention from football players. I had a good idea what they had been told based on the catcalls and mumbled comments as I passed them in the hall. Was it worth five dollars?

If I had known the future I might have paid up and avoided all the torment to come, but I just couldn't hand over my hard earned money then. I would regret it later, when my reputation was shattered, when the bruises were constant, when he held me down and invaded other parts of my body, then helped pin me while his friends forced themselves on me. Eventually I gave him money when he asked trying to avoid the abuse, but my pain seemed to have grown on him like an addiction.

#

Sugar broke up my painful reverie with her welcoming dance on this side of the door and I knew that Jonas had arrived. We met him at the door and he bent to rub Sugar's neck before he hugged me and grinned his lop-sided grin.

"Figured something was wrong since you didn't go to Hometown after church, thought I'd stop by and see." Then, he looked in my eyes and his face grew serious. His salt-and-pepper eyebrows raised and he extended both hand, big palms up, his whole body a question mark. I collapsed into a chair and scooted up to the kitchen table. I looked away. This gentle man deserved a woman with less baggage, but finally, I wanted him to know my long-ago history. After over thirty years of silence, I was scared enough to tell.

My voice rang strong even as I wrung my hands under the table. "Pull up a chair, honey. It's time I bent your ear."

And for the first time, I told my love about my brother, growing stronger with every word, opening my heart to expose secrets that I never thought I could share.

Chapter 3
May: Jonas and The Talk

If kitchen tables could talk, my scarred round oak table would have had plenty to say after that Sunday afternoon soul cleansing talk with Jonas. I've heard that materials in a house, like wood and stone, sometimes absorb the energy of the events that happen there and can be felt years afterwards. Sometimes, as I lie in bed waiting for sleep, I try to sense the energy of the woodwork in my old farmhouse and it always feels good, like only happy times and peacefulness ever happened here.

During the talk, I kept wondering if this table was going to absorb the energy Jonas was radiating. While I talked, his hands were either clenched fists, pushing on the table edge like he wanted to get up or open with his broad fingertips drumming, one after another. When I'd take a break and laugh or wipe my eyes he would hold my hands across the table.

I had started all the way back at my childhood on the dairy farm in Atlanta. I relived my dad's accidental death and my mom's craziness. I told things I hadn't thought about for years, but they just poured out. I shared the torture masterminded by Timmy Lee – although I had promised myself I would never tell a living soul how he made me feel. My hatred and my shame for hating him surfaced. I told Jonas the details of my miserable high school years and that my one life goal was to get away from Timmy Lee. Now, he was right here in Lindside and I was unnerved. I told Jonas about the bloody bruises that became so painful and so hard to hide that I chose to quit fighting and instead submitted to him and to his friends. I choked when I told about the trips over and over to the DeKalb County Health Center for pregnancy tests, but I told it, every unbearable detail. I went on for the better part of three hours. Finally, I was done, all talked out. As the words left my mouth, lead weight left my body. Chains that had bound me rattled as they fell all around. I was unimaginably exposed. Every sight and smell and sound and touch was magnified. The air moving from the door made the hairs on my arm ripple. The bird chirps from the trees were firecracker-like and the running refrigerator roared.

Jonas stood. He turned his back to me at the sink, looking out the window, the glow of sunset outlining his big body. I was exhausted and knew the next few seconds would show if I had done the right thing by trusting him. Unable to bear the thought that I might have just crossed a bridge that was burning, I sat and waited.

He heaved a sigh that caught in his throat and wiped his face with his sleeve before he turned around.

"Do you want me to hurt the sumbitch?" He was as tense as a cat stalking a bird, ready to strike and, clearly, he wanted me to say yes.

I wanted to urge him on, but I picked at the rough edge of a fingernail I had been biting, "I guess we wait and see what he does." My throat was dry.

"I'm staying over tonight." The usual question wasn't in his tone and the screen door slammed behind him. I watched as Sugar bounded after him.

Three decades of intimacy with Jonas prepared me for his departure. He had to be outside when he was deep in his thoughts, a carryover from a childhood home crowded with extended family and a subsistence lifestyle outdoors in the arctic. Jonas was an Inupiat, Northern Eskimo, who had followed his girlfriend from Prudhoe Bay to the Louisiana oil fields. He had believed her story about being pregnant and married her on his twentieth birthday. When she ran off, he had partnered up with an oilfield coworker, mechanic Ben McDaniel. They worked here and there for a few years and when Ben came home to care for his mother he found work for both of them in the mountains of West Virginia. Both men worked at the area's main employer, the Celanese plant, and both had reached the age of serious thinking about retirement.

Ben had come back initially to make arrangements for his ailing mother. I had come into their lives when I agreed to move in with the elderly Mrs. McDaniel and care for her the last years of her life. Ben had found me through my landlady at the boarding house in Bluefield, dear Mrs. Boswell. She knew someone who knew Rachel McDaniel's need for a live-in caretaker, knew that the McDaniel's were good people and I would be safe. Mrs. Boswell hated for me to leave her, but she figured this was a good move for me. She talked to me and wrote Rachel who sent Ben to pick me up and drive me 50 miles to Lindside in his old pickup. I was too scared to say a word, but he joked and talked to me all the way. The agreement was that at her death I would have the house and twenty acres for payment. She lived three more years, and I cared for her the way I would've taken care of my own mother if I'd had a chance. Ben settled in a newer house down the road and stayed and Jonas bought a little house around the mountain, but it was a few more years before Jonas and I met.

Ahhh, Jonas. I stood at the kitchen window and watched him stomp through the yard, his shaggy dark hair bouncing in layers with his steps, a little grey was showing at the at the temples, but other than that it was as black and shiny as it had been when we met. My heart soared with emotions: trust, gratitude, and boundless love for that man. It didn't seem so long ago that he had entered my life but it had been nearly thirty-five years. Where had the time gone? Sugar frolicked at his heels and I remembered another dog that had greeted him back in 1975 when a big yellow lab named Buddy was my faithful canine companion.

#

I'd been standing at the same kitchen window back then, washing dishes, when Buddy started woofing. A diesel engine rumble had brought Buddy out from under the deck, fur along his spine standing up. He began barking like he'd cornered a bear. I peeked out the screen door wiping the dishwater suds off my hands.

"Ma'am? Ma'am? Could I speak to you a minute?" a husky voice came from a half open driver's side window.

I ventured out onto the deck. "You **are** speaking to me. State your business."

"*Aazai*, call off your dog, ma'am, so I can get out. Please."

I sighed and slapped my thigh a few times. Buddy ran to me – that dog loved attention and he waggled all over for a little pat on the head. He seemed to have forgotten the intruder for the moment, but I grabbed his harness just in case.

"Thankee, ma'am. Name's Jonas. Ben McDaniel sent me." The driver stepped out onto the running board and eyed the big yellow mostly Lab rubbing against my leg. I looked up when the driver spoke and my gaze kept rising past his broad shoulders, beyond his trimmed dark beard to his sparkling black eyes. He towered over his truck roof by two feet.

I thought, *Lord have mercy, that one is all man.* There were little needle pricks in my hands like when I almost have a wreck or when my feet go to sleep, then start waking up. *Lord, what is the matter with me. I better keep Buddy close, one swat from the snow shovel might not take that hunk of man down. All man, shoot, Buddy had treed him in his truck.* I tried to hide my giggles by patting Buddy some more ...

I straightened my face. "If Ben McDaniel sent you, you're welcome, come on in. Go on Buddy, leave him alone."

I had seen Jonas around and knew he was friends with Ben, but that was the first time I ever talked to him. We visited in the kitchen for an hour before he got down to business, which was that Mr. McDaniel had sent him to see if there were any repairs needed in the old house. He also wanted to ask my permission to hunt on the place. I thought of so many repairs that I had to grab an old envelope to write a list. Teehee. Permission to hunt? He could hunt anytime day or night. And that's how that got started.

#

But in spite of my best efforts, it was two years before Jonas saw the inside of my bedroom. A bat had squeezed through a crack in the chimney into my room and I had thrown a towel over it and beat the little mound with a bath brush until I was pretty sure it was dead. I called Jonas and told him I needed help to get rid of the bat. That was the first and only lie I had ever told him. Truth be told, I was not in need of his help to toss the poor dead creature in the sinkhole. I had shot and killed a rabid skunk and a dozen groundhogs who had had the audacity to feast in my garden; I probably could have managed a bat. Anyway, he drove up the mountain in record time and followed me upstairs where the corpse lay. After the interment, I asked him to check where it got in and he nailed up molding and caulked and generally bat-proofed my room. That must've been precision work because it took three evenings. Lovely summer evenings with firm young bodies tangled in soft scented sheets. Whew, Lordy, I better quit thinking about that.

Later he explained that he had been slow moving because as far as he knew, he was still married to Lena. He hadn't seen or heard of her for five years at that point and we had just slid into loving each other in spite of the legal ramifications.

#

I inhaled and breathed out a long shuddering sigh as I returned to the present. Twilight had deepened, and I needed to turn on the kitchen light. Jonas's footsteps were soft on the deck and I stiffened, prepared for any reaction. The screen door squealed and warm air entered with him. His mood had lightened, it usually did when he tramped around for a while and he reached his arms to me. My body melted against him. His beard carried air that had been touched by wildflowers and new cut hay, but I wouldn't embarrass him by telling him how sweet the outdoors made him smell. He held me and whispered into my neck, "We'll get through it, whatever comes." Silly me, all I could do was blink back happy tears and nod. And we went upstairs for the night.

Chapter 4
June: Cemetery Security

Jonas was long gone for the seven-to-three shift when the phone rang the next morning. I debated if I needed to know who was calling but by the fifth ring I quit watching the dust motes drifting in the rays of sunshine shooting through the sheer curtains and let curiosity win out. I rolled over in the bed to check out the caller ID. It was Tisha, the clerk from Lindside Elementary School and after Anna Bradford, my dearest friend. Stretching my lanky body to get a kink out of my back, I pressed the green button. "Hello?"

Without missing a beat, Tisha started in," Somebody stole Mommy's flowers up at the Bradley Cemetery last night. I swear to my time, these fools would steal the pennies off a dead man's eyes. Joey just put a wreath of pretty spring flowers on there for Mother's Day and both vases were full of the nicest big plastic tulips."

I scooted up into a sitting position against the headboard. "You have got to be kidding me! Did they bother any other graves?" This happened at least once every summer and the low down thieves took the flowers to the flea market over at Pence Springs and sold them on Sunday mornings. The dirty dogs take the artificial flowers out of the arrangements and sell them by the bunch. One family even bought their own grandpa's flowers back before they realized it.

"Yes, ma'am, they cleaned off the whole center section, even stole the fresh casket flowers from the McDonald baby that was buried last week. Scum, that's what they are." Tisha was beyond flustered. "We've got to do something! The law knows but they can't do anything. We need us some evidence."

Chapter 4

I was mad, too, but in view of all my other problems, I thought for a minute before jumping in. "Is it time to go mark them?"

"What are you talking about? With paintballs the way you did that stray cow?" She was talking about the neighbor's rogue cow that jumped the fence whenever it stormed and tore up jack then jumped the fence back in. We couldn't tell which cow it was because all five hundred of the neighbor's Herefords had white faces and reddish brown bodies. I shot the rogue cow right in the middle of her white forehead with a neon green paintball. That had made her stand out.

"I don't think this is a paintball situation." I flexed my ankles under the sheets. "I think this is a twenty-two situation and I just happen to have one. Will you go with me?

Tisha was quiet for a moment. "I promised Joey that I wouldn't do anything that might get me sent to jail. Will you do all the illegal stuff if I cook?"

I shook my head, Even though Tisha was a hard-working clerk and community activist as well as the mother of three boys, she thought a lot about food. Maybe it was because those boys ate so much.

"Coconut macaroons, please, about three dozen. "I sighed. I was going to get fat on vigilante missions with Tisha. "How about 10:30 on Saturday night? Come up the house and we'll walk through the woods over to the cemetery with my rifle. Whoever's doing this will probably come back for the northern section – lots of flowers on that side, too. There's a storage building up there with a knothole facing north. I know that because one time when I was helping Jonas trim the graveyard when he mowed on weekends up there, the riding lawnmower he was driving threw a rock that whizzed by me so hard that it hit the wall and knocked a knot out of an old board. Sounded like a gunshot, like to scared me to death. I know exactly where that hole is. I know where they hide the key to the padlock, too. We'll wait in there with the gun in hand and if the no accounts come back, we'll aim to nick 'em, just mark 'em, so we can see who it is. And we'll eat your coconut macaroons while we wait."

"Sounds good. I guess it's the only way." Tisha sounded a little spooked, but she was ready to expose this creep and I was happy to help. I pulled open the drawer of my nightstand and admired the latest addition to my arsenal, pink and pretty there beside the Band-Aids and moisturizer. The .22 rifle and .410 shotgun had been around for years, but I had purchased the Pink Lady .38 revolver only last fall. Jonas called the rifle "Miss *Nakuruq*," the shotgun "Mr. *Nipituruq*" and the revolver my "*Utukkuu Avilaitqan*." I figured out that the revolver is my "little friend" but he just laughs and laughs when I ask him what the Inupiat words mean for the other two. It must be a pretty good joke because he still gets tickled about it. Must mean something like "Good shot" because I am. I used to worry when my dog barked at night and I was alone. Having a gun within hand's reach and knowing I could mostly hit what I aimed for sure helps me sleep better.

With the happy thought that I was going to be able to do something about somebody else's problem instead of stewing about my own, I threw my feet over the side of the bed and immediately wished I'd taken a Motrin the night before. I loosened up my stiffened joints shuffling down the hall to the bathroom. Time to take on the world, my man and my guns all beside me.

I kept real busy all week, didn't sit down except to eat. Mowed the grass, cleaned every weed from the garden, mucked out the goat barn and the chicken coop, did all the washing, stacked a truckload of wood that had been in a pile since wintertime, made a refrigerator full of desserts, anything and everything I could find to do. Missed church on Wednesday night and Jonas raised an eyebrow but he didn't say a word. I told him I needed to be home at dusk to thin out the groundhogs that were looking at my sugar peas, but I was really practicing, reminding my eye and trigger finger how to shoot true.

Jonas is a religious man, but he doesn't ever go to church with me. He says that God is easier for him to find outside. I know he goes to certain places on the mountain and he is renewed. Maybe I will need to start going with him since the invasion of my house of worship by Timmy Lee. On the other hand, maybe I can stay in church and get some divine help in working through my hatred. I guess we all have to find our peace wherever we can.

I picked cherries and made preserves on Saturday. Couldn't keep my mind on the recipe and it didn't thicken the way it should of so I guess I had ten pints of cherry syrup instead of jam, but that would still be good poured over pound cake. I wiped up the stickiness and washed the bowls and pans and tried to get in the right mood to go shoot a thief. I didn't mean shoot to hurt, but just to mark him so we would know who he was. *Wonder if we know him? Wonder if he will even come back after his big haul last weekend? Wonder if three dozen macaroons will be enough to keep us from being bored during our wait?*

Jonas's schedule had been changed to third shift for the next two weeks beginning that night. He called before he left for the Celanese plant to tell me good night. I had to change arms with the phone to pull on a black turtleneck and baseball cap as we chatted. The ninja look was what I was going for. Probably wouldn't make any difference sitting in a storage shed for hours, but it helped my confidence to be at one with the darkness.

I waited at the screen door and noticed the waxing crescent moon. The stars were out and there was enough light to make out shapes and large objects. When headlights flashed across the yard, I figured it was Tisha, but felt better when I could make out her face in the semi-darkness. "You ready, old woman?" she greeted me.

I grinned at her sass. "Born ready." We high-fived. "I'm the sheriff tonight and you are the deputy." She agreed to our crazy way of deciding who took charge of our events. I felt like taking over, tense and anxious and needing action. Also, shooting was probably included on the list her hubby Joey thought were ways to go to jail. Tisha was wearing purple, the local high school colors, which I thought was a mistake in case we had to make a run for it, but then again, everybody in Monroe County had purple hoodies so it wouldn't pinpoint our identities much. She was carrying the macaroons in a crinkly zip-lock gallon bag, but I made her put them in my only double-sized tall Cool Whip container so we could be quieter when we reached for them.

I left the living room light on and the TV playing just like it would be if I were home, grabbed Miss *Nakurruq,* and left a very disappointed Sugar inside. When I peeked through the window from outside I could see that she had hunkered down in her regular spot by the recliner and was watching TV without me.

Tisha opened the squeaky pasture gate and we set out on the mile and a half hike to the cemetery, following a cattle trail through the fields and woods. Both of us carried little mag-lights, and we had to use them every now and then to keep from stumbling. We could see the dark strip of road below us in the moonlight but there were no cars coming or going. Dew had fallen and the grass was wet but the packed dirt path felt firm and smooth underfoot. The mountain moonlight was full of the music of insects and night birds and some bawling mama cows in the distance, and we didn't speak for twenty minutes. Somewhere during those first few minutes I realized that we were overdressed for the warm night. I was sweating buckets.

Tisha's voice broke the silence. "Oh, man!" she whispered and jumped on one foot. I turned with my light and got only fragments of the action.

"What in this world?" I whispered back, but then the smell reached me and I knew.

"I stepped in a fresh cow pile and slid and nearly fell." The pitch of her voice was unnaturally high and I just couldn't keep from giggling. I was nervous anyway and Tisha was the biggest clean freak in the county. She wiped her foot over and over in the wet grass mumbling about never coming clean and bleach and all manner of words for filth.

We arrived at the graveyard about 11:15 and hurried up the hill through the graves. My fingers felt over the doorframe for the key and there it was. We spent a scary ten minutes figuring out how to unlock the rusty padlock on the chained front door of the shed, go inside and make it look locked from the outside. That problem plus the presence of dozens

of graves made me a bit shaky. Turns out there is a window on the back side of the storage building so Tisha went inside through the door and opened the window while I put the chain back and locked the lock. I didn't remember that window at all; I guess it was so dirty that it just looked like the wall. Then I was able to put a cinder block under the window, climb up on it and get a knee on the windowsill. Tisha helped me in. More like she cushioned my fall as I tumbled inside. We laughed and knocked off the dirt and dried grass we had stuck all over us.

Tisha found the knothole knee high and as big around as a fist. I stuck the barrel of Miss *Nakurruq* out it. We rattled around a bit and got comfortable on the floor among the tractor, mowers, weed-eaters rakes, scythes, and shovels. And we waited, getting used to the smells of gasoline and oil and cut grass. We were perky for the first ten minutes, alert for every sound on the gravel road, every dog barking down the mountain. Then, we started eating macaroons. Wonderful sweet, sticky, macaroons. Besides being a clean freak, Tisha was a really good cook.

We emptied that Cool Whip bowl before midnight. Tisha summed up both our conditions giggling, "I am as full as a tick." Every few minutes, we had to take a break to stretch our legs and brush the grit off the seat of our pants. Then Tisha had to go to the bathroom and suddenly we realized that we couldn't get out the window because it was too high. We were locked in the storage shed at midnight in a graveyard with no easy way out. This knowledge was met with hysteria. We laughed until Tisha begged me to stop because she was about to wet her pants.

"Stella, I am not kidding. I gotta go." Tisha danced from one foot to the other.

"Okay, okay, let's think about this, you need something to stand on to get out the window, let's look around in here." Armed with mag-lights, we searched the crowded shed, the flower thief forgotten for the moment. The tractor seat would be a perfect height for reaching the window but it needed to be moved up about a foot. We pushed and pulled and could not move that old Ford 8N an inch. As I was resting against the tractor fender, sweat trickling down the small of my back, Tisha squealed, "Look, the keys are in it!! " She turned the key to the on position. Nothing happened.

As we listened for the tractor to start, the sound of crunching gravel reached us. I squeezed my full belly by the tractor tires over to the knothole and ever so quietly picked up the gun and peeked out. There was a light colored pickup truck sitting in the moonlight and someone was getting out. I could see an outline against the truck and the driver took a big cardboard box from the truck bed. The dash lights were glowing enough to see that he was alone, but no headlights or parking lights were on. I could hear his radio playing, gospel music, of all things. I decided to wait until he actually took flowers before I winged him. I followed his movements with my eyes and my rifle until I saw him tossing wreaths and baskets of flowers into the box, styrofoam screaming against the cardboard. The sound caused my jaw to clench.

That was somebody's dead loved one he was robbing. Hard earned money was used to buy those plastic flowers to show love and respect for those who once walked on this earth. My heart was throbbing in my trigger finger. My knees ached. The gasoline fumes were making me woozy and the spot on my cheek where the gun touched it was either cold or burning; I couldn't tell. He was about seventy-five feet from me and I knew if I didn't fire soon I wasn't going to. I guess I was conflicted.

I stroked the trigger so very gently with my fingertip. I lined him up, aimed for his calf, counted to three and fired. He hollered and swore a blue streak hopping around grabbing his leg, then he pitched forward and rolled around on the wet grass a while. He kept looking at me and up higher at the roof of the shed like there was a sniper up there, but it was too dark for him to see my gun barrel and I was quite proud at how quiet Tisha and I were able to be.

I kinda felt like I should call 911 and get him some help, but it wasn't a smart time for me to be helpful. After a while he rolled over and crawled to his truck, glancing my way as he covered his head with his bent arm. I watched him pull himself up and get in the driver's side and slam the door. I intended to watch until the taillights disappeared around the bend in the road, but at that point my world exploded.

The tractor rumbled to life with a rusty muffler magnifying the sound tenfold in the night. It crashed through the shed wall. Boards ripped and wooden shrapnel flew. The tractor lurched through the chaos and lumbered on a few yards with Tisha screaming all the way. It hit Mr. William's big tombstone and tipped over. Gravels flew fast and furious as the pickup truck spun out all the way to the pavement and burned rubber when the injured driver changed gears. I guess I was in shock, what with the shooting and then the crash and sounds of splintering wood and the old tractor's engine sputtering to life and then dying again, I found myself on the floor, both arms protecting my head. I just lay there a few seconds before digging in my pocket for my mag-light and scanning what was left of the shed. I shined a beam of light out the hole and found Tisha crawling off the beast, wild-eyed, swearing under her breath, carefully placing her hands on the less dirty parts of the tractor.

She stumbled to the shed and leaned against the wall looking sheepish. "Too late," she updated me, and I noticed her pants were wet down both inseams.

"Tisha, are you hurt? " The support posts started to creak and sway about then. I grabbed the gun and dashed to the tractor with Tisha just as the front side of the shed collapsed. We let our lights play over the debris and Tisha started boo-hooing.

"Come on, you ain't gonna die from peeing in your pants. And you did it quietly, well, until the tractor took off. Just think, tomorrow we'll know who took your mommy's flowers. All we have to do is watch and see who is limping. We all have to make sacrifices sometimes. Buck up, honey."

Between sobs, she asked in phrases, "Did you think ... to get ... the license plate number?"

"No, but I would recognize the truck. I should've shot it too, come to think of it." Okay, let's get out of here." I grabbed the gun, pulled up my stretchy turtleneck collar to wipe sweat from my face and tried to absorb all that had happened.

We later figured Tisha had stepped on the starter button getting down from the seat in the dark and started the tractor which was already in gear and it took off.

It sure solved the problem of how to get out of the shed, but now we had a downed tractor, a destroyed shed, a tombstone setting catawampus, a box half full of plastic flowers, and a little tiny stream of blood from the grass to the gravel. Time to go. We were somber women as we trudged back to my house. I was exhausted and had no explanation for the scene that awaited tomorrow's visitors to the graveyard. We didn't even open the pasture gate, climbed over it instead. It was as if we had opened too many things that night.

Tisha didn't come in. I patted her car hood, "Good night, deputy." She looked relieved that I could still speak and threw up a weary hand. "Talk to you tomorrow." I went in and collapsed on the couch, but I heard a little pecking on the door. It was Tisha. She pushed the door open and stuck her head in. "Could I borrow a bath towel? I just hate to get my front seat messed up."

Chapter 5
June: Be Prepared

I figured I'd be up all night after the fiasco in the cemetery, but I slept hard and the sun was high when I finally woke up. I had a nagging feeling that bad things had happened, but it took a few seconds to come to my senses completely and remember the mission for today: to find the limping man.

No point in panicking now. I told myself. *The deed is done. I'm okay and Tisha's okay. To make all that mess worth it, we need to find the scoundrel. I know I hit his right leg, probably near his knee.'* I jumped out of bed and dressed for church with a little spring in my step. I wanted to be early so I could people watch in case the thief was coming to church. Maybe the rascal needed to ask forgiveness.

Since last Sunday, the program had reverted back to our usual Methodist routine. I don't know why we print church bulletins every week, because the order of worship stays the same except for the title of the message and half the time that gets left out. Well, and the page numbers for the hymns change, too. It was comforting for me to know when to get up, when to sit, and when to bow my head. My good friend, Anna Bradford, disagreed with having a printed agenda, though; she thought we ought to act as the Holy Spirit moved us.

I took a seat before Sunday School classes let out, just behind Anna's regular pew, and for a few minutes I was the only one in the pews. I prayed, *'God, please forgive me for my part in knocking down the shed although I know You understand it wasn't all my fault and please help grant me hawk eyes to find the limping thief, if not here, then out in the community.*

Then I sat back and waited. I thought about last Sunday and the Voices of Glory. I could get worked up into a state again if I thought about Timmy Lee so I changed mental channels back to the mission at hand. Turning that mental knob to a different broadcast of thought is a valuable skill. Anna came up to visit a minute, tilting her head and asking me what was wrong before I said a word. She knew me that well. I whispered the outline of last night's mishap and her eyebrows lifted up under her bangs.

"Morning, Stella." Jimmy Whitt stopped and shook my hand. *Why is he on a cane? Oh, yes, hip replacement surgery.*

"How is that hip doing?" My eyes looked at his leg as if I could tell something about his surgery.

"Pretty good. They say I'll be good as new in a few weeks." He lumbered down the aisle to his seat.

"Morning, Sally," I waved to Mrs. Spencer. She was limping a little, but it was her left leg.

Old Colonel Perdue came in, grabbing the pew backs for support as he shuffled by. He wasn't likely our thief, too feeble to do it, and too rich to need the money. His family was loaded even before he made his fortune.

Jon Price, a strapping young man, was on crutches. I lit up and scrambled to inquire about his health. "Jon, what in this world?" I nodded at his full cast, toes to hip.

"Horse fell on me and pinned me in the mud. He was hurt and wouldn't get off. I got 'bout a hundred mosquito bites while I waited for somebody to find me." Sure enough there were dozens of little holes in the cast so he could scratch the bug bites with the end of a wire coat hanger.

"Who found you?" I narrowed my eyes, needing confirmation of the facts.

"Dad came looking for me, thank goodness. Morning, Miss Stella." And he swung his bad leg and moved on down the aisle.

God sure has a sense of humor. Seemed like every other person in church had a limp. I was extra attentive during "Joys and Concerns" in hopes there would be a mention of a loved one with an accident or damage discovered at the Bradley Cemetery, but there was nothing. We had a lay speaker because Reverend Booth had left the day before to check on his son who was in summer school at WVU and had been in a fender bender. I sat still and pretended to listen to the lay speaker's message, but my mind was racing. I planned to go to Hometown Restaurant afterwards and check out that crowd.

Then I'd call Tisha; she was going to the Pence Springs Flea Market to see if there were flowers for sale. I folded my hands and stared a hole in the forehead of the lay speaker.

After church finally ended, I drove myself to Hometown. The place was packed. Waitresses were nearly running to keep up with all the orders. Some friends motioned for me to join them and I did but I was watching more than I was eating. Seemed to me like more than the normal number of people stumbled or limped a bit, but all of it was explainable. I left a $5 tip on the table when I was done but before I got to the parking lot, I wondered if someone at the table would take it. Paranoia was setting in and I needed to clear my head.

A nice long hike with Sugar would be just the thing. The fifteen-minute drive back up the mountain to home helped me relax and Sugar's joy in greeting me made me think that we both needed a walk. I changed clothes, threw a bottle of water into a backpack and headed for the woods, Sugar running ahead and then backtracking like she was checking on me. Jonas was working extra hours this weekend, there were power problems at the Celanese plant and I doubted I'd see him until late tonight or maybe even Monday. As much as I loved him, it was good to have a day every now and then to myself.

Even in the heat of the day, the tall tree branches high above helped keep our path shaded and relatively cool. We hiked all the way to Rice's Field on the tiptop of Peters Mountain and rested on a big rock under a tree. I took a slug of water, now lukewarm, inhaled the summer smells of wildflowers and dried grass and patted my dog, at peace with the world for the moment. The big flower blooms bobbed in the breeze and bees and butterflies danced in zigzag lines around them. The sunshine soaked into my old bones; I vowed to store up the heat and remember it in the dead of winter. Sugar would hunt a

while then come back and lie panting beside me. We watched the tall grass, some bent and broken in the field before us.

The Appalachian Trail runs from Georgia to Maine and it crosses Rice's Field right in front of our resting place. Some strange looking creatures hiked that trail. A few hikers had come down the old fire road to my house after weeks in the woods. I think they would've paid a million dollars for a good meal and a hot shower. Sandwiches, cold pop, and a water hose were all I ever offered. Well, except for the ones who wanted to sleep in the barn loft during a storm. I worried about those two all night, but not enough to trust them to sleep in the house where I was.

I leaned back against a tree and was nearly asleep when I felt Sugar bristle up beside me. Someone was coming ... more than one person because there was the sound of voices. There was no time to hide or to run back down the mountain ahead of them. I sat and fretted and waited.

Here they came, one after another, dressed just alike in tan shirts and red bandanas, carrying walking sticks, wearing little packs and knee socks all exactly the same. The grownups, I guess they were grown – they were dressed just like the boys – stopped just ahead of me fumbling with a folded map. There were two of them, a heavy one with a sweaty red face and an older bald man, looking silly in knee socks. They didn't even notice me sitting back a ways in the shadow of a tree, but a sharp-eyed little boy saw me. "Maybe **she** knows where we are," the little fellow called out nodding at me. That got the leaders' attention and they looked up and squinted my way.

Chapter 5

"Good afternoon gentlemen," I wondered how they could bear the heat in those twill button-up shirts and bandanas.

The big-bellied man tipped his hat and wiped the latest trails of sweat off his fleshy face, "Hello ma'am. Are you from around here?"

"Yes, indeed, I live in this tree, eat berries and sassafras tea year round." I heard boys sniggering; they knew wise guy remarks when they heard them. I grinned, a little embarrassed at my own smart aleck mouth and softened, taking pity on them. "Yessir, I live 'bout two miles down the mountain."

Turns out that they had missed a trail several miles back where they were supposed to hike straight down the mountain to the road where a bus was waiting for them. The access path had probably grown over this time of year and they just didn't see it, cell phones got no reception and they didn't know where they were. I debated inquiring about the "Be Prepared" motto that they were so proud of, but I decided they had enough problems.

"Just follow me and Sugar and you can go to my house and call your bus driver. Bet you miss that air conditioning." I giggled. The leader exhaled noisily and looked at his companion who seemed very glad to agree. They turned to their brood. Thumbs were all up. He took his cap off and wiped his face again. "Thank you kindly ma'am. Lead on."

And this is why I was in the middle of forty boy scouts cavorting down Peters Mountain when the flashing blue lights of a sheriff's vehicle came into view, moving from the cemetery down the road in our general direction. The car stopped at the intersection in front of my house and those lights kept pulsing. You wouldn't have been able to tell that my palms were sweating or that I was flushed from my heart beating nearly out of my body since I was so hot it seemed natural, but I was a nervous wreck. *Suppose that flower thief died? How do they know that I did it?* I focused on getting the troop the last mile, the rest of the way to my house. Sugar headed for the creek and so did the boys, whooping and getting soaked. I led the two leaders to the parlor and the phone, but I didn't leave them. I wanted to stay close, the presence of Boy Scout leaders felt protective as I waited to be arrested.

The bald man handed me the phone to give directions to the driver. I forced that tuning knob in my head to tune back in to the current business. He and I agreed that the big charter coach shouldn't come up my rutted road, as there was no place to turn it around. The boys could walk two more miles and be picked up on the hard road, US Rt. 219. I hung up and explained it to the men. Red Face had collapsed on the loveseat, taken off his boots and was rubbing his toes. The other man blew his nose long and loud, suggesting allergies or maybe tears. Clearly they did not look forward to another step of this hike.

About then, we heard sirens. I didn't move but I could see out the door. The sheriff's car was skidding into my yard.

Chapter 6
June: Boy Scouts and Cool Whip

The sheriff's skinny long legs brought him to the back door quickly, his thumb on his gun belt, fingers adjusting things, as men seem to need to do. He pounded on my screen door, "Stella, get out here!" If I had been Catholic, I would've crossed myself. The screen door squeaked then banged shut when I joined him on the porch.

"Calm down, Elmer, I have company, as you can see." I stretched my arm out and moved it side to side in my best Vanna White imitation, encompassing the yard, the creek and dozens of boys.

"I know, I know, Stella, we've been looking for 'em all day, I got medicine for one of the boys," and he dug into his pocket. I guess that was what he had been adjusting, my mistake. "This kid forgot his bee sting pen. He has a deadly allergy to bees and he forgot his epinephrine. If he gets stung without it, he'll die."

He handed me the case. While relief swept through my heart and lungs I stared at the prescription label blind and numb for a split second. Then, my smart little mental knob changed gears again and I read the name, Conrad Romanello. "Conrad!" I yelled at the top of my lungs. Conrad appeared, red hair out of control, sweat and creek water plastering it in every direction, glasses tilting and sliding down his freckled nose over a beaming snaggle-toothed grin. Not a worry in the world. I handed him the pen. "Forget something?"

"Ooops." He shrugged. "I thought Scout Master Dave had it." Conrad found his backpack, carefully stashed the pen case and tightened the straps on his shoulders. "Thanks, sheriff. " He hung his head, "Guess Mom was worried."

"That's an understatement, I better give her a call." The sheriff ruffled the boy's sweaty hair, and then wiped his hand on his pants. "Be careful out there, boy." Everyone believes Elmer is a mean old man; he is soft as a kitten.

"Thanks, Stella, I'll call the boy's mom. Now what are you doing with these guys?"

"They are walking out to the hard road." A thought hit. "Hey Elmer, could you give them a police escort?" I peeked through the door at the two scout leaders and wondered which one was Scout Master Dave, probably Red Face. "Would you have room for these two to ride with you?" Their bodies had crumpled, one filling the loveseat and one sat, knees above lap on a low flowered footstool. Heads were drooping and sweat stains noticeably spreading. They perked up at my question and looked at the sheriff, for all the world like puppies begging with their eyes.

Elmer looked them over, two grown men reduced to puppy dog status, twisted his mouth to disguise the beginnings of a smile. "Sure thing. Let's move out." I resisted the urge to watch them get up but heard the whimpers and groans from the porch as I walked away.

The boys grabbed their gear quickly and got their orders from the leaders and Elmer, mostly Elmer. They lined up four abreast and fell in behind the police cruiser, lights still rolling around and flashing. I went and put Conrad on the front row, just so he was close by and waved until they were out of sight.

I was proud to be part of the rescue. It was easier to be thoughtful when you weren't looking at a gun charge and jail time.

Anna called an hour later, after I had taken a shower and turned on the ceiling fans to get the house cooled and settled down to be lazy for a while. She wanted details about the ruckus in the cemetery last night.

"Did they steal those plastic peonies I used to decorate Charles' grave?" I racked my brain to remember if Charles was on the left or right of the maintenance shed.

"I don't think so, Anna; we interrupted his plans." Inside my head I doubted that her husband would've care one way or the other if he had plastic flowers on his grave. Anna was so sweet that I didn't dare say it out loud, wouldn't hurt my devoted friend's feelings for the world. We talked a while and hung up with a promise to talk more often.

I settled back in the recliner and the phone rang again. "Listen, Stella, I got us a clue." Tisha was talking too fast for me to even consider interrupting. "Over at the heathern flea market, I found a guy what knows the guy that usually sells artificial flowers." I knew she was taking about Pence Springs, the Sunday morning flea market, heathern because you had to miss church to get there before it closed.

"Was he there?"

"Why, yes, he was there or I couldn't have found him."

"No, I mean the guy that sells artificial flowers."

"No, I'm getting to that part. He was NOT there today and he sent word that he wouldn't be back for a while but he would still sell the flowers at his yard sales. So, all we got to do is find his yard sale." The satisfaction just dripped from her voice.

"Good job, girl" is what I said, but I was thinking we needed a few more clues like where was this yard sale or what was the guy's name. "So, next weekend, you and me hit the yard sales?"

"Yep, and I'll be the sheriff, your turn to be the deputy. This is all on the up and up so I'll drive."

Well, that reminded me of the real sheriff and I told her about my afternoon and I waited a little too long to tell her why the police car came sliding into the yard so she would gasp and whisper "Oh, my God" over and over. Sometimes it gets on my nerves, but today it just tickled me.

After that call, I popped the stool of the recliner up and pushed the back of the chair backwards and stretched out to reflect on recent events. It took me a while and I must've gone to sleep because when I woke, it was twilight and Jonas was at the kitchen table eating a turkey sandwich.

"Hello there, how come you're not at work? Why didn't you wake me?"

He chewed a mouthful down to a manageable size to talk. "We fixed the mess at work." He took another bite and chewed some more. "Seemed like you needed to sleep. Word on the street is that you saved a troop of Boy Scouts today." He swallowed and took a drink of lemonade. "Pretty hard work in the heat."

"They were lost, Jonas, I just led them off the mountain. Sugar could have done it all by herself."

"You heard about the Bradley cemetery?"

Pushing the recliner back into place, I sat up straight, all ears. "What happened?"

"Looks like somebody tried to steal the old Ford tractor and drove it into a tombstone. Left a trickle of blood and wrecked the shed." His eyes studied me.

"Reckon it was terrorists?" I leaned forward, gripping the arms of the chair.

His eyes sparkled. "Terrorists with a cool whip container. It was the only clean thing in that shed. Ben and some of the guys tried to push the shed wall back up and brace it a while ago. Looks like isn't going to work." He voice trailed away and he took another bite and chewed a few seconds. Then, he brightened up. "They found the cool whip container and a spent .22 casing."

He took another bite and for once in my life I had nothing to say. I could hear Tisha's "Oh, my God. Oh, my God" inside my head but those were the only words I could think.

"Where's Miss *Nakurruq*?" He choked laughing and beat on his leg.

Now I was getting mad. He didn't have to tease me. I hadn't cleaned the gun and my tall Cool Whip container was gone. I was busted.

Chapter 7
June: Jonas Knows

"Awww, hon, don't be that way. I know you were there and that your .22 was fired. Just don't know why ... or what caused the tractor to crash through the shed. " He looked at me and took another bite of turkey sandwich and chewed so long, my mouth got dry.

"Well, it's complicated," I murmured and I looked away, at the ceiling, the walls, anything but him.

He came into the living room and reached his hands to me, helping me out of the recliner. "C'mon in here and tell me about it." I allowed him to lead me and sat at the oak table with him.

"Well, another individual and myself knew that the artificial flowers at the Bradley Cemetery have been stolen for years, always in the summertime and usually on Saturday nights." I took a deep breath. "So we aimed to do something about it." I peeked up at him. Still eating. Guess he had fixed two sandwiches.

"And ...?" He made circles with his empty hand trying to prime the pump.

I decided to clean the slate and spoke rapid fire to get it all out and over with. "We waited in the shed until a pickup truck pulled in and a guy started throwing flowers in a cardboard box then I shot him and Tis – another individual – fell on the starter button and the tractor took off and crashed through the wall and then it all fell in slow motion and he drove away and we hurried on home."

Sensing no movement across the table, I dared to look up. His mouth was open, disgustingly full of food and he was staring, eyebrows so far down they touched the bridge of his nose. He swallowed and wiped his mouth. "You shot somebody?" I flinched at the roar.

"Not to kill him, just to mark him. We need to find out who is stealing the flowers."

"Stella, you actually shot somebody – on purpose?"

I nodded, miserable. It sounded worse in the telling. "But it was in the leg, probably only a scratch."

"You gotta be kidding me. Last week, you were terrified of your peaceful life being interrupted by your brother and this week you shoot somebody? Did you think about missing his leg and shooting him in the head? Or that he could've pulled a gun and shot back? No, you didn't think." He hung his head as if he had a weight on his shoulders, then raised up. "Didn't tell anyone that you were going to pull this stunt or get any advice or help in case things went badly either. Your hard head is gonna get you in trouble yet." He shook his head and scooted back, putting an exclamation point on his words with the scream of scraping chair legs against the floor.

"I guess I needed a project to get my mind off Timmy Lee." I was wringing my hands on the table. Jonas refilled his glass from the pitcher of lemonade on the table and scooted his chair back. I counted every bead of condensed water on the pitcher while he drank. He was calming down, smacking his lips with the last drink of tart lemonade.

"Maybe we need to change the name of your rifle. Miss *Nakurruq* doesn't fit any more. You hit what you aimed for."

"I never knew what that meant anyway." I was relieved that he was loosening up enough to kid around.

"Means 'cross-eyed.'" His smile was broad enough to squeeze his almond-shaped eyes into narrow slits, laugh lines crinkling almost to his ears. He choked on the lemonade and his secret joke. I thought it was pretty funny, too, but let on that I was mad and hurt.

"I don't much like that you made fun of me all this time."

"Well, there's something else you aren't going to like, something I heard at work. " He was serious again. Now, I could bear to look at his face, curiosity winning out over misery. "Seems one Timothy Lee Davis was at the Christian Church on Wednesday night and at the Seneca Trail Church of Christ for Sunday morning church. Not the whole quartet, just him singing solo. He's been hanging around with your preacher at the Shale Bank Restaurant, having a mid-morning cup of coffee a couple of days this week."

"How do you know all this?"

"Let's just say Timmy Lee is a man that needs watching."

I became brazen, strong in knowing that Jonas cared enough about me to keep an eye on my mortal enemy, "Let's just also say that the thief is a man that needs shooting."

Jonas sighed and stood, and wrapped his strong arms around me, kissing the top of my head. My face was in his soft flannel shirt and I could feel the heat of his forearms below the rolled up sleeves on my back. How could I resist? I promised not to plan any more shootings, ever. And I agreed to take the concealed weapon permit class so I wouldn't get in trouble with a gun in my car. I knew he wouldn't tell and eventually, when he cooled down some more, he'd help me find the thief. He cleared the table, kissed me, a good one, and headed out the door for a short commune with nature before he had to go to work. Sugar met him on the deck and they headed for the woods.

Boy, did I need to call Anna, but it would wait until morning. My mind fixed on Timmy Lee. He had to be up to something. I tidied up the kitchen and decided to make a list of the things I needed to get done this week so I would be free for the weekend yard sales.

Pencil and pad in hand, I studied on what needed to be done. My bookkeeping was getting behind. I had a dozen business accounts and usually updated the books once a week as records came in by email. I hadn't known the first thing about computers when one of my clients mentioned that computerized records were the absolute latest. A nice perk was that I wouldn't have to come to town to pick up receipts and cancelled checks if I computerized my work.

I took a class at the James Monroe Vocational-Technical Center a few years ago and learned about 'Quicken Accounting'. Immediately, I saw how much time it saved. I'd come a long way since the WV Business College classes in Bluefield. Jonas had gotten computer-smart, too. I had shown him all I knew but he had gone way beyond that, researching anything and everything. He bought and sold farm equipment online and also kept up with family members and friends in Alaska on the computer.

Some people resisted change, but I had embraced it for a long time. The changes of my life, painful as they were at the time, had led me to a good place with a home and a job and friends and Jonas. It had always felt right to me to be ready for change and willing to improve. The pencil tumbled onto the kitchen tablecloth as I enjoyed the luxury of remembering. Mrs. Boswell, who had kindly rented me a room, also nudged me to go to business college.

"Why, you could walk to downtown, without no driver's license. The WV Business College has classrooms on the third floor of the Coal and Coke Building. Pick a career: secretary, switchboard operator, office manager, accountant, just pick one. You catch on quick. Go on, learn how to do it and get a good job. It's time for you to get out and about." Blanche Boswell was nothing if not direct. Her life had been a struggle and now, in her golden years, she was fighting to just put one foot in front of the other. Guess she was tired of my ten days of mooning around, staying in bed most of the day. These days people would say I was depressed. I like to think that I was between plans.

She persuaded me. I walked up two flights of narrow dark stairs in the Coal and Coke Building and picked me up a pamphlet and a catalog. The information was on a wooden magazine stand in the tiny hallway. Maybe they knew prospective students were too scared to go in the office. I all but ran down the stairs and went to the lunch counter at Kresge's and read every word. They didn't require a high school transcript, just wanted proof of age and tuition money. I could get the money but I wasn't about to use my real name to prove my age.

I studied on that during the walk back to my room and for a couple of days fearing someone would find me if I used my own name and I that would have to go home and face Timmy Lee. By then, I had told Mrs. Boswell that I had left home in the night and a little about why. She said that she had figured something like that. We had tried to figure out how I could get a driver's license without my real name and came up blank.

When I finally told the dear lady about the problem with signing up for classes, she sat real still in her rocker. Then she rocked slowly and hummed while she thought. She stopped and looked at me, "How old are you?"

"Eighteen, be nineteen in September." I answered truthfully. She pushed her massive body out of the rocker and left the room with her cane, returning with an ancient metal lock box. With

trembling fingers she unlocked it, wiped away the dust and opened it. She went and through document after document, deeds, insurance policies, and who knows what all else.

She pressed a yellowing envelope to her chest, choking out a whisper, "Look at this. My Stella would have been a year older than you." She offered me the precious birth certificate of her infant daughter, dead of scarlet fever the year after I was born. I read it over and over. "She was a purty little girl, she walked early and she talked early. Our next oldest child was thirteen years old when the baby came. Quite a surprise she was." Blanche laughed a little then got serous again. "Frank was killed when she was a few months old and it was so comforting to look at her and see his green eyes and curly hair. The older children helped me and we got by but then the scarlet fever hit." Her eyes were blanketed over with pain or time, I couldn't tell exactly. "This ole paper ain't doing me ... or her, no good, you use it if you can. Make a proud life with her name."

I took deep shuddering breaths wrapped tight in her soft arms breathing in the flowery smell of her Avon talcum powder. I guess I was sad for her baby and for my lost life. Before she let me go, I felt differently. I felt relief. I had a chance to start over.

That's when my second life began. No longer Penelope Ann Davis, I became Stella Frances Boswell. I managed to get a social security number, holding my breath as I handed the application over the counter at the Federal Building. Then, I got a night job at in the hospital cafeteria high on the hill another three blocks away. That check combined with an early morning paper route made enough money to pay my room rent and go to classes in the fall. It was a happy summer. Someone cared about me. I was busy and hidden from Atlanta and all the horrors of home. Timmy Lee was not in my life. Finally, I was out and about.

Jonas honked his truck horn as he left and I picked up my notepad and doodled my name and the word TRUST. Trusting Blanche had been a huge step for me. My friendships with Anna and Tisha sustained me. They didn't know all my past demons, but I had trusted both of them with parts of myself. Trusting Jonas had been easier yet. The fact that all of them had trusted me first opened the door for me to have faith in them. Life was sure a sight easier when you could depend on somebody else.

Chapter 8
July: Yard Sale

I buckled down to work. Caught up on all my bookkeeping accounts, worked in the garden or picked blackberries when it wasn't raining. Made pickles and blackberry jelly. Except for going to Wednesday night church, I laid low and didn't hear anything about the cemetery or a shooting or Timmy Lee.

Tisha wasn't surprised that Jonas had figured out I was at the cemetery and wasn't worried that he would tell anyone else. She had Jonas pegged as the strong silent type. We were gung-ho to hit the yard sales early Saturday. When I phoned Anna Friday night, I invited her to come with us but she didn't feel good and didn't need anything, so she thought she'd sit this one out.

Tisha met me in the ATM machine's parking lot early Saturday morning. I drove.

Our summertime yard sale trips had led us to some unusual places and we had bought some strange stuff, but we had never been scared before. Today, we watched for poster board signs and yards full of tables and piled clothing and toys and made a few stops but didn't see any flowers. Then, we followed crudely made yard sale signs down a mountain ridge. The roughly paved road narrowed and deteriorated into gravel and old damp forests replaced sunny mountain meadows. The corrugated cardboard signs, childishly lettered, lured us on.

"Stella, where are we?" Tisha peered through the passenger window, looking for a landmark or even a mailbox for a clue.

I laughed, "I think they call this Stinking Lick, I read that they cut out the school bus route last year, just not enough kids down here anymore. We rounded a curve with cars lining both sides of the road and I whooped, "Whoa, this must be it."

I squeezed the Subaru into a space straddling a ditch as Tisha whined. "I hope the other drivers leave before we do so we can get out of here."

"Tisha, Tisha, Tisha, don't worry. I got us here and I can get us out. The sign says there's a two-family sale out back, let's go see if any flowers are for sale."

We marched around the house down a path darkened with ancient pine trees. The smell of the sale hit us before we laid eyes on it. The backyard was a network of clotheslines draped with camouflage jackets, mildewed bed linens and stained comforters. Breathtaking. Boxes and tubs of video-tapes, boots, stuffed animals matted with burrs, and soiled baby toys were piled underneath the fabric collection. A partial box of Depends undergarments, so old that the stained-with-age vinyl shattered at a touch, was priced at $5 in the same scrawl as the signs.

From between two ramshackle outbuildings, a chained pit bull lurched at us, barking. "Git down and shaddup, Diego!" thundered a man who approached the dog from the screened back porch. I don't know which startled me more, the dog jumping from the silent shadows or the man yelling, but whatever the cause, my heart was beating in my throat. We hadn't noticed that there were people on the porch but as the man walked back my eyes followed him and saw ten or so silent adults and children seated there facing straight ahead, fair-haired boys and men in white tee shirts under faded over-alls, blonde women and girls in washed out plain dresses. They looked so much alike I imagined that they must be members of the same family, maybe here to watch or help with the yard sale.

I nodded a "Good morning!" to the group but no one changed expression or spoke.

"Where are all the other customers?" Tisha whispered as she glanced around.

"I do believe it is time to go," I answered.

A quick movement caught my eye. The dog silencer was coming our way quickly. "Lady, you ain't going anywheres ...."

We both froze as he reached for me.

"... until you hug my neck, Lord have mercy, Miss Stella, don't you remember me from your Sunday school class?

Come on in and see Maw, she still laughs about that time I set Kimberly's hair on fire in church and you took my lighter."

I hugged him hard, mainly because I was so relieved. "Tisha, this here's little Bill Conley. He came to my church a few times when he was a boy."

He shook hands with Tisha. I could tell she was holding back a little away from his dirty hands and clothes. "Only time I ever went to church was when I was a ward of the state." His tone was proud, then he added, I guess to explain the conditions that landed him in church, "That was back when Paw was in jail and Maw couldn't make ends meet." He looked at me, "We sure had a good time there!"

I remembered that some of us had had more fun than others, but I kept my mouth shut and then it clicked. Bill would know who sold artificial flowers! Bill could actually be the thief so I looked him over while he chatted with Tisha. On two legs, no injured knee or leg.

"Bill," I chose my words carefully, "we are looking for a man who sells artificial flowers over at the Pence Springs Flea Market. We heard that he was going to sell at his yard sale today but we don't know where he lives." I tried to seem like I didn't care one way or the other but I held my breath waiting for his answer.

Bill motioned for me to step behind an outbuilding with him. My sandals squished in the mud, at least I hoped it was mud as I followed. He bent his head down to mine so close I could see his snuff trickling out of the corner of his fat bottom lip. When he spoke, I could smell his dip, too. "He's a crook and a ... " he struggled for a terrible enough word fit for my ears, "... a sinner, Miss Stella. Even the mountain mafia is after him."

"Well, who is he, Bill?" I said but I was reeling. *Mountain mafia, what the heck?*

"I don't think he is gonna be stocking up on flowers anytime soon. He done robbed the wrong grave and the mountain mafia shot him." Bill tensed, rubbed his foot in the mud and studied the highest pine branches.

My blood ran cold at the fear in Bill's voice. It took me a few seconds to remember that **I** was the one who shot him, so I need not be too afraid of the mountain mafia, whoever that was ... and if they even existed. Smacked of too much cable TV here in Stinking Lick, I thought. No point in insulting

Bill's intelligence by pretending to want flowers, can't say that I know he is a thief because it might connect me to the shooting. I chew my lip and study Bill's face as I think. The silence works better than anything I could've said.

"People call him Sugar Bowl and he might be one of them Miller grandsons." Bill spit into the mud. "But I didn't tell you that."

I nodded and wanted to solemnly reassure Bill that his information was safe, but I was just so happy to finally have a name that all I could do was hug him and pound him on the back. He hugged me back, moist with sweat and reeking of snuff. "We gotta go, Bill, take care of yourself. Tell your maw I said hi, we'll stop by another time. And thanks." I waved as we neared the corner of the house where, as soon as we were out of sight, we ran to the car. Not a word was spoken until we were down the road a piece. Then we exhaled and whooped and hollered and high fived. We had the name of the thief!

The Dairy Queen was calling our names as we drove by on the way home, so we giggled through the drive-thru lane and took advantage of the $5 special: burger, fries, pop, and a mini-blizzard. The challenge was eating the burger and fries before the blizzard melted. "Oh, hell," Tisha muttered and wrapped up her half eaten burger, " forget the dry ole burger and let's eat the blizzards now and have fries for dessert." So we did. We sat in the ATM parking lot a few minutes enjoying the cold sweet stickiness in the blizzard cup and happily anticipating the crunch of French fries.

"Wonder where Sugar Bowl Miller lives?" Tisha mused. "You ever heard tell of a boy named 'Sugar Bowl'?" I was savoring a mouthful of chocolate covered cherry blizzard and couldn't talk at the moment, but Tisha didn't mind a bit. She just kept right on wondering things. "And why do you think they named him that? Is he fat like a sugar bowl or because he eats a lot of sugar? Maybe he's a diabetic. You know not too many people even use sugar bowls anymore." By then, I swallowed and could speak.

"Tisha, the main thing is to find where he lives or where he hangs out."

"Then what? You gonna shoot him again?" She pointed her finger out the window and pretended to fire it which inspired me to make a revving motor noise and hang on to the steering wheel, then fall over in the seat, my rendition of Tisha's cemetery support. Tears flowed as we laughed and laughed.

"Really, what are we gonna do when we find him?" She managed to straighten up long enough to be serious. It was a real good question, too.

I thought on that one. "The only way we can prove he is guilty of stealing flowers is to tell that we caught him red-handed, but then we would have to also tell that I shot him and that isn't going to look too good. I can't see any way to bust him without busting us. What are we going to do with him?"

Tisha leaned against the passenger door, still stuffing cold French fries in her mouth. "Well, we know he is alive, which is a plus. When we find him, we can keep an eye on him."

I was instantly irritated by all the time this was taking and thumped the steering wheel in frustration. "I don't have time to babysit this creep, I want him in jail. Let the sheriff babysit him."

"I thought you *was* the sheriff that night," and Tisha slapped her leg breaking into giggles again and sputtering bits of chewed potatoes on the dash. She used the wet wipes she always carried in her purse to make the dash look better than it had pre-sputter. I waited until she was done.

"Tisha, you ever heard of the mountain mafia?" She hadn't. I told her what Bill had told me and watched her jaw drop and her eyes grow wide. Tisha prided herself in knowing all the local legends and current topics of gossip, but she didn't know this one.

"Well, think a minute, no mountain mafia shot Sugar Bowl because we did. But he thinks they did and he is pretty scared. Shoot, *I'm* scared of them since that mean Bill is and I never even heard of them before. May be fear of them will adjust Sugar Bowl's attitude. May be that we don't have to do nothing else."

We agreed to keep on looking for him, at least figure out where he lived from a distance, but the pressure was off. We would keep checking the graveyard to be sure the flowers stayed put, but Miss *Nakurruq* was staying at home. Besides, I had promised Jonas. Tisha crumpled up all the DQ trash and put it in the bag. I thought she was going to take it with her, but she tossed it in my back seat and grinned. *Keeping her own car clean, good grief.* I waited in the ATM lot until she had started her car and it hadn't exploded or anything before I pulled out.

On my drive up the mountain to home I reviewed my happy thoughts: no murder charges, no suspicion directed my way, and we now knew the name of the thief. It had been a very good Saturday. I started feeling a little lighter and turned on the radio to sing along. One burden was lifting.

Chapter 9
July: Late For Church

I slept well that Saturday night and came to life quickly as the first rays of sunlight danced across the end of my bed. Sometimes I forget to pull the shades and the sun hits my bed early. Seems a pity to close the shades on the portraits of nature that my windows frame, plus the house is so far from folks that no one is likely looking in. Anyway, a beautiful summer Sunday morning was dawning and I threw on a terry housecoat and went out to greet it. I had been on the deck listening to birds and sipping on strong cocoa for thirty minutes when Jonas came creeping in, his truck crunching gravel. He was on his way home from work.

"Morning."

My voice startled him as he ambled up the walk and he grinned. "Didn't expect to see you up so early after a day out with Tisha. Did the yard sales survive you two?"

"Pull up a seat and I'll tell you what we found out. Want some cocoa? "

"Naah, water would be good though, long night at work." I stepped inside for a tall glass of ice water. When I got back, Sugar was at his feet getting a good petting. I interrupted to hand Jonas the water, just dying to tell him about our news.

"We found out the flower thief's name ...." I waited for him to show interest.

He didn't even look up from his long strokes of the dog's front legs. Watching his hands move kind of made me lose interest in my own story. "Not in the obituaries, I hope." He finally looked up and slapped final pats on Sugar's sides. He drained most of the water in one swallow. "Okay, okay, tell me," and he grabbed me and pulled me to his knee. I wrapped my arms around his neck and pressed my forehead to his and stared blue eyes-to-dark brown eyes.

"Sugar Bowl Miller." I enunciated clearly. He kissed me and I kissed him back. *Good grief, I was distractible.* We giggled and tickled each other then went indoors and up the stairs. Sunlight was flooding my rumpled quilt before we spoke again.

I used one arm to prop myself up, "Have you ever heard of the mountain mafia?"

He rolled over to face me, eyebrows knitted but a smile playing on the corners of his lips. "What? What are they supposed to be? And where did you hear of them. Tisha? Is she the Godmother?" He tossed his pillow at me. I ducked and told him about Bill. Jonas remembered him from my stories as a Sunday school terror. Then I explained the fear in Bill's voice and how he thought that Sugar Bowl had robbed the wrong grave and got shot by the mountain mafia.

"Well, we know that isn't exactly accurate information." His grin broadened and he sat up like he was getting up, then settled back against the headboard. "C'mere and let me tell you about *Imanaraqs*." I nestled into the crook of his arm and lay my head on his chest.

"My *Aaka*, Grandmother Kippi, told me about little people who live on the tundra. Inupiat people call them *Imanaraqs*. They have glowing red eyes and they live underground. Whenever storms come in the arctic, a door might blow open, maybe the back door or the door to the porch and grandmother would always gasp, cover her mouth and then say, 'An Imanaraq has been inside. You kids better be good.' We were not to wander too far out onto the tundra or play on the frozen lagoon or throw rocks or talk back, oh and a long list of other things." He chuckled, and then grew somber. "When we misbehaved, we were told that the *Imanaraqs* would get us and take us away from our home and family and make us work underground forever. Those wicked children were never found again. Sometimes a hair ribbon that a sassy little girl was wearing would be found blowing from a tiny willow or a toy would be seen that was dropped from a bad little boy's pocket when he was kidnapped. I tell you I was scared of *Imanaraqs*." The silence hung heavy.

"Sounds kinda like our booger man." I was caught up in the apprehension of it all, just like a child. I could feel my heart racing at the memory of the booger man of my childhood.

Jonas stroked my hair. "I think kids need *Imanaraqs* ... and a booger man or something like it to help enforce their goodness. The upstanding citizens of Monroe County may need a mountain mafia for just the same reason." He let that sink in then reached under the covers and pinched my behind. We jumped out of bed on either side squared off, ready for a pretend fight. He ended it unfairly. "You better get ready for church. I'm going home to sleep."

I looked at the clock and squealed. It was 10:15. I would just about have to teleport to get there on time. I hurried to the bathroom and heard him whistling down the steps just before I turned on the water.

#

Not much feels as guilty as slipping in late for church. It is a temporary guilt, though, forgotten immediately as I join the congregation. The guilt I once felt for being with Jonas was long term but had grown fainter over the years until it was just a shadow. I still hated that Jonas was another woman's husband, but the guilt was nearly gone. We had had many discussions about a divorce and our marriage, at least, I had discussed them, but Jonas mainly hung his head. As much as we wanted to live together, he was married and I felt as the Lindside United Methodist Church Treasurer that I shouldn't live with a man without a marriage certificate. Jonas and I took our commitments seriously. Ben McDaniel had confided once that Jonas wanted to locate his wife, but couldn't. Ben had shrugged and mumbled that it was hard to divorce someone you couldn't find. And that is where that had ended.

Mercy, it was hot that morning. The wet edges of my hair felt cool against my skin. I helped myself to a bulletin from the basket outside the sanctuary, knowing I'd need a fan, and waited until the first hymn was in progress before I slunk down the center aisle to my seat. I hoped that all eyes were on their hymnals but I knew better.

I was in place with hymnbook open in time to sing the fourth and final verse then parked myself in the pew and listened to the joys and concerns. I was stirring the air using the bulletin as a fan but my hand stopped in mid-flutter when Reverend Booth spoke, "In addition to the prayer list on the bulletin, please remember our brother in Christ, Timmy Lee Davis, who has not been able to find a place to rent or a job. Spread the word, if you know of a rental unit, apartment, house trailer, or a small house, he's looking." I craned my neck to follow the preacher's eyes to see if Timmy Lee was in church, but he wasn't there. I was reeling.

My throat burned from swallowing over and over. That at least kept me from screaming while I tried to blink away the big white spots I kept seeing. *Was I having a stroke? Wouldn't Timmy Lee love it that the stress of knowing he was near caused me to croak?* The spots eventually faded during the children's sermon. The message was about patience. It was somewhat calming and led me back to where my swallowing was more normal. I hoped that I wasn't giving away my feelings and I must've covered them well, because no one called 911 or came to see about me.

The service progressed with scriptures and the sermon and another hymn and the offering and benediction.

After church, a bunch of us went out to eat at the Hometown Restaurant. The preacher sat at my table and Sally Spencer asked him the question that was burning in my mind. "What has possessed that good looking gospel singer to look for work here? Doesn't he know that a third of the county is laid off?" I speared some green beans as if I wasn't hanging on every word.

"He feels he has some special talents and there is a niche here that they would fit into nicely." The preacher laid down his fork, during the meal, a rare event, indeed, and called across the table to retired military strategist, Col. Perdue, "Colonel, do you think we need Brother Davis in our church?"

"Yessir." Col. Perdue was deaf as a post. If Reverend Booth had asked him if he wanted to hike to the North Pole, the Colonel would have probably said the same thing.

"See, Brother Davis has a lot of local support. I, for one, hope he lands a job soon and becomes part of our community."

If they could've seen beneath my skin, they would have watched all my blood stop flowing and my fingers and toes become white and cold. My speared beans were doomed to remain on the plate. I looked up and asked, haltingly, "What special talents does he have? Besides singing, of course."

Reverend Booth took up this praises again, "Finances, like fundraising, and campaigns. Did you know that he has been a stockbroker and a financial advisor and has managed several congressional candidates?"

Well, butter my butt and call me a biscuit, he has the preacher snowed. Special niche my eye. Timmy Lee has found a bunch of new folks to trust him. Suckers are what he would consider these good people. I looked around the room and Sally Spencer seemed to be thinking the same things I was thinking and sprang into action.

"Whose money is he gonna manage in Monroe County and how does he figure to raise funds when there are pitiful few dollars extra around here? And just which candidate does he aim to get elected. Elmer Johnson has been the sheriff for forty years and Judge Ballard will be elected until he dies. What job is there that has a niche he can fill?"

Reverend Booth was squirming. "Sally, the board is going to discuss this at tomorrow evening's meeting. No need to borrow trouble." He turned to talk to someone on the other side.

Sally looked at me. "We sure don't have to borrow trouble, we have a snootful of our own. The church parking lot needs paved, all the youth want to go to church camp, and we are three months behind on the power bill for the Fellowship Hall annex." She pushed back from the table and gathered her purse and sweater. "Our board needs a backbone when it comes to money. " I knew all this from my role as a long time board member and church treasurer, but I didn't let on, didn't even agree with her, "Stella, could you give me a ride home, my daughter Betty is using my car this week since theirs broke down. I have become a bum." She shook her head.

"I could use the company, let's blow this joint." We picked up our checks, told everyone goodbye, and paid the cashier on the way out. I could barely think, but managed to calculate the tip. Sally's presence was a treat and I hated to let her out when we reached her house. It was going to be a long Sunday afternoon facing the fact that Timmy Lee was here to stay.

Chapter 10
July: Fundraiser

Sunday afternoon was more relaxing than I had supposed. I took a nap. The last few days had been busy with the garden all coming in at once plus the added stress of Timmy Lee. Guess it was too much for me to handle. Refreshed, I got ready for the Sunday night services.

I wanted to relive the dinner discussion with Sally, but she was not at church, in fact, there were a lot of empty pews. *Summer vacations,* I thought. *Several families camping or gone to the beach before school started back up.* There was an update about the big chug holes in the parking lot: on the first Sunday of each month a special offering would be taken for pavement until we raised $30K. The youth group had been offered the concessions for a big auction sale and we were asked to donate bottled water or pop or any kind of foods so they could make enough for everyone's camp fees. *Good deal, let them earn that money.* I folded my hands. And finally, the last announcement, a fundraiser was planned for Friday night. I guess I had missed it at the morning service. There would be a bean dinner, a bake sale, an auction of donated items, and a talent show. The children's choir was invited to sing and any other entertainment that wanted to perform was welcome. It wasn't clear just what the money was earmarked for – probably the power bill for the Fellowship Hall Annex. I mentally marked my Friday calendar to help in the church kitchen.

As I followed the short line of worshippers out of the sanctuary, I felt a tug on my sleeve and it made me jump because I thought I was the last one in line. "Stella, I need some help." Anna Bradford was on tiptoes whispering towards my ear.

Chapter 10

"Why, honey, I am here to do anything you need." I meant that, too. Anna had always been the big sister I had never had, she knew some of my secrets and egged me on to believe in myself. She was about twenty years older than me and was visibly starting to slow down.

She led me to the front corner of the fellowship hall. "Stella, I don't know what to do. Somebody was walking on my front porch last night. This morning all my flowerpots were turned over and dirt and flowers were all over the place. I was so scared that I couldn't move until the sun came up." Tremors shook her hands as I held them. " I just stayed still in the middle of my bed, couldn't even call out to see what they wanted." She studied my face. "Can you help me, Stella?"

I thought, *Oh, Lordy, I told her about me shooting that thief. I promised Jonas I wouldn't shoot anybody else. Lordy, Lordy, Lordy!* but I said, "Well, now, Anna, have you had any trouble with raccoons lately? It could be a fat ole coon on your porch."

"Yes, I am having some trouble with raccoons." She was thoughtful as if she wanted this to be a raccoon problem but she knew better. Her eyebrows were down and she blinked a lot. "They **are** eating the cat food, but they are not leaving big muddy boot prints on my steps. It was a man, maybe a boy, but somebody walked around out there, just under my bedroom window." She put both little hands on my arm. "Could I borrow your pistol, Stella, for a few nights? I'll take real good care of her, will put her under my pillow at night, just keep her handy."

Her eyebrows went up and she looked at me with such pleading eyes, I hugged her tight and whispered, "Don't you worry another second. Stop by any time this week and get her." I was suspicious, though. This was not the Anna I knew and loved.

Anna clung to me like a baby until she quit trembling and I straightened up. Her hair was a gorgeous white and her scalp glowed pink through her thin waves. She had lost some weight lately and was frailer today than I remembered. I walked her to the door holding her hand. *Wonder if this is something that I need to tell Jonas?* I decided it wasn't. Wish she would've asked me to wait up for the prowler one night, like a stakeout situation, but maybe it is best that I just loan her the gun.

Anna hasn't been as strong since her Charles died. She says she doesn't want to move closer to town, maybe the girls are bugging her to go. I bet that is why she came to me, she didn't want them to know she was afraid, it would give them more ammunition to intrude on her life. Still, it wasn't at all like her. Charles had a big cabinet of guns, why doesn't she use one of them. Maybe she needs a pistol, something small enough to hide. I definitely don't need to tell Jonas. Anna needs to have some power over her fear. She isn't herself and just needs a little boost. I am overdue a visit to Anna's house. I'll get up there this week.

I spent most of the week in the garden and kitchen. The number of tomatoes getting ripe at the same time overwhelmed me. Gorgeous red and yellow slices graced my table every meal, I had canned 56 quarts of quartered tomatoes and 21 quarts of spaghetti sauce. At the end of each canning day I turned my hot sweaty face to the heavens and said a silent thank you to Rachel McDaniel who had coached me in the kitchen during the last months of her life. I was ready to try something new, though, and read in a Mother Earth magazine about drying fresh foods. The food dehydrator that I bought at a yard sale seemed to work so I spent a morning slicing a basketful of tomatoes and loaded all the trays of the dehydrator. The hum of its little motor was comforting as I baked muffins and pies for the Friday fundraiser.

The back seat of my car was plumb full of baked goods by mid-morning on Friday and I had on a new pink apron over my jeans and shirt, the smock kind with big pockets. I decided to slide my pistol, *Utukkuu*, into a pocket so to be ready to give it to Anna. I hadn't taken time to visit her during the week. Surely she would be at the fund-raiser.

When I arrived, the fellowship hall at the church was an anthill of activity, workers scurrying here and there. I made three trips carrying all my pies and muffins, then rested a second and surveyed the scene.

The plastic folding tables and chairs had all been set up and decorated with canning jars full of wild flowers, a temporary stage had been set up at one end of the huge room and a podium, microphone, and speakers were all in place. Children were chasing one another around the tables and women were carrying food to the long buffet line. I saw Anna in her Sunday best dress, laughing and wiping tables. Good that she was here, I needed to catch her and give her my little friend if she was still scared enough to be interested.

I washed my hands to help, turned for a towel and saw him. Timmy Lee was talking to Reverend Booth. I wiped my hands on my apron and moved closer, pretending to straighten flower arrangements.

"We sure are blessed you are able to help us out. I never dreamed that our little church could expand our outreach to include a media director." Preacher Booth shook Timmy Lee's hand, then slapped him on the back.

"It's me that's blessed, Preacher, bringing the Good Word through the power of radio, the miracle of television, and the wonder of Internet. There is so much untapped," he paused, "strength ... strength in God's children that has not been awakened in our community." The men embraced powerfully thumping each other's backs. Preacher Booth walked away, wiping his tears.

The words numbed me. *When had that been decided?* Not at any board meeting that I had attended. I fumbled with the delicate chicory blossoms but my mind was too scattered to know what I was doing, so I edged back to the kitchen and spent the next hour washing pots and pans and wiping any countertop that had an exposed inch. From the bits and pieces of conversation in the kitchen I came to understand. Some people think that hardworking churchwomen don't gossip, but I think it is fair to say that they **are** observant and that they share what they observe. I imagine that the church kitchen walls hear more news and decision-making than the walls of administrative offices. What I confirmed was that the proceeds of this whole fundraiser were committed to the salary of the new media director, that handsome gospel singer. Red spots danced over the dishwater suds as I washed and washed.

When everyone had eaten and the music ended, the preacher and I counted the money. It was a surprising amount. He couldn't wait to announce that the benefit dinner had raised over $11,000, the first of several fund-raisers to provide a salary for the church's new media director. I took the deposit and stashed it in the usual hiding place in the kitchen, the dishtowel drawer, until I finished working. I looked for Anna but she must've slipped away while we were counting the money.

Finally the crowd thinned. The folding tables were all cleared and wiped and stored. Every dish and spoon was washed, dried, and put away. The last of the cleanup crew was rattling around in the kitchen; they had spread their damp dishtowels out to dry and were heading out the back door. Good-byes and thank-yous filled the room before it was silent.

I looked around for something else to do and noticed the choir robes children had tossed in the floor near the rack in the corner. I went over and began hanging them up when I saw Timmy Lee. Alone in the kitchen. Timmy Lee and I were alone in the fellowship hall. Something inside me, something that had been stretching tight over the last few weeks, snapped. I tossed the silky robe in my hands into the pile watching it slip and slide into a resting place on the others. It seemed to fall in slow motion. Then I levitated across the room. He was walking through the kitchen door, out into the hall and I met him head-on.

"Timmy Lee, you look at me," I reached up to grab his flabby shoulders and square his body up to mine. "I know you, you dirty dog. I have spent a lifetime trying to forget you, to erase the terrible things you did to me."

Timmy Lee stepped back from me, "Who are you woman? Are you insane?" He studied me squinting as if to see underneath to understand the rage. He looked around the room for help but we were alone.

"Don't remember me, Timmy Lee? The girl you tormented through childhood and pressed against the wall every time you wanted something ... then shared her with your friends ... but wouldn't speak to her in front of them ... think Timmy Lee ...." My voice raised a decibel, the volume so loud that my throat was dry. I swallowed and dug my hand through my apron pocket for a piece of hard candy or gum. There, forgotten, was my little friend. *I hadn't even remembered that I had it, too preoccupied with this snake.* I got louder and pushed him with my free hand.

"... the same girl who knows that you stole all the money from the senior class and probably from the bank until you lost the summer job, and from everybody who ever bought a car from you, the girl that you lied to and about ... your lies forced me to leave home three states away and thirty years ago on my graduation night to come here and start over. I have a good life here, a decent life with honest people and you dare to spread your filth and lies over me and these good people." I felt the moisture from his breath and worried about mildew or diseases that he may be spreading. *I'll wash later.*

I stopped for a moment, not sure what I was going to do next. I fixated on the sweat stains growing under the armpits of Timmy Lee's shirt. He had backed up against the block wall. *Good, got him where he used to have me.* I inhaled hard. "Still a salesman Timmy Lee? Selling God these days?"

It seemed natural to pull the gun out and point it at him; maybe I'd watched too many NCIS episodes. I held the gun pretty steady considering my bad mood. Timmy Lee waved both arms with hands spread. *He still had no sense at all – like that would stop a bulle*t. He was babbling something but I could only see his mouth moving. I guess I wasn't real interested in what he had to say.

Everything slowed again and I hesitated. *If I kill him in here, the church cleanup crew will have to clean up the mess ... Oh, drat, I'll help.*

I sighed, tried to remember if I there were rubber gloves at the church. *Yeah, I think there's a pair under the sink. OK, no problem.* I backed up two giant steps, enjoying the groveling but trying to distance myself from his venom, aimed quickly, then hesitated. My fingertip pad just touched the trigger, so slight a touch it could have been a dream.

In that quick moment, Timmy stumbled back against the wall. His waving arms hit the only wall decoration in the fellowship hall, a big heavy metal cross made of braided rebar. It dislodged some cement and cinder block as it fell and hit him hard on the head. He fell against the wall. At first he was kind of leaning, then his heavy body settled into itself like a collapsible cup made of rolls of fat. He slid all the way to the floor. When he stopped only his head and shoulders rested against the block wall. The cross lay crosswise over him, the short part cushioned on his stomach and the long part on the floor.

I was stunned. I knew I hadn't pulled the trigger and there had been no explosion of sound. What in the world? I resisted the urge to blow across the end of the barrel of my seemingly magic gun, then put it safely away in my pocket. I didn't understand it but I was starting to feel relieved. *Is this what miracles feel like?*

I tippy-toed up to him, leaning down to look him over, but ready to run in the other direction if I needed to. His eyes were shut but he was breathing. His shirt was dark and moist but it was sweat not blood. I reached way out and touched his damp pants and checked out my fingers, not blood, maybe urine. I looked up at the wall and saw a ragged dent in the cinder blocks where that big cross had been hanging. He must've been knocked out when the cross conked him on the head. *It served him right. Guess this is how it feels when things are meant to be. It felt good, respectable or something. And I really didn't shoot him, so there wouldn't be all that worry that you get when you shoot someone.*

I straightened up and tucked a tendril of hair back into my bun and looked around the room. I didn't much feel like hanging up the rest of the choir robes. *Think I'll go home and put my feet up.*

I grabbed the money to deposit from the dishtowel drawer and headed out. The whack of the wooden screen door was the last sound I heard before I started my car and headed by the bank then home to my drying tomatoes. My feet hurt and my temples throbbed like a headache was beginning. Church fundraisers are so exhausting.

Chapter 11
July: Daughters and Husbands

I hated that I didn't get a chance to give the gun to Anna at the benefit dinner. Then I wouldn't have nearly shot my good-for-nothing brother, which I didn't really regret, but I was a little worried that I could do something stupid regarding Timmy Lee and end up in jail. Also, if I could've given her my little friend, I wouldn't be worried about Anna. She had been upset the time I last saw her, but I knew that she was tough as a pine knot. Her life had been hard, even when Charles was alive, and even harder now. As I tried to relax at home that Friday night, I couldn't get Anna off my mind.

She and Charles had been 'bout as different as two people can be. For every time Anna blushed shyly, Charles bellowed a wild story to anyone that would listen. He was happiest leading the cavalry charge in Civil War battle reenactments, kicking his horse with both feet and waving a saber in the air. Anna was teeny and fair, could still wear girl sized dresses; Charles ducked through inside doors, he was that tall and had a big beer belly. He was vain about his black hair and combed it into a DA, a style last popular in the 1950s. He thought he looked like Elvis. Good grief! Anna worked up a garden, made clothes and rugs and quilts at home and worked part-time at the senior center. I knew for sure that Charles didn't work at the Celanese or in the school system and when I asked what he did, Anna had heaved a sigh and said, "Let's call him a farmer or ..." she hesitated, " a handyman." I remember that she looked upward and I think she said a little prayer. It was clear that they didn't have much. And whatever she had now was less than they had had together.

Anna and I were friends at church but we were also mountain friends. We swapped recipes and weather reports, daffodil bulbs and starts of forsythia and irises when we thinned the flowerbeds. We talked on the phone or in each other's kitchens, sharing juicy bits of news about the people we knew and little secrets of our lives although I always knew there were things she didn't tell anybody. I guess we were more than mountain friends, almost like we had grown up together. Sometimes, we rode together to church events and sometimes, rarely, we just rode around to get out of the house. I felt like an auntie to their two daughters, but Charles was not one of my favorites. He and Jonas got along pretty well, but I didn't pretend to understand it.

Charles had been a jerk about having girls instead of boys. He yakked about how disappointed he was that there was no son to "carry on his name" and how that was so hard on him. He called his beautiful little girls "split-tails" until Anna threatened to crack his head with her skillet. She had fire in her eyes even though he acted like lord of the manor most of the time. I heard him say time and again that it would be nice to have someone to go fishing and hunting with him, or share his interest in the Civil War. Of course, I would've loved to have had Jonas's child, any gender, so I was pretty disgusted with Charles's whining.

Charlene and Brooke were pretty little girly girls, and they started early trying to please their daddy. Anna dressed them both like china dolls, even ironed the ruffles on their baby bonnets. Charlene was the quiet one. She would stare at Charles with his own brown eyes and cuddle with him in the recliner when he would let her. The art projects in school she made were always for her daddy. He tossed everything she made for him in the trash, but Anna rescued everything and smoothed out all the cards and drawings and kept them.

Brooke was born when Char was seven. By the time Brooke was toddling along, Charlene had about stopped trying. All the attention was on the baby who was a precious thing, outgoing and cheerful. Anna worried that Brooke's need to please her daddy would carry over to adulthood and her own relationships. Anna was a wise woman.

Charlene wasn't as outgoing as her sister and her quiet ways gave Anna other worries. Char listened to strange sounding music in the upstairs bedroom and dressed like the dead, according to Anna. As a teenager, she wore all black and used dark lipstick. "Goth," Anna explained to me, " is the latest teenage craze." Charlene took it a little far out of her mother's comfort range, though. Just after finishing high school, she planned a Goth wedding down at the campground at Glen Lyn on a Friday the 13th with a justice of the peace officiating. She had sent her mom a black corsage to wear. Anna just couldn't do it. Anna stewed for a week about the decision to go or not to before deciding to stay home. She begged me to go so I could report back. Charles never considered going. His contribution to the wedding was to thoroughly cuss everyone involved and leave that weekend on a fishing trip.

Charlene's gown was purple trimmed with black lace and the groom wore a tattered black Cure t-shirt and low slung pants with chains hanging from his belt loops into his pockets for the ceremony. Both the bride and groom had eyebrow piercings and Charlene wore thick black eyeliner and had black fingernails and carried black roses. It was not a Barbie doll wedding. Anna worried about her daughter's immortal soul. Looking back now, we should have been more worried about that no good boyfriend, Jeremy.

We all knew Jeremy Boyd; he lived on around Dunkard Church Road at the base of Peter's Mountain. Bless his heart. He and his family lived in a tiny house without running water until he was in high school. Jeremy's role was peacemaker, the middle son of five boys. All that horseplay and wrestling may have knocked him in the head too many times because he grew up with empty eyes. His parents had good hearts, I guess, but they were kinda funny turned.

Anyway, after he graduated high school, he skedaddled off the mountain and disappeared for a couple of years. When he came back, he had a job in the coalfields, a motorcycle, greasy hair down to the middle of his back, a drinking/drug problem, and an eye for Miss Charlene Bradford. They married, at least we guessed the Goth ceremony counted as legal, and moved to the "patch," the great and glorious free State of McDowell County to an apartment over the Kozy Kountry Kitchen near Bradshaw, WV. It was a rough place and I didn't trust him as far as I could throw him but I figured he'd take care of Charlene.

The number of times Charlene and Jeremy had been home in the last two decades could be counted on one hand. They had managed to drag in just before Charles' funeral, looking older than their parents. There wasn't enough make-up to cover the dark circles under her eyes and the bruise on her jawline, but she was there. They had no children, we didn't read about them in the magistrate report, and they didn't seem like they needed money. All good news, but I wouldn't call it happily ever after.

Ten years after her sister's wedding, little sister Brooke married a mobile home salesman who had more money than she had ever seen. He worked and she stayed at home. They seemed real content in their almost-new double wide just outside of Lynchburg, about a three-hour drive away from Lindside. Brooke didn't know that he kept his old single wide in the next county after they got married and had supported another woman there since the wedding. She had learned of it about two years ago in a classic wrong number phone call from his mistress.

She just smiled and got pregnant, a desperate failed attempt to save the marriage. Anna didn't know of the trouble until Charles died last fall and Brooke came in for the funeral with three kids and no husband. Baby Ethan's daddy hadn't even shown up for the boy's arrival. We all assumed that he lived with the other woman now, but a couple of months back, when Brooke was about to go under, he had started paying the utilities, the house payment, and had promised her $500/month for the kids as long as she didn't file for divorce. I knew Anna had sent her every dime she could scrap together. It could have been a lot worse, but it could be a lot better.

#

I decided to ride around the mountain Saturday morning and check on Anna and take her my pistol, but I left it under the driver's seat until I was sure Anna wanted it. Her voice greeted me when I stepped on the porch, "Come on in, Stella. The door's open." The house smelled like pickle relish from her canning that day, but the stove and counters had been wiped clean and everything was put away except the glass jars glowing bright green with their contents. Also, there were some half-gallon jars of grape juice that she had made a couple of weeks ago. We labeled the jars and I carried them down the basement stairs to her pantry shelves, telling her that I needed the exercise, but truth be told, I was afraid she'd stumble and fall.

Chapter 11

It turned out that she didn't really need my gun; she just needed a strong shoulder to lean on. I had shared everything about Jonas and me years ago, and now I found myself finally telling her the truth about Timmy Lee. I knew she was a vault of secrets and that anything I told her would stay put. She told me things about her life that I had suspected. Her health was not good. She was broke. Charlene and Brooke were heavy on her mind. And Timmy Lee had been bugging her to go to assisted living at the place that took your social security check for expenses. He wanted her to sell the house to him. He was a monster, still up to no good. What had brought her to the point that she was scared were the noises and muddy footprints on the porch. They were bothering her a lot and she couldn't sleep. We prayed together and she asked if I would stop by again on the way to church on Sunday morning. I agreed, and heavy hearted, I left her.

Chapter 12
August: A Diversion

Summer was fading and nights were finally getting cooler. Tomatoes filled my kitchen counters, and the corn was getting ripe fast. Vegetables were taking a lot of my time, and I was grateful because that kept me from fretting over Timmy Lee or Anna Bradford or the Mountain Mafia.

Tisha thought I was working too hard. "You gotta get outa that kitchen and off the mountain," she told me Saturday afternoon when we had our regular phone time.

"For what?" I asked.

"For your sanity." Tisha went down a list of things I could do: "Go shopping at the Mercer Mall or get on an AAA bus tour or drive out Route 100 and go to White Gate to the Amish store, or get Jonas to take you out to dinner. When was the last time y'all had a romantic dinner?"

Hmmm, I thought. Jonas didn't come up with these ideas himself. I had to plant the seed, water and warm it and then, sometimes it didn't grow what I intended. Like the time I wanted a new kitchen floor and I hinted and hinted about how the floor showed every blade of grass and bit of mud that we tracked in. Jonas bought a mat for the back porch so we could wipe our feet. Another time I asked him straight out to hire a private detective to find Lena, his skinny little wife, and he did absolutely nothing, just said, "Let lying dogs sleep." He drove me crazy reversing things, but they still made sense.

"Nothing sounds too inspiring to me." I sighed, a sigh so long that it turned into a yawn and Tisha must've felt that the conversation was over, which was correct, and we hung up.

Tisha was right. Timmy Lee, Anna, and the garden were overwhelming me. I needed to do nothing for a while. I turned off the water bath canner, left dozens of tomatoes in the sink and headed outside. Sugar had her nose in the short grass of the yard like she was sniffing out a mole or a vole. I watched for a while, enjoying the little breezes that were growing cooler every evening. She started tossing something up in the air, letting it hit back in the grass and doing it again. I went to rescue the little mole or whatever it was and snatched it off the grass. A sickly green pod tapered to a point on both ends. What in this world?

It was about the size of a long skinny pine cone and was enclosed in tight scales. Sugar bounded around me wanting it back. I tapped my fingers against it. Was it solid or hollow? I couldn't scratch it or pick the edges of the scales. I sure hadn't ever seen such a thing before or handled the lightweight material it was made from. How did it get to my backyard? I looked around to check if it came from a tree or from underground. No branches overhead. No holes nearby. The dog could've drug it in, but from where? If it was not from nature, where did it come from? Must've dropped from a plane. Russians? Terrorists? Was it a canister of poison gas? An electronic sensor? Was I being watched? I stumbled to the deck to sit down after I realized the logical truth; it had to be from an alien space ship.

I held the pod gently now. It would probably be best to keep it outside in case it exploded or released poison gases. I went inside to get something to keep it in and settled for a Ziploc bag and an old metal lunchbox. I zipped and clipped it safely inside and put it on the top shelf in the shed with last year's Mason jars. The goat barn would've been more convenient, but if it could hurt me it might hurt the goats and they were fainting goats, high strung and all that.

I needed to call Elmer. Someone in the sheriff's office might could identify it and disarm it. At the very least they would know someone who could. Along with my current worries about the Anna and who might have found that no good Timmy Lee in the fellowship hall conked in the head by a cross, I now was facing the possibility that the fate of the world was in a lunchbox in my shed.

The sky was clouding up and a light drizzle was beginning so I bustled to the garden and picked a few dozen ears of corn. Just in time, too, the sprinkles were solidifying into a steady rain. By then it was 4:30, and I couldn't stall my worry any longer. It was time to call the sheriff's office.

"I don't know where it came from," I repeated to the deputy who took my call. "It was in my yard this afternoon and I am pretty sure it is not from this planet."

There was some coughing and sputtering at the other end of the phone and my call was transferred. I was glad that I worked at home so I wasn't exposed to folks who came to work sick. Elmer came on the line.

"Stella, what is going on up there on Peters Mountain?" His voice had a happy ring to it and I was glad he was able to talk to me. It was calming to talk to a competent, healthy person.

"I found a pod in my yard a while ago. I've never seen anything like it and I am worried sick that it might be dangerous. I s'pect that it may not be from here."

"Where do you think it is from?" I could tell that the sheriff was not as worried as I was. "Did Sugar drag it over the mountain from Virginia?" I could hear him smiling.

I felt he needed to get serious. "I think it landed in my yard from the sky, probably from a plane or maybe a spaceship." There, that should wipe that smile away. "Can you send someone from the extension office or the FBI to come and identify it?"

I could hear him clear his throat and blow his nose before he answered. Colds must be going around up there at the county seat. "We are covered up today, Stella; there's a report of a load of turkey manure that overturned over at Ballard near the Dairy Bar and people are complaining because they can't eat for the smell. Officers are on the scene there and in Peterstown where there is a rabid skunk call in progress. As soon as they finish up, we'll send an officer to your place." He asked about my health and how I had been doing and I felt better. *Well, good. I would have some help in saving the planet.*

After we hung up, I got back to work. In my basket were several dozen ears of sweet yellow corn still dripping wet from the rain, so I straightened up and organized the kitchen. I was energized, ready to shuck and cut corn all evening then maybe work on the tomatoes. The first shuck ripping had begun when Jonas's truck roared up into the yard. He burst in the back door a few seconds later, wet from the rain and a little wild eyed. After he looked around the room at the fixings for corn canning, he settled down then sighed and started muttering under his breath. "*Aazai* ... hells bells Stella, I thought you were in some kinda trouble." He stood with his hands on the back of a kitchen chair, shaking his head. "I was listening to the scanner and the dispatcher sent a deputy up here to check on an alien something or other."

I kept right on shucking and wondered if he would figure out that he could help, too. "Good, I will be glad to get another opinion."

"On what?"

"On the thing in my yard that I think dropped out of a space ship." He moved to the door and stared outside.

"Where is it?"

"In the shed, where it can't hurt anything or anybody."

Jonas bolted out the door. I had just finished an ear of corn, so I put it in the pan to wash, shook the silks from my apron into the basket of corn shucks, grabbed a windbreaker with a hood and headed off into the rain to show him the pod.

The shed felt cozy, rain pattering on the metal roof and the gasoline, grassy smell of old lawnmowers. Tension from Jonas was ruining the mood though as I felt around on the top shelf for the old metal lunchbox. I opened it and held the Ziploc bag by one corner to show him. He walked around it looking but he didn't offer to take it.

"Do you think it is a bug of some sort?" he asked, studying it intently, one hand on his chin.

I jiggled the bag a little to tease him. Jonas didn't like bugs. "No bug here, big man. I really don't know what it is. It sure doesn't look like anything I've ever seen with my own eyes or even read about. Wanna touch it? I opened the Ziploc and dumped it in his big cupped hands.

"Looks like petrified dog *anak*." Jonas rubbed his thumb over it gently. "But these scales are weird." He continued to handle it then brought it up to his nose to smell it. I was afraid he might taste it too and I thought that was taking too much of a chance so I interrupted.

"No, it's not dog poop, too light weight. What does it smell like?"

Jonas thought hard. "I have smelled it before but I can't place it. Not pine or laurel, but something from the woods."

About then, a police car rolled up to the open shed door and young Deputy Long waved before he dashed through the rain to join us.

"Hey Stella. Jonas." He nodded. "What do we have here?" We showed him and he turned it over and over, listening to our ideas. "Guess I better take it to Dave Dalton, he's the MoCo extension agent and he might recognize it."

I doubted it, but it would be a good start. "Be careful with it, it might be dangerous," I warned. The lunchbox was offered up as a secure container but he declined, zipped the baggie shut, and was on his way.

Jonas put his jacket over both our heads and we hurried through the pouring rain back to the kitchen. He shucked corn and I cooked a big supper. All was right with the world in my kitchen, at least for the moment.

Chapter 13
August: The Threat

I dreaded getting up Sunday morning, but I drug out of bed anyway and cleaned myself up. I dressed in yesterday's clothes to feed the dogs and goats, enjoyed a cup of cocoa on the deck, then headed upstairs, put on my Sunday best and left two hours early to go see Anna.

The mountain road glowed like a wet watercolor painting. It was a moist, balmy morning and a few red and yellow leaves were showing off their new fall colors brightened by the rain. The dark, wet tree trunks on either side of the dirt road stood out in contrast. I stopped once in the road where sunlight was streaming through the branches like arrows and thought that this was a better place to worship than church. I sat there a bit before heading to Anna's house. I figured I'd be late for church, but it didn't seem important.

Anna's front screen door was rattling around a little in the warm breeze, but she heard me and called out her usual "Come on in, Stella." She was all dressed and ready for church but I couldn't persuade her to go with me. That little woman was hard headed. We talked for a while and prayed again and I helped her as best I could. I was truly glad to spend time with her but I didn't stay long and I left in a hurry for church. When I left, I glanced around the porch and noticed some of her potted plants were knocked over and dirt had spilled out. *Raccoons or Timmy Lee?*

I sat at the steering wheel a long time with my head on the steering wheel, maybe ten minutes, before I turned the key and backed out in the road to head in the direction I had come. My body ached and my head hurt. I tried to tell myself that I was thinking about Anna, but I was also stalling because I didn't want to face Timmy Lee. I sighed. What was done was done and it was time to move on. My body didn't agree. I was shaking and my stomach was in knots when I pulled into the church parking lot. My mind overruled my body and I charged right on into the sanctuary, grabbing a bulletin on the way in.

Reverend Booth was reading the scripture. I had only missed the call to worship, the joys and concerns, and the opening hymn. I was there in time for the sermon and the offering. The Methodist Church services stay on the agenda. I opened my Bible to follow along and figured most everyone else was, too. As the preacher started his sermon my eyes searched around the room for Timmy Lee and found the back of his head way up front. I could see a little shaved place stained red with Mercurochrome around a centerpiece of thick black stiches. I smiled but had the decency to cover my mouth with my hand pretty quick. The sight of him didn't cause white spots to appear or stomach cramps but I wouldn't go so far as to say I was glad to see him. I was pretty happy that our confrontation, well, it was mostly my confrontation not ours, hadn't ended up with me facing murder charges. I tried to be sorry that the cross had busted his head but figured God saw right through that phony confession. Then I stared at his head. It was shaped like my Daddy's head, with the same hairline, a little point in the middle of his neck. It set me back to think of Timmy Lee as being part of my beloved father. I studied my hands and wondered if my Daddy had lived to be as old as I was, would his hands have looked like mine?

Chapter 13

I thought about the day of Daddy's accident. I could still see the red Formica kitchen tabletop where Timmy Lee and I were eating breakfast, well, I was eating and my ungrateful brother was complaining because he wanted donuts and we were having cream of wheat. Daddy insisted that we have warm food in our belly before we took off down the hill to the bus stop. Timmy Lee never whined to Daddy but as soon as he was alone with Mom and me he invariably moaned and pouted for something he wanted and couldn't have. I don't think Mom cared what we ate but she followed the rules Daddy set, at least until that day.

Daddy was in the barn milking just like every other day, the difference was that he hadn't come in to tell us goodbye before we left for school. He didn't come and he didn't come and I was watching the clock, real nervous because I didn't want to miss the bus, but I had a heavy feeling, too, like things were never going to be the same.

"Mom, I'll go check on him," I offered and she nodded, looking out the door towards the barn. I ran over the frosty ground to the barn and called, "Daddy, Daddy" over and over but only contented chewing and shuffling of cows answered. I darted by every stall and finally found him in the last one; his body mangled and bloody stuck under the skid-steer loader bucket. I guess he was already dead, but I hugged him and screamed and tried to get him to speak or squeeze my hand, but there was nothing. Then, I begged him to take me with him because somehow I knew my life was going to get tough real fast. I remember looking at the yellow machinery to see how I could get killed, too, but I didn't try.

Ages later, I stumbled to the house, all over blood and told my mom that he was dead, to please call the police. She went screaming upstairs and Timmy Lee just sat there, I guess what you would call "in shock" these days. I took over, interrupting a conversation on our party line, "Excuse me, could I please call the police. My daddy is dead." And the two early morning gossipers hung up. The police came and then the coroner and they took Daddy to the funeral home.

Mommy wouldn't come out until the next day even though I pounded and pounded on her bedroom door. I sat in the floor leaning against her locked door, crying until I hiccupped myself to sleep that afternoon. Timmy Lee woke me up because he was hungry and I fixed sandwiches for us.

That night, some neighbors came with more food. It was the end of my childhood, that day was. Timmy Lee was 12 and I had just turned 9.

#

I refocused when the choir sang and was alert for the offering and the hymn of invitation. During announcements, Timmy Lee thanked everyone for helping with the fundraiser and nodded as his head swiveled all around the congregation. Our eyes met and I stared him down. No one else would've noticed the recognition, but I saw it behind his eyes. Shadowing the friendly expression for the church people, his eyes held a dark promise for me. If he were in a place where he could've, he would have detailed his threat aloud. Instead, he started rubbing his thumb against his other fingers and flashed a circle at me over the pew then stretched his arm and scratched his head with his middle finger. The warning was there, in his eyes and in that finger motion. He told the details of the upcoming Fall Festival and urged each of us to contribute time, crafts, food, and prayers. I began breathing again as he sat down. I hadn't realized that I was holding my breath as he spoke. '*Why don't we just give you everything we have,* I thought as I rose for the musical benediction.

"Surely the presence of the Lord is in this place, I can feel His power and His grace. I can hear the rush of angel wings, I see joy in every face, surely the presence of the Lord is in this place." I hoped so. The words I heard at the end of services every Sunday usually empowered and lifted me, but today I knew that there was another power on the move in my church.

Chapter 14
August: Making Money

The threat in my brother's eyes was burned into my brain, but I was coping pretty well. I can't say that I felt good after church that Sunday, but I didn't feel like shooting anyone, always a plus. Exhaustion had settled in and was bordering on paranoia. I needed to believe that my church and community and friends would insulate me from him.

The bookkeeping was piling up so I buckled down and got my customers' accounts updated by mid-week. I went to the Wednesday night services, deciding to darn sure not let Timmy Lee's warning keep me from my routine. *And I am going to do it with a smile,* I vowed to myself on the way to church. Like a cowardly biting dog, my brother sniffs out fear and preys on it. I spoke out loud as I drove. "As God is my witness, I am never going to run away from him again." I shook my fist at the sky. *Shades of Scarlett O'Hara,* I thought and laughed at the self-made drama I was starring in.

The service was unremarkable; the only news was reminders to stop in the alcove outside the sanctuary as you left. There were lists of items needed for the fall festival and sign-up sheets for those who were willing to take responsibility for a church activity booth or those who had their own merchandise to sell but would pay a fee for the space.

I needed a boost and decided that it would be fun to rent a space with Tisha again this year and so I stopped afterwards in the foyer to sign us up. I would need to be there to count the deposit anyway, so I might as well take part. Tisha made delicious baked goods and colorful wreaths from ribbons. Our area was torn during football season between Virginia Tech and WVU fans so there were many "houses divided" with two school loyalties in the same family. One of Tisha's specialties was a wreath with WVU blue and gold loops on one side and VT's maroon and orange ribbons on the other side. She completed the decoration with logos for both schools. Many football school wreaths graced front doors during autumn. She also made fall wreaths in orange and yellow and brown with little scarecrows and acorns.

With my extra apple butter and applesauce and baggies of dried apples, we'd have a nice variety of items. Maybe I could make some old timey cornhusk dolls before the festival, too. I leaned over and added our names to the list. I glanced at the names already on it and saw homemade bread, dried flowers, painted gourds, and fried apple pies. It was going to be a wonderful afternoon and as I laid down the pencil, I hoped Timmy Lee was taking his "media" job seriously and advertising the event properly. When I looked up, there he was at the door watching me.

I swallowed down my shriek and met his angry eyes with a sugar sweet greeting, "Well, hello there Mr. Davis. How is your poor head? I noticed you had stitches. What in the world happened?" Others stopped to hear his answer and I breathed again waiting with them. Oh, he was so caught, wanting to be evil, but he couldn't in front of others with a lady inquiring so thoughtfully about his injury. He only hesitated a moment before flashing a big toothy smile – and a gold crown that I didn't remember, "The Lord works in mysterious ways, ma'am." He took my hand in both of his and I nearly passed out. "Would you please pray for me?" All I could think was *Oh, hell, no!* but I was quick witted enough to stammer, "I bet the Lord already knows just what you need, but I'll pray that he takes care of you quickly." The way he was bullying Anna came to mind and I slid my sweaty hand out from between his. He nodded his head at the little group heading out the door and turned tail. Score one small victory for me. I visited as long as I could fake my usual conversation with the other ladies before I hurried on trembling legs to my car.

The next morning, I was cleaning up in the kitchen and I showed Sugar the door so she wouldn't be underfoot. Comet and Windex were lined up on the counter and I was reaching under the sink for a bucket when I heard Sugar barking like the devil himself was in the back yard. I peeked out between the venetian blinds on the back door and lo and behold it was

Timmy Lee, just sitting in his car. Sugar had her front paws under the driver's door and was baying like only a redbone hound could. Timmy was motioning her away and pounding on the window under her paws but she didn't catch on. She attacked most every movement that Timmy made, pouncing on his window with big muddy paws.

What to do? If I went out and called Sugar off, he would get out, and then what? What did he want? I hadn't taken the gun permit class yet, so I didn't want to shoot at him because Jonas would be even madder but maybe if I shot in my own yard it wouldn't matter.

It seemed cowardly to ignore the whole situation, but that is what I did. I took the steps two at a time like I was a teenager and wondered if I would be sore the next day. I stretched out in the upstairs bedroom floor where I could raise up every now and then and see what was happening. Really didn't have to look much, just listened to Sugar howling and heard Timmy Lee's muffled cussing through the crack in the window where he was trying to reason with that dog. Should've videoed it and put it on YouTube so the world could see what a devout man of God he was. Anyway, I got stiff and cold lying in the floor after a while and tiptoed back downstairs and started scrubbing the sink, very quietly.

Finally, Timmy Lee gave up and turned the car around in the yard and sailed on back out the road, spewing gravel and dust behind him. Sugar trotted back to the deck and collapsed, she was exhausted after howling and bothering him for twenty minutes. I shook my head at her, just like me, she was getting old.

After I finished in the kitchen, I relaxed on the recliner for a few minutes with some Fritos and a cold Dr. Pepper before calling Tisha. I needed a change in mood. "Hey, girl, we got ourselves a money making opportunity on Saturday week – my church is having their Fall Festival."

"Saw it on the evening news on Channel 6, I think it was on Monday. You Methodists are working the TV and the radio. Joey heard it announced on KNRV, too. I figured we would do it again, so I bought my stuff today and I'll bake tomorrow night and until late on Friday."

"How about wreaths? You got any extras to sell?"

"Oh, honey, have I got wreaths?! They are everywhere in this house, can't stack them up or the ribbons'll get squashed. I probably have two dozen ready to go, even a few for Christmas in case anybody can think past football and Thanksgiving. So, yes, I am so ready. Jesse needs to buy new tires before he comes home for Christmas so every little bit helps. What is your *spe-she-al-e-tee* this year?"

"Nothing too exciting, apple butter and applesauce, and dried apples. What do you think about corn husk dolls?"

"I wouldn't bother. They take too long to make and everybody oohs and ahhs but nobody buys them. How about lemonade from real lemons? That sells good at the state fair. We paid $3 for one big Solo cup, of course it was real hot that day and we would've drunk creek water if it had had ice in it."

"Hmmmm." I thought about loading lemons and sugar and lemon squeezers and pitchers and buying cups and cold temperatures and came up with another idea. "Cider! Tisha, I could buy it in those gallon jugs and just pour cups as they order, could have ice for cold and a crockpot for warm, maybe throw in some cinnamon to make our table smell nice."

"That's a good idea!" She caught my enthusiasm, or maybe I was just high on having faced down Timmy Lee. "And how would you feel if I invited Eliza to join us? She made some cute birdhouses from barn wood this summer. I bet she would share a table with us." Eliza worked with Tisha at the school. She was good company and had wonderful problem solving skills, a good thing because her job was full of difficulties, not to mention her life, most related to her thirteen siblings. Suffice it to say Eliza knew her way around the court system and all the other local government agencies. And she shared what she knew; she was a veritable reference book of practical information.

"Oh, yes, bring Eliza. That will cut back our share of the table fees, too." I was truly looking forward to Saturday afternoon now, the camaraderie and the little bit of money we would make. We ended our conversation and I started my list – ice, cider, cups, cinnamon, crockpot and ladle, apple stuff, and a fall tablecloth.

Chapter 14

I unscrewed the cap on my bottle of pop for another swig in preparation for the next phone call. Tisha didn't know about Timmy Lee or much about my life before Lindside although she had been asking little questions about my high school and family for many years. I needed to hear Jonas's voice now, needed to let him know that I had stood up to Timmy Lee and get his take on the action.

The next decision was which phone to call. We were having a time with our belated entrance into the Star Trek world of cell phones. When we were home we both used the landline, but when we left the house we tried to carry our cells. I was even slower than Jonas to catch on. My phone scared me half to death every time it rang, and I forgot it at home on the charger as often as I remembered it. I did have it in my pants pocket that time I fell in the sinkhole, thank goodness, or I guess I would still be stuck there. If Jonas was working outside, he might be carrying his cell, so I tried that first.

He answered on the fourth ring. "Hallo."

"Hey sweet baby," I cooed. He chuckled.

"Might wanna make this snappy, helping Ben McDaniel vaccinate cows and there's not a lot of time for sweet nothings in the mud here." I could hear loud mooing and squishing of muck and could almost smell the steamy cows.

"I'll call later." I laughed as the phone clicked without another word and imagined it sliding into the pocket of his soft worn Carhartt coveralls. I sighed contentedly. My life was so good, why in the world was I so afraid of Timmy Lee?

Chapter 15
August: Jonas and the Pod

I pulled the lever on the side of the recliner, pushed the back of the chair with my rear as far as it would go and stretched out. Must've fallen asleep because I jumped awake as the wooden screen door slammed shut. Jonas's grinning face peered from the kitchen and he extended a bouquet of goldenrod in my direction.

Yawning, I gathered my wits and went to meet him. The flowers were just about done, seeds were dripping off, but I carried on about them and found a big crystal vase and filled it with water. If they had been hothouse roses, they wouldn't have been treated any better.

"Thought you were going to call .... " Jonas came up for air after we kissed.

Still in his arms and resenting the lull in the action, I nuzzled his neck noticing that his hair was damp and fragrant. He had showered after working the cows. "I went to sleep," I admitted, "but I'd rather see you than talk on the phone so it all worked out."

We moved to the oak table in the kitchen, the second best place for us to talk. I found some sausage biscuits left over from breakfast and reheated them. "I stood up to Timmy Lee this morning after church." I served up two huge biscuits. "Do you want some gravy or apples with those?"

Jonas already had a mouthful and he held up one finger. I understood that meant he could talk in one minute. He swallowed. "Yes, please, gravy AND apples." I scurried around stirring up some gravy and opening a jar of canned apples. No doubt about his priorities. In our early years together it would have hurt my feelings when he clearly thought more about food than whatever current obstacle I faced. Now, many hurt feelings and cross words later, I knew that I would have his full attention once his belly was full. At this point, I even think I throw things in the conversation just to watch him percolate on them while he eats. Not really payback but entertainment.

And so it was. He squirmed a bit in thought and ate two plates of biscuits while I wiped up crumbs and ran the dishwater then flipped on the ceiling light. Summer was over, it was getting dark early, not yet 6:30.

He pushed back his chair from the table and his plate, sopped clean of apples and gravy with the last bite of biscuit, "Stood up how?"

I replayed the scene from church and he chuckled. "So you've settled on a happy medium, somewhere between shooting him and hating him from afar? Just going to aggravate him until he gives you hateful looks?"

"Yep." The kitchen was restored, dishes drying in the rack. I sat down at the table and continued, "That look scared me. When we were kids that angry look was always, and I mean every single time, just before something very bad happened. I knew something was going to happen but the thing nearly always surprised me. Like when he killed my cat ... he loved that cat, too, but it was worth it to him to give it up to hurt me. He was cruel and I don't think that has changed." I shook my head.

"A concealed weapons class is being offered at Dove Gun Shop in Princeton next weekend." Jonas's eyes were steady looking into mine.

I snorted.

"It lasts two hours and cost $50." His tone was so serious that I sobered up.

"But there's the Fall Festival. You know I'm planning to sell all day with Tisha and Eliza."

He did know and didn't miss a beat. "There's another one at the Glen Lyn Church of Christ the weekend after next at 9 AM. Same length of time, same money."

"Pretty sad state of affairs when churches are hosting gun classes. What is the world coming to?" He had no answer for that, so I changed things around. "Why do I need a class? I can shoot pretty well."

"Bad side effect of carrying a gun illegally is jail time." He leaned back in his chair and crossed his arms still looking at me. I knew it would be best to just do it. White-haired old lady in a gun class would stand out, no doubt.

"Okay, okay. I'll go." Once I gave up the fight, I actually looked forward to the class. I thought about the kinds of characters might I meet taking the class and felt strangely excited.

I must've shivered because Jonas pulled me to my feet and hugged me. He whispered, "All that ends well is well." When he twisted old sayings around, I didn't know if it was because English was his second language, if he was teasing me, or if he was so smart that he could change the words to seem wiser. Tonight he seemed like a very wise man.

We walked up the stairs, arms around each other's waist.

My cell phone's musical ring woke me the next morning. I was so proud to be able to figure out and set ring tones. "You Can Leave Your Hat On" played when Jonas called, although I tried to answer before the lyrics start when there were others around. Anna's calls rang the Golden Girls theme song, "Thank You for Being a Friend," and "Born to Be Wild" played when Tisha called. I didn't know if they would like the songs I chose but I did; it tickled me when they played. For everyone else's calls, there was a snappy little beach tune. It kept on playing while I scrambled out of bed. I didn't leave it on my nightstand because I had read that cell phone vibes could cause cancer if they stayed too close to your head for too long. I used the speaker button a lot.

Anyway, I looked at the caller ID and the clock at about the same time, a split second before answering. Eight o'clock on the dot. It was from the Monroe County Sheriff's office.

"Stella, this is Deputy Long."

"Good morning, everything okay up there in the big city of Union?"

"Yes, ma'am. Just calling to let you know we got a report back on that pod that you found a while ago."

"And ...?" I enjoyed the delicious pause, re-imagining all the possibilities: space junk or a tiny Russian warhead were my best two guesses.

He cleared his throat. I stopped breathing.

"Stella, it hatched."

"What?" I gasped. "Into what?" Again, my mind did cartwheels. Alien life forms, killer bugs, poison snakes ....

Mercifully, he continued. "Says here that it was a Sphinx Moth pupa. 'Extremely large specimen.' Said they are found near tomatoes."

"Well, my, my, my," was all I could come up with.

"Will you be wanting a copy of the report?"

"Oh, yes, please." We continued on with jibber jabber and I thanked him but truth be told, I had a little trouble digesting the news. I pressed the red button to end the call. It had taken me weeks to remember to do that after each call and I felt lucky I hadn't said anything about any caller that they had mistakenly heard.

Jonas's side of the bed was empty, but I knew he hadn't left. I found him in the kitchen fixing a tray of toast and hot cocoa to bring to me in bed. Bless his sweet heart. I knew I would be in for a razzing when I told him the pod from outer space was a moth cocoon, so I didn't bring it up at first, just enjoyed supping the warm chocolate at the table. I guessed this was how old married couples felt, as cozy in the kitchen as in the bedroom. Before I knew it, I blurted out, "Jonas, I want to marry you."

The room became as silent as the grave. I swear that birds quit singing, Sugar stopped snoring in her corner spot, the icemaker in the refrigerator decided it had enough ice and we all waited for Jonas to speak, to do something. Instead, he hung his head.

I nibbled on my toast and the crunch sounded so loud that I swallowed that bite whole. Then I choked and ran to the sink for water. Tears, from being choked, ran down my red face as I stared at the man I loved. Too many conversations had ended without me being satisfied and I was ready to stand my ground. He looked up sheepishly.

"You know I want us to be together. Aren't you happy?"

"Oh, no, you don't. I've heard this one before. Asked and answered. Lessee, we had this talk in 1995, 1997, 2004, and 2010." I really didn't know the years, but figured I was close and he wouldn't question them.

"Stella, honey, you know I'm married. I can't marry you."

"Well, get unmarried. I'm getting old."

Those words hung in the air. He rubbed the back of his head.

"I can't find her, Stella. I've tried. I hired a private investigator and paid him to travel all over the country, to Alaska, to Texas, to Louisiana, even to San Diego, California where her family was supposed to be. No records, no voting, no debt collection, no warrants of criminal charges, no Facebook page, no income taxes filed. Nothing."

This was news to me and I was somewhat gratified, but my heels were dug in. "So, get a divorce anyway. Can't you file and post notices in the papers where she last lived?" I knew he could because I had just about worn out a computer researching this very thing. I kept staring at him, but he had turned and was looking out the window. I could see the frost in the grass outside and it strengthened me. It was the time of year for frost and it was time for us to quit living as if our love was wrong. Nature requires certain order and we were not in step; we were living unnatural lives. I saw that my knuckles clutching the back of the chair were white but I dared not relax.

He turned and spoke so sadly that my heart broke. "I can't. I can't divorce her without telling her. Myself. Yes, I know she wronged me. I know that she probably used me for a ticket off the slope." His face softened and his eyes glowed. "I stopped loving her a long time ago. I love you, Stella Francis Boswell. And I want to marry you, too."

Then he talked some stuff about doing what he had to do and shooting sick dogs yourself, but I didn't make any sense of it because I was in his arms holding my breath to will tears away. When I could talk again, I whispered, "The pod hatched." He held me at arm's length and I got tickled, plumb hysterical then he started grinning and we collapsed on the couch until we were spent from laughing. Then, we went back to bed.

Chapter 16
September: Fall Festival

I hit the floor running the morning of the Fall Festival with faint memories of a scrambled dream of money floating just out of reach. Must be worried about my own flat wallet. Anyway, in spite of my crazy dreams, I was primed and ready for festival day. The car was loaded, the dogs and goats were fed, and I was ready to go when I had a nagging feeling that I might need the gun. Couldn't imagine why, so I shook it off and headed to the church. Maybe the feeling was a reminder to sign up for the concealed weapons class, which I had not yet done. I wrote myself a mental note and hoped I would remember.

Tisha and Eliza had both arrived before me. Tisha stuck her tongue out at me above the stack of boxes in her arms. "Love you, too," I laughed.

Eliza hailed me in the parking lot, "Could you carry one box to empty my car so I can lock it?"

"Sure thing." She piled it on top of my load.

"Just look at those clouds, hope it doesn't rain and keep people away."

I nodded as we went inside. "Half the fun is socializing."

From out of our boxes and bins, the colors of autumn appeared. We smoothed pumpkin and maize patterned tablecloths, adjusting them neatly. The table filled with wreaths, birdhouses, baked goods, and apple products. We had a three-column system in a composition notebook for collecting money, one column for each of us. Finally, we taped prices everywhere and unfolded chairs to sit a spell before customers showed up.

Looking back on that day, I wonder how I could've been so blind. Maybe I was too caught up in the frenzy of the details of running a booth, having every little thing right. Could be that I was hungry for female companionship and was looking forward to Tisha and Eliza's company so much that I was oblivious. Also, as much as I hated to admit it, I was aging (or possibly maturing) and I tended to ignore things that were not on my priority list. Whatever the reason, I was missing out on reality.

Our tables were colorful, our merchandise was good quality, priced right, and there was plenty of it. The three of us were friendly and attentive to customers. The reality was that people that I knew were ignoring me, walking by without a word or a glance at the wreaths or applesauce or birdhouses. When my apple products sold, it was to people that I didn't know. Tisha and Eliza had lively conversations with several friends, but not me. I stayed busy, though, rearranging items, making change, and readying the bags for sales. Between customers, we visited and got everything talked about.

Late in the day it was the usual thing to trade goods with other vendors. I spied Regina William's table of homemade baked goods early and was hoping to trade any leftover apple butter for loaves of bread if she had any that didn't sell. As folks were starting to pack up, I went over with two jars of apple butter to offer for bread, but I couldn't get her attention. Regina was talking to someone and didn't seem to notice me so I retreated back to my table, but I watched until she was free then I hurried back across the room. Someone must have caught her eye in the distance because she walked right by me as I approached her.

"Oh, well," I thought, "It wasn't meant to be." At least Timmy Lee wasn't there. I figured the media director or fund-raiser or whatever he was, should be at all church functions, but he was strangely missing. Not that I missed him. All the logic in the world didn't seem to change my fear and anger. Jonas was trying to change my thinking. He had put a bug in my ear about facing down or letting go of my hatred of Timmy Lee. Jonas's idea that Timmy Lee was the only living person who shared my DNA and the memories of my childhood was good food for thought. I'd love to reminisce about the few happy childhood times, if only he wasn't so dang mean and I wasn't still scared of him.

Chapter 16

All in all, the Lindside UMC Fall Festival was a good thing. We all earned a little spending money and the church made a pile of cash. I counted the church money with the preacher, the procedure done by the book, as always. One real positive note was that Tisha and Eliza and I planned a lunch date for Thursday and I could hardly wait.

It wasn't a romantic dinner with Jonas, but it would be fun. We were going to Pearisburg to eat at "The Bank," a swanky place in a remodeled version of the old stone bank. Funny how the new banks in Princeton were sprawling, two story modern buildings. I'd rather put my money in a little stone building. More secure to my way of thinking.

The bookkeeping went real quick on Monday and Tuesday and by Wednesday, I was raring to gussy up and go out to eat after school on Thursday. The garden and the apples were all put up. I had black walnuts to crack but that could

be done anytime, no rush there. I decided to pick up a few things at the grocery store Wednesday morning and maybe get a haircut at the Curl Up & Dye if Julie, my regular haircutter, had a time available today.

At Grant's Market, I saw several regulars from church and I waved at each of them but no one seemed to have time to chat. Probably for the best, I could get wound up and take too long to shop. On the way home, I stopped at Curl Up & Dye and Julie was her usual bubbly self, and she had time to cut my hair right away. She gave me the entire local scoop, including the fact that the mayor had refused in advance to scrape any snow in the beauty shop parking lot this winter. He had done it for free for years but was bowing out this year unless they decided to pay him. I understood the business end of that, but Julie and the other beauticians were downright cranky about it. Then we talked about the town moocher and her opinion had not changed – poor ole Sandra who asked everyone who parked downtown for a dollar was pitiful. The latest was that she had even asked a man carrying a fresh baked custard pie from Hometown Restaurant for a piece of that perfection. We had heard that her husband locked her out of the house until she brought back her daily quota of money and she was probably hungry. So sad. Then Julie reported that a Monroe County church had suffered a big theft and we both *tsked* the ornery people in this world that would steal from a church of all places.

The next morning I washed and blow-dried my short hair. It always felt nice to get rid of all those tiny hair clippings after a haircut. My clothes were clean and mostly wrinkle free and I put them on and headed to the Lindside School mid-afternoon to pick up the girls for our evening out. We giggled and told tales all the way to Pearisburg, a thirty-minute drive on a glorious sun-drenched afternoon.

"Tisha, tell Stella about that volunteer that got caught stealing from the library's bazaar," Eliza prompted as we neared The Bank.

"Oh, my God," Tisha gasped, "You would not believe how bold he was. And I was there and I watched him. A customer gave him a twenty and he laid it by the cash box and made change, then he slipped the twenty in his pants pocket."

"So what did you do?" I pulled into a parking place and Tisha kept telling the story.

"Well, I tell you what, I wasn't gonna stand there and watch a thief take money from the library. They don't have enough money to pay the heat bill some winters and it just wasn't right. So I told him to sit down and I yelled for Colette, you know the new director, to come and search the no-good thief."

"Yes, there's three of us," Eliza told the hostess, a cute young thing with her blond hair in a tight bun wearing a crisp white shirt and perfectly fitting black slacks. We followed her to our booth while Tisha yakked on.

"And then that sucker had the nerve to tell me that it was his twenty which was a dang lie and then Colette just put out her hand and he dug down deep in his pocket and pulled it out and gave it to her. That woman stared him down until he turned red and started to cry and it seemed that her angry switch was flipped on went he started blubbering. She pointed at the door and screamed 'GET OUT, YOU ARE FIRED.' Whew! I was so traumatized that I didn't know what to do. I was afraid that he might have a gun and would hurt us. I just acted without thinking and applauded and chased him out the front clapping behind him like I was shooing a puppy or something."

Tisha was pretty excited reliving the whole experience but she calmed some when we got our elegant six page menus. "What are y'all gonna get?" She read through the entrees.

"Do we want drinks, oh, how about a glass of wine? Stella? Eliza?"

It was really hard to read the menu, make a decision and get in a word edgewise, but we finally decided on a white wine, duck breasts, wild rice and butternut squash stuffed with cranberries and apple bits.

Tisha kept us laughing with stories from school. "Remember Stacy Williams? He was a foster child in his aunt's home and she got paid to keep him and his sorry mama came and fought her sister for the money because he was her kid?" Yes, we remembered and both of us shook our heads at the memory, but Tisha plowed on. "Well, he went on the fourth grade field trip to the movies over at Beckley and the teachers were waiting for the students to get their popcorn and pop for the movie but they weren't allowing them to go into the arcade right there in the lobby. So they keep shooing the little things back to the theater, but Stacy and Andre are fooling around the change machine. Somehow those two have come up with a few dollar bills and they are struggling to put them in the slot and get their quarters. Old Miss Dunbar goes over and tells them to get back to the theater, that it is time, and they beg to stay. Stacy says, 'Miss Dunbar you gotta let us stay here and play this game.' Little fat Andre is nodding his head behind him. Arms outstretched and stomping his little work boots, Stacy begs, 'We are winning every single time!' Oh, Lord, Dunbar says she had to put on her mad face and point to the theater but she was about to burst out laughing as those two high rollers trudged down the hallway to join their classmates."

I laughed and laughed. "Poor little boys, I bet they spent all their concession money playing the change machine. Oh, but they still had their money, didn't they. Well, poor little boys with no sense."

That just got Tisha wound up again. "Let me tell you about a third grader who brought the spelling bee word list back to the teacher and asked for another list 'cause her list was in Spanish,' that her mom said so. The teacher asked for her list and looked it over. It was in English, that girl's mom just couldn't read the hard words. Oh, mercy ...." I cracked up and so did Eliza, but we ended up feeling sad because how are children ever going to get ahead when their parents can't read the 3rd grade spelling bee list?

We hushed long enough for the duck to melt in our mouths. The food was so good but the servings were smaller than our usual, so we had room for dessert, two pumpkin fritters for Tisha and me and an apple cinnamon cheesecake for Eliza. We ate those in silence, too. By the time my plate was clean, I was so full I just leaned back in my chair. Both women were waiting for me to finish up.

"We need to tell you something," Eliza began. "You need to know what people are saying." I can only imagine how blank my face looked. There was not a concern in my empty head. I licked a tiny smear of fritter filling from my lip and raised my eyebrows in interest, face and heart open for the next news report.

Tisha joined the mission, "A bunch of money is missing from your church, like several thousand dollars' worth."

"What?" I felt my face start to flush at the proximity of this event. "Why, where is it?" I looked from Tisha to Eliza.

"People are saying that you took it." Eliza rested her forehead on her hand supported by her elbow on the table. I had a fleeting thought that she shouldn't have her elbow on the table, but mostly I was sick.

"We know that isn't true, but that is what is going around town. We didn't know if you knew, but if you didn't, we wanted you to at least know about it." Tisha brushed crumbs off the table with the linen napkin.

"I didn't know." I managed to mumble while an icy shard of hate and fear grazed my heart.

"I told you so." Tisha pointed at Eliza "She had no idea in this world why those goody-two-shoes church members were giving her the cold shoulder on Saturday."

"Honey, we are so sorry." Eliza took my hand in hers. "Anybody that knows you knows that this is just a big ole lie."

I allowed myself one long, stuttering sigh, wiped my eyes with the fancy napkin, figured it wouldn't stain, and realized in the same moment that I felt the pain that Timothy Lee Davis was setting me up.

After the ride back to Peterstown, I waved good-bye to my friends and allowed as how my world had slowed down. I drove home slowly. Even the rhythm of my blinker before I turned up Wilson Mill Road to the mountain seemed to be in slow motion. Partial paralysis had set in.

Chapter 17
September: Facing Facts

That night I lay in bed reliving all the things I had done to get away from Timmy Lee. *Trudging through the summer fog to the Atlanta bus station when I should've been at a graduation party. Riding a bus through the dark to anywhere to get away. Leaving my crazy momma and my dear grandma and grandpa. Taking a dead baby's name for mine. Learning how to do for myself and make a living all alone.*

I put my arm over my forehead and felt sorry for myself just long enough for common sense to kick in. *C'mon Penelope Ann,* I reverted to my birth name for the first time in a very long time, *quit yer whining. Your body is sound and mostly, your mind is, too. Figure out how he stole the money. You knew he was going to, think about how he could've and prove it. The truth will come out, just give it a nudge.* Once I sorted it out, I relaxed, rolled over, and went to sleep.

The sun rose again and I was not awake to greet it. Nope, no church for me today, 8:00 AM found me on the deck, my fleece robe belt pulled tight around my waist. I would not need to dress; this day was devoted to thinking. Planning and plotting. Gathering information. I had an empty spiral bound notebook that I had bought at Wal-Mart during their back-to-school sale and I was taking notes and making lists.

Every now and then I threw the notebook down. Sometimes I stood gripping the deck rail and stared off into the trees on the mountain. Sometimes I hung my head and groaned. Finally, I went upstairs and grabbed my dependable cold steel friend, the Pink Lady, little *Utukkuu,* and fired off a couple of shots at a target nailed to a tree on the edge of the mowed grass. The noise startled the dogs and the chickens and the goats all fainted and I was sorry, but it made me smile. Just what I needed, a big roar that I controlled. Now maybe I could think.

A self-improvement book had caught my eye in a bookstore once and I had read a few pages on the subject of not worrying about what others thought. The actual quote was something like,"What other people think about you is none of your business. "That was strengthening right now because I really did care what my church friends thought of me and I had to save the pain of facing them for later. From experience I knew my will to survive was strong but during this long morning after, it seemed like the urge for revenge was no small part of my spirit either. I reasoned that if I didn't care what others thought, I wouldn't need payback. But I did. Surely that need would lessen as time went on. Surely.

I made a list of questions.

1. How much money was missing?
2. Who discovered it missing?
3. What event earned the money?
4. What debts did Timmy Lee have?
5. How did my name become involved?

Then I marked out the last one because I would never know, Timmy Lee wasn't that dumb. When he spoke, I knew he would arch his eyebrow or pause at the right time just so the listener thought they had come up with the idea that I could be the thief. He didn't have to ever say my name, just choose which word he said a little harder or slower. Yep, he was smart, but he would eventually mess up.

The money couldn't be stolen from the Sunday offering. The Methodist Church doesn't even allow the offering plates to rest on the altar for the rest of the service; they have to be removed right now. If the ushers were thieves, they would have to pocket the money in the hallway between the sanctuary and the nursery classroom where two adults count the money. Most of the offering is personal checks anyway. No large amount of money could be missing there.

There had been a number of benefit dinners during late summer and fall. Plus the big fundraiser that was supposed to help with Timmy Lee's salary. That was the evening I had tried to shoot him. *Oh, my* I thought as my blood ran cold. Eleven grand, give or take, I had counted it and deposited it myself. But who had given it to me? Think, think, think. The cash bag was in the towel drawer when I left. Timmy Lee was passed out cold in the floor. How could he have shorted the money? It had to have been before I took aim at him.

I sighed with a bit of relief. *He was stealing before he knew I was his sister. His revenge was just sticking me with his crime. I didn't cause him to steal; I just gave him a convenient scapegoat. Shoulda shot him when I had the chance.*

Looked at my watch; it was 10:30. If I hurried, I could make church on time, take my seat, and focus on Godly things instead of wanting to shoot Timmy Lee. Plus, I could investigate the missing funds, confront the preacher about it and find out more about the situation.

My robe flew one way and my gown drifted to the floor in the other direction. I could dress and clean up in seven minutes when I tried. Even had time to dab on some lipstick and rip out my page of questions and stuff them in my purse before I dashed to my faithful Subaru and headed down the mountain.

Church was just a-buzzing when I entered and self-centered fool that I am, I thought it was all talk about me so I ignored it until Sally Spencer grabbed my arm. "When is the last time you talked to Anna Bradford?" I blinked and tried to make sense of the question.

"Why, here at church. No, wait, I drove over there a couple of Sundays ago on the way to church. Why?"

"Oh, honey, Anna is dead. They found her body in her bed last night. Been dead a while."

"Oh, no." I needed to put my hand on the back of the pew for balance. After a few deep breaths I found my way down the center aisle and slid over to my seat. The preacher opened with Joys and Concerns and a request for prayer for Anna's family. The Lord only knows what the rest of the service was about, I just rose when everyone else did and sat down when everybody else was seated.

Afterwards, I sought out Sally again. Anna's death was foremost in my mind now, but I did have a list of questions about the theft and a need for answers. "Has the administrative board dealt with missing church money?" She looked away and that was my answer. "Sally, how much is missing?" She held up three fingers and looked around as if it was a secret and she didn't want to be caught telling it. I thanked her, avoided the crowd and spared Sally the embarrassment of being seen with me by ducking out the side door. My mind was reeling with the discovery of Anna's death and Timmy Lee's dishonesty. It took two days of pondering before I connected the two.

Actually, it was something that Jonas reported that drew the unspeakable line between Timmy Lee and Anna. We were heading down to Wickline's Funeral Home for Anna's wake when he mentioned that Anna had left her little house to the church. That spun my head around. "What? She has two daughters and one of them with kids and in the middle of a big ugly divorce. Her girls need that house and she knew it."

"Just telling you what I heard. The ambulance guys said that her will was on the kitchen table, had just been changed in her own handwriting." Jonas maneuvered his big Ford 350 into the parking lot. "Anna must've been feeling badly before she died."

"Huh," I grunted, "most people do." I was aggravated at this turn of events and was taking it out on Jonas. He unbuckled his seat belt and opened the door with one smooth movement, slammed it, and was almost to the funeral home by the time I caught up and touched his arm in apology.

"You know what I meant was that she must've known she was going to die, felt different or something," I said. "But she wouldn't have given the church her house when her girls need it," I paused. "And she wouldn't have asked me to borrow a gun or ... maybe ... she needed it for something else ... oh, my goodness, could she have wanted to shoot Timmy Lee, too?" We stopped at the podium where guests sign the book and stared at each other.

Just then, Brooke, her younger daughter, greeted us. "'Preciate y'all coming. Momma sure liked you Stella, and you too, Jonas." Brooke's eyes and face looked like she had been crying for the two days since her mom had been found, but she was doing a good job tonight greeting her mother's friends. She had gained a little weight since I had seen her last, but every curl was in place, her dress fit nicely, and she looked like the small town girl who had conquered the world and had returned home victorious. Her black shiny hair sure reminded me of her daddy. She ushered us into the viewing parlor where a pink metal coffin was surrounded by baskets and sprays of colorful fall flowers. The lid was closed and a framed 8 X 10 photograph of Anna was set on the lid beside the family flower blanket. Guess being dead for several days in the warm days of fall doesn't give the undertaker much to work with, beauty-wise. I was disappointed, though, I wanted to see her, whatever was left. Made me doubt she was dead or something. The flowers were real nice, and I walked around and checked who had sent every arrangement.

I spoke to Charlene, the older sister, who was sitting alone by the wall rubbing her legs constantly like she had poison oak. I tried to comfort her, but she turned away from my attempt at a hug. The long sleeves of her wrinkled blouse mostly covered her tattoos. Tattoos don't seem to improve much with age, I was noticing in those I could still see. When I asked her how she was doing, she snapped, "Just great." But that was all I got out of her. It was startling to see how much she looked like her mother when she raised her eyes, full of pain, to see us. Anna hadn't had the dark circles and bruises that Charlene had tried to hide with make-up. Jeremy wasn't there. I figured that he was partying at his brother's place.

After we had made our rounds, we took a seat in a folding chair in the front room and visited with Calvin Weikle. "What was the official cause of death?" I asked softly. I knew he wouldn't think that it was really my business, but I had known Calvin since elementary Sunday School and had paddled his little rear more than once, so his black undertaker suit, shining shoes, and aloof solemn manner did not much intimidate me.

Calvin shook his head. Well, she was seventy-seven years old; she was in bed with no signs of struggle, no sign of forced entry. The front door was locked. The law didn't see any reason for concern, so no autopsy was performed. Probably a heart attack." He shrugged.

I felt like he didn't agree, something in the shrug was rebellious. "What do you think?" I whispered. He looked around the large room and hesitated before he spoke.

"I don't know, Miss Stella, something just wasn't right. Brooke had broken a window to go in and find her mom, and she said she didn't touch her or anything just touched her forehead, blew her a kiss, and called 911. Said the smell was pretty bad. When our boys and I got there, we found her with her cheek on the pillow in that big bed, covers pulled up to her shoulder."

"That's sounds normal."

"Yeah, but when we moved the blankets to put her on the gurney, she was wearing a nice dress, stockings and everything. Course it was pretty messy." He rubbed his neck. "But, I thought it felt funny." He stared at the floor them looked up at me. "I've said too much. Just getting suspicious in my old age. Keep that under your hat, will you? I know you and Anna were close and I've no right to stir things up." I nodded and thought, as I did at every wake or funeral, how hard it would be to be the undertaker in a small town, where you knew most everybody that you buried.

We stayed a while longer, some church folks came over to visit and I was grateful, knowing the rumors going around about me. Old Colonel Perdue was speaking loudly in the entrance and we all turned to hear him. "Well, there is a silver lining to poor Anna's death." He seemed to be trying to make his audience feel better, "Just as soon as the girls can get their mother's belongings out of the house, the church takes possession." He leaned back and smiled and spread his hand on his chest to orate further. "And the preacher has suggested that we lease it, at a very reasonable rate, to our media director, that nice Mr. Davis, so he will stay on."

Well, that confirmed the rumor Jonas had heard. I sat back so hard my head hit the wall. How had Timmy Lee pulled this one off? I didn't know how he did it, but I knew, to the core of my being, that he had done wrong.

Chapter 18
September: Madness and Mafia

I thought Jonas would drop me off after Anna's wake, but he marched inside. He unlocked the door and held the storm door for me, "I can hear those gears spinning in your head." His eyes met mine and I looked away. "And I want to know what's going on." His voice was firm.

The kitchen smelled delicious, barbequed pork chops were simmering in the crockpot; comfort food helped me cope with stress. I breathed in the welcoming smell as silence filled the kitchen. I just couldn't talk. My heart was too full of feelings. I was sad and mad and afraid all at the same time. Funny thing about fears, they eat you up from the inside, ruin your sleeping hours, shadow your daytime hours, keep you from life. They had me whipped at that moment, they did.

"I don't feel well, I am going to head on to bed. Oh, and thanks for the ride, glad you were with me tonight." That was good-bye, in case he hadn't noticed.

He lowered his eyebrows, "You are so full of bull, not a thing wrong with you that we can't figure out together. Miss Anna is dead. Money is missing from the church. It all smells bad. You know something. Or you think you know something. Tell and show time." Was he teasing me or did he do that without thinking? In the middle of his serious, boot-stomping mood, it tickled me, and broke my tension. I giggled on the inside, but I dared not smile yet at him. Lordy, he was serious.

"Well, you go first, Jonas, tell and show what you have and then I will." I pulled myself up against him, almost touching him but not quite. I could sense the cold of his Carhartt jacket and his warm, cinnamon gum-flavored breath. He reached for me and as much as I wanted to be held and reassured, I needed to get this ugly stuff sorted out first so I backed off and pulled out a kitchen chair and flopped down.

He tossed his jacket aside, eased into a chair across from me and took a deep breath. "When I was a little boy, I was scared of the northern lights. You say aurora borealis. We say *kiuguyat*. They stretch across the skies, sparkling in greens and yellows and purples. They look like bright ribbons unfolding against the dark or like psychedelic draperies." His eyes closed and I knew that he was seeing them inside his head. "My *aapa* told me about *kiuguyat*, how they would come down when people whistled. He said that they would scoop up naughty children and that I should never whistle because it brought them near. My ancestors carried knives to fight the lights in case they came down to get them. They said that heads were severed and taken to the sky." He pushed back from the table. "Inupiat people are survivors, they fight the elements, they live from the land and the sea, they go whaling and hunt in the worst conditions in the world and yet, something they did not understand scared them to the point that they made up horror stories. I understand worrying about the unknown and keeping children safe, but this lack of logic among a practical culture is weird." He looked at me. I didn't get it.

"What are you talking about?" I got up to serve pork chops, shaking my head at a northern lights legend just pulled outa nowhere.

"Talking about you."

I turned and paused with the crockpot lid in midair. "Talking about fear, how it changes people's logic. You are half crazy trying to figure out your brother, trying to survive the pain he has caused in the past, and focusing every bad thing on him. You doubt the good people in your life, those who you have lived and worked with for thirty years. You are missing the beauty of life and those people who have never hurt you. And you want me to go on home?" His eyes were angry now. "Well, I'll go Stella, and I know that you are messed up right now, but you need to look at your life – do you enjoy always thinking the worst, carrying a gun to fight some imagined enemy?" I couldn't meet his eyes and turned away, angry and righteous. He stood, grabbed his coat, and shoved his chair forward. It tipped and balanced on the table edge before the door slammed and the screen door popped afterwards. He was gone.

Drops of hot condensation dripped off the crockpot lid onto my leg and brought me around as I started to serve myself a pork chop. My appetite was gone. I replaced the lid and went upstairs to bed and got in, clothes and all. *Just like Anna, she went to bed without undressing.* I pulled the quilt over my head but it was a long time before I went to sleep.

#

My cell phone woke me with the little ding-ding that rang when I got a text. It was from Tisha. "CALL ME," was the message. I felt rotten. My eyes were weak, my body sagged, more than usual, and a dull throb pounded in my temple. I needed caffeine and I needed it faster than the time it would take to make cocoa, so I trudged down the steps and grabbed a cold Dr. Pepper from the fridge. *Wonder why this hasn't caught on as a breakfast drink?* The cold drink burned my throat and made my eyes water. Back in bed, I called Tisha.

"Morning, Sunshine!" greeted me, "Joey talked to a guy who is in the mountain mafia!"

"What?" I sputtered and took another hit of pop. It sounded like I was going to need it.

Tisha was so excited she was yelling. "There really is a mountain mafia." I rescrewed the lid and put the bottle back on the nightstand.

"Do tell."

"They are not violent or even mean, but they are thieves. Their network is huge, covers hundreds of square miles clear through West Virginny, Virginny, Kentuck, and maybe the Carolinas. All up and down valleys and mountaintops. Tisha was reverting back to her first language, hillbilly. She did that when she got enthused. "Joey says it might be connected to a bigger den of thieves, a big city ring, don't know for sure."

"How did Joey find this all out?"

"He stopped down at the Old Sportsman's Roost just outside of Peterstown, to see a man about a truck for Eddie and starting shooting the breeze with a old man who was three sheets in the wind. He said he was a looker for the mountain mafia and Joey bought him a drink to hear his story."

"Was Joey drinking?"

"Stella, you know that Joey ain't drank since the bass boat sank in the lake over at Hinton. All those drunk fishermen sobered up when they had to swim for it and not one of the four have had a drink since. They were lucky they were so close to shore. The emergency room nurses thought they'd been in a wreck, all muddy and bloody and half drunk. Remember how mad I was? Anyway, he was drinking a lemonade, takes a big man to go in that joint and drink a lemonade, when this guy starts talking to him."

I was sure that Joey was a lot more afraid of Tisha than anybody in a bar and I know he worshipped their three sons. Eddie was the youngest, I couldn't believe he was old enough to be driving.

Tisha kept right on, "He said there were hundreds of 'lookers'. They spend a lot of windshield time on dirt roads just looking at what people have. Sometimes they hike around to get a better look. The best lookers have a vehicle that nobody notices and either a fantastic memory or a fat notebook to keep up with items and locations. This guy was a 'looker' but he had wrecked his car and so was outa work."

"Go on, go on." I was unscrewing my pop lid for another nip but I didn't want her to stop.

"When the action starts, they get a phone call from a 'finder' who gives them a certain item that is needed. Could be anything, a hood for a '85 F-150, a kayak, two dozen propane tanks, a TV antenna, or even ginseng plants. Anything. If they've seen it, they report the location, and then their job is done. Stella, you still there?"

"Yep, right here. Do you think that artificial flowers are on that list? Do you think Sugar Bowl was a 'finder'? Do you think they are mad at me for shooting him?"

"Nope, this is bigger than that, these guys don't care about the lookers or the finders. Besides, nobody knows what happened in that cemetery but you and me."

And Jonas, I thought. *In the mood he is in, he may just turn us in.*

"There's more, Stella, they make a deal, the 'finder' and one of the big dogs called the 'needer'. He knows the biggest dogs, the 'sellers' who sell this stuff for high prices up north or in Atlanta or Charlotte, you know big places. Then the 'getter' gets a call from the finder and they pick up the stuff and deliver it.

The man told Joey that they do a lot of work just before sunset and just before daylight when decent people are asleep but they can still have enough light to see. Sometimes they work on Sunday mornings when people are at church. The secret to success is that they are not greedy. Lookers don't push what they find – they wait until there is a need, if they don't have it they may offer a close substitute. After the sale is made, money trickles down to the finders and lookers. Not big money, but enough to help out an SSI check or a disability check real well. Besides, it's a good reason to get out of the house."

Tisha was out of breath, and I was just amazed at the details she had so we were both quiet for a few seconds.

"Wowee, Tish, I never knew any of that. Are these guys around here?"

"Yep, this guy was from Talcott, not far from here, just over the Summers County line. Kinda creeps me out that people are looking at other people's stuff all the time."

"Me, too, but it makes some kind of twisted sense, like running a business. I bet the books are complicated ...."

Tisha whooped, "Yeah, you *would* think about the bookkeeper. I thought about stealing stuff that other people touched and thought that I would need to wipe it down before I stole it." She giggled some more. "We are probably not going far in the mafia."

I laughed with her, and then refocused, "So did Joey get the truck for Eddie?"

"Nope, he let the mafia guy have it, said the body was pretty rusted but it would fit in real well with his line of work. Said Eddie would probably rather walk than drive that ugly truck."

Tisha knew about Anna, she and Joey had sent a beautiful wreath to the funeral home, and she told me how sorry they were. She wanted to talk about it, but I couldn't yet. I didn't tell her about last evening at the funeral home or about Jonas because I needed some time to clear my head and put things in order again, but I filed the mafia information away. *Kinda like a looker would do,* I reasoned.

Chapter 19
September: Good-Bye Anna

After Tisha's explanation of the mountain mafia I got out of bed, took off my rumpled street clothes, and showered. I pulled on a bright blouse. Anna had once said that it showed my gypsy blood. She was always feisty like that, sometimes laughed that I was looking "ready for market" when I put on a little weight. I had sighed yesterday when I dialed her number before thinking. Oh, how I was going to miss her.

My dusting ended when I lost my dust rag. I fixed a cup of cocoa and thought I'd heat up a pecan twirl to eat while I retraced my steps to find the missing dust rag. That thing was here somewhere. When I opened the microwave there was the dirty cloth! I just grabbed it out and stuck in the little pecan cake. Tisha would have been disgusted but I figured the heat would kill the dust germs.

Housework was becoming a lost cause, so I thought I'd get in an hour of accounting work. The secretary from Boggess Hardware had just scanned and sent their ledger, so I entered amounts onto their computerized spreadsheet. My mind still wandered. I double-checked them, saved them, and exited the program. Not a good time for numbers, either.

Anna's funeral wasn't until afternoon, but I wanted to bake some butterscotch brownies for the family dinner at the church and devil some eggs. My hens were about to stop laying because of the cold so the number of eggs I had was dwindling, but there was still an extra dozen eggs to spare. It was a nice tradition to feed the family of a deceased member at the church after a funeral. Everybody pitched in and there was usually way too much food. Memories and tall tales floated around the tables and probably made it easier for friends and family

to go home. Anna had loved my butterscotch brownies, called them blondies. Course it didn't make a lick of sense to make them since she wouldn't be there to eat them. I started wondering if friends of the dead person thought about that when they were cooking for the funeral meal. Would make more sense to cook what the dead didn't like. Well, no time like the present to get started in the kitchen. Before I started cooking, I checked the coop for fresh eggs. The metal chicken waterer glittered in the sunshine, but the air was getting colder.

By one o'clock I was ready to load my dishes up and head down to the church. A bit early, but I was too restless to stay home, maybe I could help in the church kitchen before the funeral started.

There was a respectable crowd at the church already. The parking lot wasn't full but almost. I had to park a good distance away and balance my eggs on top of the Tupperware box of brownies while closing the car door with my elbow. Sally Spencer met me at the back door of the kitchen and held it open for me. "C'mon in here, Stella, it's getting chilly out there."

"Yes, ma'am, it is, winter is on our doorstep; must be Mother Natures's telling us it is time for a rest." I was happy that Sally had spoken to me, I had almost forgotten my own troubles during Anna's passing until I saw her. I knew that others might not be as nice. We were the only two in the kitchen for a few minutes and we arranged the food that had already come in and stirred the crockpots that were plugged up around the room. The eating tables were already set up and we wiped them down and put some little harvest centerpieces on each one.

"I can't think of another thing to do. Stella, you go on in the sanctuary and I'll be right behind you." Sally was drying her hands on her apron before she hung it up. We could see others coming from the window and she was hurrying along to get me clear before they hit the door. Or, that's what it felt like, anyway.

I took my regular pew and had a fine view of Anna's flowers and her coffin. Lots of nice flowers, obviously store bought, though. Bet Anna would have loved some fall wild-flowers. I'd have to remember to tend her grave with wild-flowers when I can. Anna buried in the Bradley Cemetery with the snow and wind whipping across her grave. I hung my head and felt awful sad. Along about then, a man slid in beside me and put his arm on the pew back behind me. I didn't look up but I knew it was Jonas and I didn't want him to see me cry and then I got choked up worse because I was so glad he was there. About the time Clarence Price got up to sing, "Be Still My Soul" I got the waterworks under control, but when the song was over, hiccups started. I was a mess.

The preacher talked about Anna's life and her devotion to the church. He mentioned all the volunteer work she had done over the years, all the dinners she had helped with, he obviously didn't know that Anna was no cook. She liked to eat, and she didn't mind washing dishes. And as if a funeral needed a finale, he said, "I've saved the best of Anna's good works for last. The very day of her death she deeded over her home to her church."

He waited for an amen and sure enough, Timmy Lee, the snake, jumped up and shouted "Praise Jesus!" Others mumbled agreement and some said "Amen." I saw the shoulders of Anna's younger girl, Brooke, bending forward and shaking as she wiped her eyes and blew her nose. Then I got mad. As the preacher preached, I started explaining to myself why my blood was boiling:

1. Both her daughters were struggling financially. Brooke, was in the middle of a divorce and had three little children. I don't know if she would've moved back here but they could've sold that little house. Charlene was living in an apartment clear over in McDowell County, heard tell the neighborhood was like the trailer park down in the Orchard before that place got cleaned up. She kept the details from Anna but it was pretty well known that Jeremy was a drug addict. Both of them could have used a little money and that house was the main thing Anna had to give them.

2. I was crazy, sobbing mad at her other friends for not checking up on her sooner. For her to lie there dead for two weeks was not right.
3. Somehow Anna's death was an advantage for Timmy Lee. I don't understand why or how he got her to sign over her house to the church. This part of my anger was pure frustration.

I lost my train of thought when Clarence sang another song, a modern, upbeat song that I didn't know, something about being serenaded by angels. It was beautiful and took the raw edges off my anger. Then the services at the church ended and we followed the family out.

Jonas led me by the hand and helped me up into his truck to go up the mountain to the Bradley Cemetery. Just his coming into the church was unexpected, not to mention touching me in public. We had always been private about advertising our relationship. But I was too torn up about Anna to focus on Jonas.

The graveside part of the funeral was short. The sun had come out for a last few minutes' glimpse of Indian summer but the air was cool. Pastor Booth told a good story about his mother's death, talked about Anna a little more, read the Twenty-third Psalm and said a prayer. The girls each took a

rose from the blanket of flowers covering their mother's casket, and stepped back to shake hands with those who didn't see them at the wake. People lingered, seeming to want a few more minutes with Anna before they headed back to the church for the meal. I didn't feel like helping with it, didn't much want to face people at all. But, while we were sitting in the truck waiting for the line of cars to move forward, Brooke approached my window, all hunched up in her thin jacket, eyes weak and runny. I opened my door and climbed down to hug her.

"Oh, Stella," she cried into my ear as I held her, "what happened to my momma? Will we ever know?" Choking sobs grew into a wail. I could feel her sadness in my bones and something else that gave me goose bumps. Guilt? Fear?

"Honey, honey, your mom loved you and your sister more than anything in this world. She would not want you to shed one tear. Besides, she's with your daddy, bet Charles is holding her tight in his arms as she watches down on you right this minute." Then I added, "She had a full, happy life" hating myself for using that threadbare phrase but hoping it would be of some comfort to Brooke. I held her at arm's length and wiped her wet cheek with the back of my hand. I didn't know how fragile she was right now, so I decided to act like her mother would have. "You gonna have to move on, take care of your kids. Can you sell some of your dad's guns and all that Confederate stuff he was so proud of?" She started crying again but I continued. "There was an old uniform and guns and Confederate money and belt buckles and all kinds of junk stored upstairs. Charles was real proud of his old stuff, must be worth something." Then the wailing began again.

"It's all gone, all of it, Stella." Brooke whispered and collapsed.

Chapter 20
October: Thieves and eBay

Brooke came around when we splashed water from a bottle in her face. By then the sun had all but disappeared behind a cloud and it was flat-out chilly. She had to be freezing. She started crying all over again when she was at herself, but she was okay. I reckon there is something to the idea that mind and body are connected cause her mind had just about shut down. No money, no hope, and no mommy left to turn to. No wonder her spirit broke.

The kids were sitting in the back seat of her Toyota Corolla; the oldest one, seven-year-old Rose, was taking care of the two younger ones. She was playing patty-cake games with the three year old, while the baby slept in his car seat. Jonas helped Brooke to the passenger seat, and I took the wheel. He stood by the car like he didn't know what to do, so I rolled down the window.

"Jonas, go on down to the church and tell her sister Charlene that she's taking the kids to Anna's and oh, get yourself some dinner."

Brooke interrupted weakly, "Charlene left already in their car. Seems like she couldn't take being alone any more, Jeremy spent the whole time at his family's house, drinkin' and druggin'. She said she was leaving him as soon as the graveside service was over." Jonas nodded.

"One less to feed." I remarked and turned to Jonas with a new thought. "Why don't you get some platters and load up enough food for Brooke and the kids for a couple of days? We'll meet you at Anna's house." He nodded again.

When the car started after grinding a bit, it was obvious that it had passed its prime. The muffler was either rusted out or missing entirely. The warning lights on the dash were all on. They didn't bother me at all; my engine light had been on for months. Ben McDaniel called them "idiot lights" because by the time they came on it was too late anyway. He got Jonas calling them that so I picked it up and quit paying any attention to them. The left rear window was missing and had thick plastic held in place with duct tape. It was not too cold but the plastic fluttered when I picked up speed and vibrated so loudly that we couldn't hear each other talk. In spite of all that we made it back up on the mountain to Anna's place. Brooke had gotten herself together but was shivering. She was pretty wet; a bottle of water goes farther than you think.

She got the kids inside out of the cold and changed a diaper there in the downstairs bedroom. I guess she had been sleeping in her mother's bed. The living room was messy with pillows and blankets and children's clothing. Looked like her sister had camped out on the living room floor with the kids.

"Stella, could you please fix a bottle for the baby? They are in the refrigerator."

"Sure thing," I called through the door. I didn't want to tell her that I didn't know how, but it was all ready, just had to warm the premixed bottle in the microwave for a few seconds so I didn't have to admit I knew nothing about baby bottles.

She settled the children on a comforter spread out on the bedroom floor, gave Rose some crayons and a coloring book from the diaper bag and told her to share. The older two were playing happily and the baby was attacking the bottle when Brooke and I sank on the couch where we could watch them.

"I am so sorry about your mother. Did you talk to her near the end?" Brooke shook her head no. "She was having a hard time, Brooke, and she was worried about money, and about you and Charlene. She loved you girls more than life." I had bitten my lip to keep my voice even.

Brooke's green eyes got big and she leaned forward to talk. She motioned to the bedroom, "I can't even take care of my own family. Mom was sending me money every week or two until I could find a job and day care for Ethan. The only reason I risked a trip in that old car was because I hadn't heard from Mom, no calls, no letter this week or last ...."

"... and no money." I finished the thought aloud.

"I broke a window to get in and there she was, dead." I expected another crying jag, but Brooke was her strong perky self again. "I knew not to move her until the funeral home guys got here, but I blew her a kiss and said a little prayer for her. Then, I ran back to the car. It stunk in here." Brooke may have dressed up fancier than Anna, but she got to the point exactly like her momma.

"We slept upstairs that night after they took mommy's body. We pushed up the windows until the smell finally left. What little food was in the refrigerator was spoiled, but we found some canned beans, and some fish sticks, and rolls in the freezer. We've eaten pretty well for the past four days. Then, Charlene bought some groceries: hotdogs and buns, chips and bread and cheese and peanut butter." She shook her head. "My kids think this is heaven."

I winced at Anna's grandkids going hungry. "Have you looked in the cellar? Your ma put up grape juice on Labor Day and grape jelly and a lot of chowchow back in the summer."

"I didn't think of the cellar, Stella. That will be some good eating for my babies." Then she spun around real quick, "Will you help me pack it up? The new man at the church says we need to be out of here in a week, and that's just three more days." Then it hit her all over again. Here came the sobs. Good thing Jonas started knocking on the door, 'cause that gave us something to do and I was fresh out of things to do. Frustration and depression were big obstacles and it seemed to me that Brooke had every reason to be entertaining both.

"Well, looky here, kids! Mr. Jonas just found something for your dinner." Brooke had opened the front door. The two older ones ran to see and Jonas led them to the kitchen table like the Pied Piper with a big cardboard box of foil covered Chinette platters. I heard him tell those children that dessert was better served before the meat and vegetables and gave them a piece of peach pie to eat right then.

By the time Jonas and Brooke reappeared in the living room, Brooke was smiling and thanking him. I had gathered my wits a little. It was hard to sit on Anna's couch and see her bedroom through the door and her kitchen, even though it was all topsy turvy from the grandchildren visiting, it was still Anna's place, so I started to straighten it up.

Jonas took his cap off and held it on his knee, and then smoothing his straight hair down in the back with his other hand turned to Brooke. "When you going back, Miss Brooke?"

Chapter 20

She paused in her efforts to pick up toys and pillows and pulled over a kitchen chair, filling her lap with all the things she had picked up from the floor. "Jonas, I might as well tell you the truth. My man has left the kids and me. He says he will pay the rent plus $500 a month if I won't file for child support or alimony. So, we have a double-wide and a little money, but I need a job and a good babysitter to keep baby Ethan."

Jonas straightened out the fold in his cap and folded it again. "Well, I don't know how all that works, but I think somebody in this room knows a good lawyer." I felt him looking at me before I looked his way. I had been neatening up blankets from off the floor and stopped mid-fold.

"Well, yes, I know a lawyer, Lawyer Dillon. She is a good woman, too." I went back to folding.

"But she IS a Baptist." Jonas offered, eyes twinkling at me. I made like I was going to swat him with the blanket.

"Oh, hush, nothing wrong with being a Baptist."

"Probably wouldn't care much about whether the Methodists were getting a new piece of real estate or not." He got up and went to the window and raised the shades. "Nice lot with your momma's house, Brooke, flat and dry."

I gulped. He was right. Darlene Dillon could tell us if the will was legal, if the claim on Anna's house was real. She wouldn't be looking at it from the perspective of my church board. She would be objective. Plus, she could give Brooke some divorce advice, too. Jonas was brilliant. I'd probably never tell him that and he smiled all smug just like he knew what I thought and knew, too, that he'd never hear it from me, but he knew all the same.

"I reckon you and me need to go down to Peterstown tomorrow and see Lawyer Dillon just as soon as she has time to see us." Brooke had gone back to cleaning and straightening out clothes. She nodded.

"We're gonna go on around the mountain, now. I laid the blanket in the pile on the coffee table. "I'll come and get you tomorrow after I make an appointment. And, I'll talk to you then about your daddy's Civil War stuff." I gathered up my coat. "Jonas, Brooke says all his artifacts that were upstairs are gone." Jonas whirled around.

"What?" He had just replaced his cap and we were heading out the door but he whipped it off again and whacked it on his thigh. "Miss Brooke, did you tell the police or the funeral home men?"

Brooke collapsed onto the couch like a rag doll. She sat limply beside the pile of clothing for a second before she answered, shaking her head. "Nope, I didn't know until yesterday when Charlene went upstairs looking for something valuable to sell. Both Daddy's wardrobe and trunk where he kept that stuff are empty." She kept on smoothing clothes, but I could tell she was getting sad again.

"Miss Brooke, would you mind if I went upstairs and looked – your dad showed them to me years ago and I, well, I just want to see for myself." He spoke haltingly, like he really wanted to go upstairs but he didn't want to bother her right now.

She waved towards the stairs, "Have at it Jonas, but I can tell you that there is nothing there worth anything." Jonas headed towards the steps and took them two at a time. I couldn't keep up on those steep little wooden steps and had to stop to catch my breath at the top. The room was plenty tall in the middle but the ceiling followed the rooftop so both sides had short little walls with built-in doors that led to under the eaves, attic storage space. Anna had kept her girls toys there after they grew up, especially pretty baby dolls, and I swallowed down a lump in my throat. The big iron bed still had a white chenille bedspread with tufts of pink and blue from years ago when the girls had lived there. I knew Anna hadn't climbed the steps regularly since Charles had died. She still used their bedroom downstairs, hadn't changed a thing.

Jonas had rummaged through the wide wardrobe drawer and was staring at the inside of an empty steamer trunk muttering, "*Athigaa* ... makes no sense, no sense at all. The padlock is unlocked, not forced open. Nothing is bothered except the things from the War Between the States that are missing." He looked at me. "Did Anna ever talk about selling them?"

"I don't think she even came up here in the last year, she was feeling her age and those steps were hard on her."

Jonas grunted, "Well, somebody did!" And he stomped back down the stairs, turning his big feet sideways to fit on the treads.

"Did your mom ever talk about selling your dad's war collection?" Jonas was already asking Brooke before I got there. I thought he was being darn insensitive being that this was the very day of Anna's funeral, but he seemed determined.

Chapter 20

Brooke looked Jonas dead in the eye, strong and unwavering. "No sir." Then her voice broke a little and she looked around blinking back tears. "Mom treasured that dumb stuff just because it was Daddy's, not because it was worth anything. I even looked in the outbuildings, but there's nothing there but rusted folding chairs and flower pots." Her forehead wrinkled but she shook off the confusion to go tend to the fretting baby.

"Well, you all sleep good tonight and I'll call tomorrow as soon as I know something about when the lawyer can see us." My words were hurried. Jonas had his cap back on and was impatient to get out the door, but he waited long enough for me to hug the children and Brooke.

Once we were in his truck and heading to my house, well, I supposed we were heading there, he started drumming his fingers on the steering wheel and staring real serious-like at the road. Then he didn't turn at the forks of the road to my house but went straight on to his little pre-fab house and got out and went in, never mind me. I almost thought he had forgotten me and I was getting a little miffed.

I straightened my good clothes and followed him inside as soon as I could get down from the truck "Now, just a minute, Jonas, you might still be mad at me, but ...."

I shut up as I found him already turning on his computer to search Craigslist and then Ebay and finding Confederate belt buckles. He looked and looked and read and reread then jabbed the screen with his finger. "That one belonged to Charles! I know it, the buckle has initials on it that proved it was his great-grandpa's. He showed it to me the summer before he died." Then, with anger clouding his black eyes he stared at me but he seemed to be seeing something else. "Stella, someone is selling Charles and Anna's artifacts online."

He spent most of the evening tracing the sale of the belt buckle, turns out the person selling it had bought it from another online seller who had bought it from a private dealer. Jonas searched and searched the internet and took page after page of notes. I was confident in his computer skills and his determination. Jonas would find that dealer and ask a few pointed questions before he quit or handed it over to the sheriff. I stirred around in his kitchen and fixed a bite to eat and then he took me to my car at the church and followed me home and came on inside.

Chapter 21
October: Lawyer Visit

Long after midnight, I lay with both hands behind my head staring at the ceiling. The wind howled outside and I could hear rain or maybe sleet pinging against the metal roof. Jonas was asleep beside me, warm and smelling like Ivory soap. We had made up, I guess, since we were together all afternoon and he had decided to spend the night. I hadn't taken time to ponder our relationship any more. My life was getting in the way.

Even as I exhausted myself reliving all I knew about Anna's life and death, I still had a few of my own problems to solve. *How could I prove that I didn't steal any church money? Who did take it? What does Timmy Lee have to do with it all?*

Then there was Jonas. I turned onto my side and watched his chest rise and fall as he breathed deeply in his sleep. I needed him but I was too proud to say so and tired of wanting to be married. Maybe I should break it off with him. No, I knew better than that, I would never do it. That was so crazy, I knew I was feeling the anxiety that came to me sometimes in the darkness.

There was a heaviness in my heart about church. I felt like I was on the brink of a deep canyon and I could tumble in or I could turn around and walk safely away. Would the people from church look the other way or worse, push me over the cliff? Or would they save me, lend me a hand and pull me back to safe ground. What if they had to choose between Timmy Lee and me? I was no saint, but I didn't take from others and I tried to always do the right thing.

I wanted to wake up Jonas to see what he thought but decided I had pushed my luck far enough for one day and snuggled against him instead. When sleep finally came, it was deep and dreamless.

#

When my feet hit the floor the next morning, I reached for the phone and made arrangements to see the lawyer at ten o'clock. The next call was to Brooke to tell her to be ready by 9:30 to go to town. She seemed glad to have a purpose.

Jonas was starting to move around when I came back in the bedroom to warm my fingers over the radiator. The temperature had fallen overnight and I had just scraped my frosty windshield. He had to work late tonight and needed to get his hours right side up, so I resisted the urge to warm my fingers against his warm armpits; he needed to sleep longer.

I left early and swung by the parsonage on the way to get Brooke. Preacher Booth's car was there so I stopped in. He answered the door in a tee shirt and jeans. That sight, the preacher without a tie and jacket, took me a minute to get used to, but he was his regular self and welcomed me.

"Get on in here out of the cold, Miss Stella." He took my jacket and hung it in the hallway and ushered me into the living room. The Today Show was blaring from a big flat screen TV and he turned it off. "What can I do for you this morning?" He sat down on the piano bench after I settled in his recliner.

I didn't even have to get my nerve up or choose my words carefully. There was no time for niceties. "Preacher, it seems like there's those in the church who doubt my honesty. No one has told me to my face, but the rumors are snaking around me. Can you help me? What do you think's behind these lies?"

He rubbed his face with both hands and moved the bench nearer to me. "Stella, there is a difference between the amount of money we counted after the benefit in September and the amount you deposited, right at $3,000." He looked at the fidgeting hands in his lap. "The administrative board officers are aware but no one else has been told."

I closed my eyes and tried to remember the events after we counted that money. I was working in the kitchen and had put the fat zippered bag in the dishtowel drawer. A few ladies were cleaning up with me and, oh wait, Timmy Lee had been there late because I had almost shot him. I grimaced and wished I had done better with that little job.

"Stella, Stella, are you alright?" When I opened my eyes, the preacher was in my face so close I could smell the coffee on his breath. He may have been touching my shoulder.

"No, I am most certainly not all right." Anger seeped into my brain and I shooed him away. "Someone has robbed our church. Have you called the sheriff, Pastor Booth? Have you talked to the other ladies helping in the kitchen? Did you even tell me about the missing money? No. No. No. There's the answers." I had raised my voice and I tried to calm down by folding my hands and looking him right in the eyes. "I tell you what, Preacher, there is a thief in our midst, and it is not me!" I couldn't stay calm, instead, I got riled up again.

I grabbed my jacket on the way out but didn't need to put it on because I was red hot. I had the sense that Rev. Booth was following me and clucking or mumbling but I had no more use for him and didn't look back. I cooled down some as I drove on to Anna's house.

Brooke was ready when I pulled in. Her hair was shining and she had on a touch of red lipstick that looked real nice with her dark hair and fair complexion. She loaded her three kids in the back seat and we headed to Peterstown with time to spare.

Down near the fountain, an artesian well that serves as a local landmark, the road has a long straight stretch. I was driving pretty fast when a deer jumped across the highway right in my path. It crashed into Brooke's side of the windshield leaving blood and hair on the glass. Brooke screamed and the kids cried. The deer twisted her body off the hood and stumbled into the ditch. Brooke unbuckled her seat-belt and turned around to calm the children in the back set. I pulled over to check out the damage to the car and the condition of the deer. Thank goodness there were no cracks in the glass and just small dents in

the grill and hood. Deer accidents were the number one insurance claim in West Virginia, just about everyone has hit at least one. The adult doe was still alive but at least one leg was broken and her head was laid open. She lay panting between clenched teeth in the dead grass of the ditch.

"Better call the law, Stella," Brooke suggested after she took a look. The kids had recovered and were listening to the radio, but she didn't want to leave them long.

"Humph." I shook my head. "It'll take them 30 minutes to get here. And for what? All they'll do is shoot the poor thing and call the state road to put lime on the body," I sighed. "We don't have time to wait." I remembered that I had my little buddy under the seat. "Brooke, I need to get something from the car, then you drive the children up there to the golf course entrance and I'll catch up." I pointed and she looked bewildered but nodded.

I grabbed the .38 and Brooke did like I asked. I said a little prayer beside the deer then shot her between the ears, pushed the pistol down the back of my pants to hide it but it was real warm so I had to tuck my shirt tail in between it and my bare back. My jacket still hung over it so it was out of sight. Then I walked up the road to the car. How easy it was to end a life with a gun. No pain for the victim, no struggling, no fighting for life. Just ka-boom and they're dead. It crossed my mind that the game warden would probably arrest me for doing his job and I frowned. Things were not always logical, but I liked practical, myself. I had just started wearing pants with elastic in the waist. They were just the thing for holding the gun in place. Good fashion choice, I thought.

We made it to the lawyer on time. She looked at the will Brooke dug out of the diaper bag and could find plenty wrong with it. "In West Virginia, a holographic will must be handwritten by the deceased. The only two exceptions are medical personnel in a hospital can write a patient's will for them and rarely a preacher at a deathbed is allowed to do so. This will was typed and the only handwriting is the alleged signature of the deceased, so it will not stand in this state. Your family could contest the will on a number of other irregularities. The signature was not witnessed, a handwriting expert must match it to Anna's writing, your mother's mental state may have been fragile, and in light of her unexpected death, there may have been coercion involved." She studied our faces. "If there is doubt about Mrs. Bradford's death being natural, we need to contact the authorities." Brooke nodded and the lawyer continued, "Most unattended deaths do require an autopsy."

"I'll get the death certificate from Wickline's and ask for an inquiry, if that is what you want." Brooke kept nodding but tears were starting. "You will need to make a statement to the sheriff." I left to find a box of tissues; when I returned they had moved on to a discussion about divorce. Miss Dillon told Brooke that she needed to go back home and either mend her marriage or file for divorce in Virginia. As we rounded up the kids, Darlene motioned me to follow her back into the conference room.

She whispered, "What does the Methodist Church want with Anna's house? It's older and in this market, it is not very valuable. Is there much land?"

I sighed. "Just two acres."

She made clucking sounds. "Stella, I'm not seeing the whole story in this. What am I missing?"

"We are both missing it, Lawyer, but I hope you can figure it out." My face was surely blank, at least that is the way I felt.

On the way home, I told Brooke about Jonas working on the computer to find her daddy's Confederate stuff, but not to hold out much hope. She swore to keep it to herself, secret even from her sister and to stay in touch.

All in all, it was a productive morning.

Chapter 22
October: Internet and Teeth

Things happen fast online. Jonas had traced the belt buckle as far back as he could last night and had called the collector this morning to find out where he had gotten it. The guy managed an antique store and had priced the belt buckle sky high because he didn't really want to sell it, but a dealer of Civil War artifacts was willing to pay so he let it go. He said that he had purchased it at an Atlanta gun show from the Mountain Antiquities booth. He had added that the Mountain Antiquities guys were known for their large stock of unique merchandise and super-fast turnover.

Now Jonas was searching for Mountain Antiquities and devouring every entry. He grumbled and swore as he typed, and after some intense minutes, leaned back and pointed at the screen. "That might be it."

I leaned over his shoulder to see that he had happened upon comments posted on a small town Georgia Topix website where Mountain Antiquities was blasted for selling stolen items at high prices. I gasped and covered my mouth. At the bottom of the website was a reader named TeeLee defending the company with scripture and righteousness. "Let any one of you who is without sin be the first to throw a stone. For the time is ripe when the world as we know it ends and only those who speak with God will survive. Render to Caesar what is Caesar's."

The insanity from this post seemed extreme in answer to entries like "Bunch of thieves, coming and going." "These guys are trouble." and "What happens at Mountain Antiquities stays at Mountain Antiquities."

"Oh, Jonas, it looks to me like Timmy Lee is behind all of it. What are we gonna do?"

"Hang on, Stella, we don't know any such thing. We know of a company who sells Civil War artifacts. We know it is based in Atlanta. We know it has a defender who quotes scripture who just might have the same initials as your brother. We don't know how the company got Anna's things. We don't know that Anna was murdered. We don't even know that she was robbed. So settle down there CSI woman." Then he grinned and grabbed my hip as I stood by him. "The truth is out there, girl." Then I had to grin, too and there we were like two possums in the muscadine vines, drunk on information yet wanting more.

"Brooke gave Lawyer Dillon permission to start up an inquiry into the cause of Anna's death. She thinks the death might not be from natural causes. What do you think of that?"

Jonas squinted at me. "I think you are a little late getting started since we put Anna in the ground day before yesterday, but it's good to get somebody official involved." Just then the phone rang with the normal beach song and I dug through the inside pocket of my purse for it.

A very excited Brooke was on the line. When she told me what she had just found, I gripped Jonas's arm so hard that he swatted me off as I finished the conversation.

"Oh, my gosh, Jonas, I don't know what to do first. We've gotta call the law, Brooke has found evidence. Here, use my phone. Tell them to meet us at Anna's house right now." I struggled into my jacket changing my phone from one hand to another. I had never expected these new cell phones to be so blamed useful and for the first time, was grateful to be able to travel and use the phone at the same time.

Jonas and I scurried across the crusty frozen mud to my car and I roared around the mountain road while he called the sheriff, probably setting a new record for getting from my house to Anna's. Brooke had barricaded the children in the kitchen with two chairs laid sideways and was pacing the floor. She threw herself into Jonas's arms and I raised an eyebrow but didn't have time to think much about it. She had been cleaning, getting toys out from under the couch cushions and there in the middle of the backside of the worn plaid couch cushion was a dental partial plate, three false teeth and some wires, still hanging on. "Are they my mama's?" Brooke asked, more to herself than to us.

I clasped my hands together at the small of my back and bent over to look, the middle cushion of the couch still standing on end and against the couch back. "Looks kinda like Anna's smile," I said. "Why didn't we notice she didn't have her teeth in?"

Jonas and Brooke separated as Jonas spoke, "We never saw her in the coffin, Stella, it was all closed up, remember?" Then he turned to Brooke and asked if she had noticed them missing when she found her. She shook her head no and big tears threatened to roll from her flooding eyes.

"Mommy never slept with her teeth in, I just didn't think about that. Her skin was thin and mushy and she ..." now she wailed "... stunk so bad." Jonas held her again when she reached out to him. I didn't really like them hugging like that, emergency or not but I never thought I was the jealous type.

We heard the sirens before the deputy's car pulled over in front of the house, and then we could see the flashing blue lights bouncing through the front porch window on the living room walls. If flashing lights were designed to get your attention, they sure worked. Between the screaming sirens and the pulsing lights, my heart was racing. Jonas opened the front door to greet Deputy Long as the young man's hand rose to knock. I had seen a smaller version of that fist before, at Vacation Bible School when he was a boy, not too many years ago. A rush of cold air and the scent of stale cigarette smoke entered with him. I would have to remind him how bad smoking was, but maybe not today.

"Afternoon, Jonas, what have we here?" the deputy looked around the small living room and kept his hand on his holster. He nodded at the children and at Brooke and me and scrutinized every piece of furniture until his eyes stopped on the couch cushion, out of place, standing on end. "What in the world?"

"It's .... We think they are ... Mommy's teeth. She died in bed here." Brooke brushed away the first tear.

Ivan Long knelt and looked carefully, but he didn't touch. "Gonna need some pictures, let me call the sheriff." He stomped out to the car, talked into his two-way radio and hurried back in. "The sheriff is coming with our digital camera. He says that there was a request for an inquiry into

Mrs. Bradford's death just today. We'll get the death certificate and a report from the boys at the funeral home ASAP. Didn't seem funny until this." He gestured to the couch, hat in one hand and a clipboard in the other. "Sure am sorry, Miss Brooke, I didn't know your mama, but I heard tell of your daddy all my life. People said she was a good woman."

Brooke looked at Jonas and then at me, seeming like she was questioning his words, but I just shrugged. "Hard to tell what he heard about Charles; your daddy was a catbird." All four of us stood around in that sitting room, the baby pulling up on the horizontal chair legs, his brother crawling after a toy, and Rose focused on coloring as if she were alone in the room. It was kinda awkward then. I finally got Brooke to sit in her daddy's lounge chair and Jonas and Ivan stepped across the barrier to get the last two kitchen chairs. Jonas offered me one and leaned in the doorway to Anna's bedroom

Jonas broke the silence, "Deputy, have you worked unsolved murder cases before?" Well, there it was, the elephant in the room, drawn and quartered right there. Got to give Ivan credit, he barely flinched. About the same time, the smell of a dirty diaper wafted from the kitchen and Brooke crossed the room and straddled the sideways chairs to grab up the baby. She looked so pretty, so full of love, with the gurgling infant reaching for his mother's curtain of long curly hair as she crossed back to the bedroom to change him. It was as if time had paused and I wondered if Anna looked that way carrying her babes.

Ivan Long scooted to the edge of his chair, his voice strong with the sincerity of youth. "Yes sir, but both of them were solved pretty fast. A co-conspirator in the Davidson murder made that one pretty cut and dried, and a flat out confession from the man who killed his wife and boyfriend ended that investigation the same afternoon. Not saying that this IS a murder you understand, but it does seem a bubble off of level." I saw sweat beading up on his smooth forehead and understood that his glances out the front window were in hopes the cavalry was coming soon.

Seemed like it took forever for the other Monroe County police car to show up. Finally, it pulled in without lights or siren, just a faint sound of crunching gravel. Sheriff Johnson gathered up a black bag out of the trunk and shuffled to the door. Jonas, holding back the drapes at Anna's front window to watch the arrival, muttered, "No hurry, all right."

The weather had turned colder, the sky was steel grey and the mountain wind bit. Elmer was so bundled up that he looked like he'd put on weight but when he came inside and tipped his hat at Brooke then started peeling off his jacket I could see that he was still a bean pole. He looked one way and the other for a place to put his hat and jacket down. Brooke rushed to rescue him and took his things so he could open the black backpack he was carrying. He pulled out a camera and started taking off lids and adjusting knobs as he talked.

"Mrs." He paused and looked at Brooke. "I am sorry I don't know your married name, Brooke."

"Pruitt." I thought I could hear her thinking *but not for long.*

"Pruitt? Is he from around here? There used to be a Pruitt played football up Union. Did his daddy play ball?"

"Naw, sheriff, he ain't got no daddy." Brooke giggled. That girl had loosened up fast. I had forgotten that Elmer could be charming. "Raised by wolves, best I can tell. I thought I could give him the family he had missed and he'd be a better daddy than his was. He left me before Ethan here was born, so that plan didn't work out so well. But, I got me a network now, talked to the lawyer yesterday and Stella there, she is helping us, too."

Elmer stopped fiddling with his camera, looked at me, and grinned his approval. "Stella as a legal advisor, that works for me."

I might have blushed, but was too much on edge to fool around. Elmer didn't seem to get how serious this all was. Then, to Ivan, "Are you writing this down?" Ivan fumbled in pockets and came up with a pen and began to write. "Get her full name and an address and phone number when I'm done."

"Yes, sir."

Elmer leaned over the couch. "Mrs. Pruitt, did you find this object?"

Brooke put her hand over her heart. "Yes sir."

"When?"

Brooke waited until Ivan had time to write down her name. "Today. Just now. Well, 'bout two hours ago."

"What caused you to turn the cushion over?"

"I was looking for Legos. Ethan was stuffing them everywhere." She choked once like her cleaning or parenting was under investigation and Elmer looked up at her.

"I 'spect this is difficult for you. Don't you worry, honey, we are nearly done." He snapped more pictures and examined the wires intertwined with the worn yarn in the orange plaid couch fabric. Then he untangled the dental work and it fell into his hand. He fished a zip lock bag out of the pack, zipped the false teeth in it and handed it to Ivan to label. Then he set the cushion on the floor, leaned it against the couch and removed the other two cushions.

When I saw what was uncovered, my knees buckled and if I wasn't upset enough at the false teeth stuck to the pillow, I was now weak as a newborn baby.

Chapter 23
November: Stella Knows

Jonas grabbed my waist when he thought I was going topple over, but I pushed him away to stare at the bright blue silk pocket hankie lying on the webbing of the couch where the middle cushion fit. The only men I had ever seen wear such a gaudy thing were the Voices of Glory singers. Timothy Lee Davis had worn the blue shirt and matching hankie.

My chest constricted like giant hands were squeezing my heart. At the same time, my body temperature must've dropped several degrees; my blood ran cold. When I could speak, my voice came out in a whisper, "Dear God, Timmy Lee was here at the same time Anna lost her partial plate." I got louder as I got angry. "Anyone want to argue that?" I looked hard at Elmer. He looked away. "What do you say, sheriff?"

Sheriff Johnson was pale. He massaged his forehead and then his neck right at the hairline and got a little color back in his face. "Stella, Stella, let's not go jumping to conclusions." He picked up the camera again and starting clicking away. Again, he found a zip lock bag and put the hanky in it, still folded with a little pointed end. Deputy Long reached for the bag and began to label it.

"Who is this Timmy Lee? Is he the new man at the church? Is he the one who said I had a week to get out of mommy's house? Why would he hurt Mama?" Brooke was purt nigh on to screaming by then but it seemed far away to me. Her children toppled over the tower of empty pop cans they were building in the kitchen floor and the clatter sounded like machine gun fire.

"Calm down, Miss Brooke." Elmer avoided eye contact and cleared his throat. "This may change things about your mama's death, but we don't know that for sure. We'll be in touch with you in a few days." The Sheriff was putting away his camera and acting like he wanted out of the house, but I was not quite done with him.

"Go get him right now, Sheriff. Right now. Put that good-for-nothing behind bars where he belongs. He paid me no mind. "Elmer, this is wrong, just wrong, to know he was here and not act." He kept packing without a word. "If you don't arrest him, you are misusing the taxpayers' money." That was my final shot, the worst thing I could accuse him of without just outright saying he killed her himself. It all fell on deaf ears. Elmer Johnson put on his police jacket, then his big ole Smoky Bear hat, tipped it at us and went back out into the cold. His deputy scrambled and scuffled around until he had all the evidence Ziploc bags labeled. He dropped the sharpie twice trying to put it in the black case with the bags then he scurried out the front door, too.

I flopped down on the other side of the couch. I thought I was going to be sick but I started mentally wailing, "Anna, I am so sorry that you are gone, I **hate** that you are dead ... and ...." I couldn't put my thoughts into words, even in my own mind.

Jonas headed out the back door and the kids stared at me before they went back to the task of building a new pyramid with the empty cans. Guess I looked like the tired old lady that I was. I sighed, washed my face then felt a little better about it all, resolved to hunt Timmy Lee down and really help Brooke out in her time of need because I owed at least that much to Anna. With all that settled, I was starting to get hungry and I wanted something sweet to eat.

"Jonas, I guess we better hit the road." I went out on the back porch and patted him on the chest, bold of me, I reckon, but I wasn't thinking clearly about the little things, just the big one. Brooke needed what they call on TV shows "debriefing" so we stayed long enough to relive the whole mess with her. I told her I was sure that Timmy Lee Davis must've been here with her mother and she just nodded and rocked in the old rocking chair. I had some questions but it wasn't the time. We all had a lot to think about.

#

It was a week to remember. We visited with the sheriff up at his tiny office in the Monroe County Courthouse four different times. One phone call to Darlene Dillon got her stirred up and asking questions. Calvin Weikle called me to see if Brooke would allow her mother's body to be exhumed then had to explain what that meant. I purely hated to tell her what it was and get her blessing but she didn't mind a bit. She seemed shell-shocked.

By Friday, Timmy had been questioned and released; he is at his best when guilty, the lies flow like New River in the springtime floods. Even when he was ten years old, he could lie brilliantly looking you right in the eye. I wondered what his alibi could be but Elmer wouldn't tell me.

Anna's poor little body had been disturbed and desecrated and not much could be determined because of the condition of her body. Shoot, I could have told them that, she was probably practically mummified from lying there in a hot house. Her little throat was probably too dried up to tell that she had been smothered. But, they did find bruises on her mouth where her false teeth had been loose and pressed against her lips and they found orange fibers in her nose. The undertaker's report showed that there was vomit in her mouth, which seems to happen when asphyxiation happens. They even found her lipstick smeared on her dental work. Finally, Anna's death was officially an open murder case.

Jonas kept busy throughout the week on his computer every night. He found two more of Charles' Civil War things traced back to the same source, Mountain Antiquities.

#

Jonas and I spent some time outdoors on Saturday. We took Sugar and hiked up to the top of Peters Mountain crunching frozen leaves underfoot. We had to unzip our jackets and pocket our gloves when we got too warm. Winter was having a hard time deciding whether to stay or whether to give Indian summer a few more days. We could see for miles through bare branches and took our time absorbing the views. I rested on rocks and thought a lot and yelled every now and then when frustration and anger at Timmy Lee choked me. I had pictured Timmy Lee bullying Anna so many times that I was beginning to breathe hard myself.

Both my companions were feeling frisky. Jonas and Sugar faked and jumped at each other and rolled together in the leaves. Jonas threw sticks for her to fetch and yelled *"Kiita,"* the Inupiat version of 'Let's go!', over and over. They were both

pretty happy in the weak sunlight of late afternoon. At last, Jonas flopped down beside me on a log to catch his breath. He tossed a stick to get Sugar away from him for a minute, "You remember that story Tisha told where she would get on the PA system up at the school and ask whose pop money was on her desk? Several forgetful employees would claim the dollar bill? I did remember something about that. She was sincere but sometimes people seemed less than honest. Sugar came back and dropped the stick in Jonas's hand. "Well," Jonas continued, "I think we could use that same idea and flush out whoever took the Civil War artifacts."

"How would we do it?"

"Easy. Just let folks know that there were some Civil War items in the attic that Charles may have borrowed and see who shows up to claim them."

I didn't get it. "But we don't have anything to give them."

"I just want to see who would come forward, maybe a greedy thief who thinks he missed something, or maybe a murderer. I dunno." He got up and dusted the leaves off his pants.

In the back of my mind, I was so busy trying to figure how to outsmart my wicked brother that I didn't give this plan my full attention. I told him I'd talk to Tisha and Brooke about it. We walked down the trail together, my toes pushing painfully against the toes of my boots. When we got back into the yard, Jonas hugged me and headed on home. We had been together so much during the last few days, I sure missed him right away, but after a few hours of pacing and reading,

I started to relax, made myself some peanut butter fudge and ate it with a spoon while it was still warm.

#

Tisha called first thing Sunday morning. "Hello, Miss Thang!" she hollered. Mind you, everyone else was respecting my privacy and pain, but Tisha called at daybreak on a Sunday, no less. I cracked up.

"Good morning to you, too, Tisha."

"What's up, buttercup?" She didn't wait for an answer just charged on. "You wanna meet up with Eliza and me after church and go down to the Palisades for the buffet?"

"Why not?" I heard my own voice, at least it sounded like me.

She snorted, "Looks like I win that bet. Eliza said you wouldn't go. High noon thirty at the ATM machine in Peterstown?"

"I'll be there."

Tisha started singing her Cyndi Lauper theme song, 'Girls just want to have fun," and I hung up on the crazy woman. I laughed out loud and got out of bed and got dressed for church.

When services started, I was seated and ready, quiet in my soul and prepared to worship. Even seeing Timmy Lee didn't upset me, but I did wonder for a split second if I could shoot him in church and get away with it. Wasn't there a movie where the police couldn't get the criminal because the bad guy was seeking sanctuary in a church? Hmmm, probably shouldn't believe everything I see in the movies. Plus, it would be messy; I was developing into a clean freak when I thought about shooting something. It was at least a slender thread to reality.

The young woman who served the church as an acolyte wasn't confident in her footing as she climbed the steps to the altar. The preacher helped her up the steps so she could light the candles. I thought about that for a minute, a man sensitive enough to help a struggling person and too naïve to recognize that his media director was a very bad man.

I tolerated Timmy's honeyed voice, reminding us during announcements of the Thanksgiving feast and inviting everyone to participate in the program or at least attend. The Joys and Concerns segment was brief, we heard about college kids coming home for the holidays and prayers requested for their safe travels, we listed all those in the hospital or recovering from one thing or another at home. Just as the preacher bid us to bow our heads to pray, an older man sitting in front of the church struggled to his feet, holding on to a cane with one hand and the pew back in front of him with the other. His skin was as grey as his hair and he was sporting a comb-over with a little freckled bald spot in the back that shined right through the strands of hair. His blue eyes squinted and deepened the crows-feet at the outside corners. He wore a soft knit pullover shirt stretched tightly over his shoulders and biceps

"Preacher," his voice broke, "brothers and sisters, I have a concern to share." He was overcome and looked at the floor for a few seconds seemingly composing his thoughts. "The doctors say I need a kidney transplant soon and I have to prove that I have enough to pay twenty percent of the surgery before they will put me on the list to get an organ donor. I need five thousand dollars." He remained standing, swaying a little until he caught his balance.

It was quiet for a split second and then the buzzing began. Now, here was a worthy challenge for our fund-raising church. Various amounts were offered from different church organizations and, of course, a dinner was planned.

When the heat of discussion died down, and Reverend Booth was ready to pray again, an attractive blonde woman jumped to her feet and raised both arms high and waved them around. She was very eager and when I turned around to see what was going on I thought maybe she was having a seizure. Her dress was bright yellow, form fitting, and low cut. Her earrings were giant pearls dangling from other giant pearls. She was talking to the ceiling, "Oh Lord, you know I don't have much material wealth ... but I do have two healthy kidneys. Praise God." She looked around the room, tears trickling down her cheeks, then upwards again and cried "Yes, Jesus." And then to us, "I am being led to give one of my kidneys to our Christian brother. Sweet Jesus, I trust and obey." The buzz picked back up.

I wondered who the hell these people were; I had never seen either one of them before.

Chapter 24
October: Scam and Gun Lessons

Church couldn't end fast enough for me that Sunday. People were just humming around afterwards in small groups intent on who could come up with the most money for Mr. McKidney, which is the name I gave him because I still didn't know who he was. Reverend Booth preached on honesty. The sermon started with a story about his uncle and I didn't know until the end what the point of it all was. Reverend Beauregard Booth was about as good a storyteller as I have ever heard. His messages had a spark and a twist to the ending like O. Henry's stories. This gave me hope that he was brighter than he seemed and would figure out Timmy Lee and his lack of honesty before it was too late or maybe he had already figured him out but was just beating around the bush with him until the time was right. At the very least the preacher still trusted me to make the offering deposits and I was grateful.

I apologized to Sally when she asked me to come to dinner with her, was glad that I really did have other plans because I didn't want her kindness to hurt her reputation with people who might not trust me. Then I rushed to my car and drove as fast as I dared, crunching out of the gravel parking lot without spinning my tires. Tisha and Eliza were waiting at the ATM in Tisha's van and I knew she would want to drive, so I grabbed my purse and walked through the drive-through to shove the locked deposit bag in the bank's night depository.

"There you go Tisha Butler, you are now a witness that I did not open the Methodist offering before I slid it through the slot." I giggled as I slid open the side door and popped into the back seat.

Tisha and Eliza were good therapy for me; they were full of fun and fresh ideas. Eliza explained the plan to order an appetizer. "The Palisades food is real good, but it takes a while, so we need to order an appetizer that is filling. I think we should order a small goat cheese pizza so we won't be dizzy from hunger."

You mean we should order one because you love goat cheese." Tisha had her number.

Eliza took out a mirror to check her lipstick, "I'm just saying that we can decide now and order it first thing and then we have something to eat while we are deciding what we want for dinner." She clicked the mirror case closed. Eliza always looked nice and she checked on her looks every now and then. Maybe that was the secret.

"Do you not remember that there is a buffet on Sunday? Or do you think we need to have pizza in our hand before we get our butts up from the chair to get a plate?"

"Oh, you're right, Tisha. I'd forgotten. But I do love goat cheese. Next time, then."

It was almost an hour's drive to Eggleston, Virginia and The Palisades, a fancy restaurant there in an old general store building. The shelves and counters were still there and so were the original worn smooth wooden floor planks. It was homey welcoming place and we looked forward to our meal. The temperature was near freezing but the road was dry, so we relaxed and used the miles to tease one another and catch up on the latest. They already knew about Anna's death being ruled a murder and were full of ideas. It was painful handling all their speculation but they were smart and I was determined to hear them out.

"I tell you one thing," Tisha pounded the steering wheel for effect. If Charles Bradford were alive, he would've been my number one suspect. He never treated Anna or the girls right."

"What are you talking about? Charles didn't gamble and he didn't smoke and he stayed at home most evenings. Plus he ate Anna's terrible cooking." I defended my friend's husband in principle although I didn't believe myself. Maybe because I still felt so badly about Anna's death.

Tisha was quick to reply and spit words like darts, "Well, he <u>did</u> drink and he <u>didn't</u> work regular and he took what Anna made at the Senior Center and spent it to go to those stupid Civil War re-enactments. I remember one time Charlene needed something for school, a composition notebook, I think. Mean old Mrs. Benson required one for a journal for all sixth graders. Anna did not have a dollar to buy the notebook and couldn't get it from Charles and that kid took a whooping from the teacher rather than admit that she couldn't buy one. Said she lost the money on the way to school. I never had anything for Charles after that."

Not much could be said to that, so we changed subjects to the man who stood up in church and asked for $5,000. Eliza turned in her seat, "I heard that happened in the Holy Christian Church over in Beckley and the guy got the church check, cashed it and was immediately healed."

"Praises be to God." Tisha added sarcastically. "Oh, those Methodists will be mad if that happens in Lindside. There will be those who trusted him and those who didn't." Tisha took her hands off the wheel to rub them together mischievously. "Sounds like there's going to be a fuss. I just love a good church fight." We all chuckled, not realizing that, at least in this, Tisha was a visionary.

The Palisades buffet was glorious and we all ate until we were nearly foundered, but we couldn't relax long because other Sunday diners were waiting in line. We reluctantly left our window seats and the view of the grey-green river and railroad tracks framed in bare branches.

On the way home, I shared the fact that all Charles' Civil War artifacts were gone and that Jonas thought they were stolen. "Jonas was thinking that we might force the thief's hand if we acted like they missed some of the Confederate pieces and advertised them around town. He got the idea from you and your pop money announcement, Tisha. What do y'all think?"

Eliza was worried, "Stella, these people KILLED Anna, they are not school teachers who forget to pay for their pop. They are KILLERS."

"Well, thanks for reminding me, Liza, but Jonas wanted me to ask. He feels like he's got to do something. What if we just made a few careful comments and see who comes out of the woodwork?"

"I'll help." Tisha was a doer; I'll say that for her. "And Joey'll help. We'll just put the word out and give a phone number to call, probably your phone, Stella. Then, you make an appointment to meet them and we'll all go with you and see if they could be suspects."

"I am telling you that you are heading right straight to trouble." Eliza was digging in.

I figured we would be perfectly safe, but I played along. "A phone call won't hurt us. The thing will be safety when we meet them. How about if we meet in a very busy public place, take a look at them, get contact information and then check them out?"

Tisha drummed her fingers on the steering wheel. "If I was a thief, I would want to see the merchandise, which will not BE in a busy public place. How are we going to show them the goods, which, by the way, we don't have?"

Eliza said, "When my brother sells big stuff like tractors and cows on Craig's List, he meets up with the buyer at the Shell station and then leads them around the mountain the back way to the farm, makes the deal, then leads them out." She sighed, she might be weakening. She added, "Not that this is a good idea for this situation."

"The killer is probably local or knows somebody here, so if we say that there are Civil War items in Anna's attic, the location is not going to be any big secret and we are going to have to meet there to show them. How do we catch this guy and still stay safe?" I was faking my concern. I wasn't a bit worried. Timmy Lee was not going to ever hurt me again.

"They have killed once in that very house, so I think you two are dead ducks if you go through with this." Eliza, the sensible one, shook her head, trying hard to stop this plan. "How about you do it all online and trace the contact information and then go to the police?"

Tisha pulled the van over beside the narrow road and turned around to talk to me eye to eye. "Nothing loosens up a crook more than someone's innocent honesty. Someone they think they can swindle. Let's get Brooke to do that part; she's pretty and seems innocent, we run the ad and she handles the face to face meeting."

We sat there in the cold for another twenty minutes, debating and ironing out the details of the scheme. When we pulled out, I realized that I hadn't even paid enough attention to understand how the plan would work, but I would tell Jonas that they wanted to help.

They could set it all up next week. *I wished them luck.*

#

Chapter 24

I signed up for the Glen Lyn Church of Christ concealed weapon permit class. On the appointed day, this Saturday morning, I took $50 out of my egg money, which wiped out that fund, and headed to Glen Lyn. I didn't know if I was supposed to take my gun, but I knew it wasn't legal until I had the permit, so I decided to take it but not let on until I had the card to make it legal. Little Miss *Utukkuu*, my pistol, fit nicely under the carpet that covered my spare tire.

I resented getting up early for this nonsense, but I did it. I parked and was following signs from the parking lot to the side door of the church when I met one of my future classmates, a loud young woman with a thick head of curly hair and tight blue jeans. She had arrived in a lifted pickup truck, one that was so high you'd need a step ladder to get in it. Bet it would flip over in a sharp curve doing much speed. This one was so loud I bet it caused babies to cry. It had what we used to call cherry bomb mufflers. I thought that they were illegal but that might've changed. Anyway, she was dropped off just after I got there and we walked together as soon as she finished wiggling and waving at the young man driving. His ahooga horn played the opening notes of Dixie just like the General Lee from "Dukes of Hazard" as he spun out of the parking lot. She hollered and waved some more then she blew a big pink bubble with her gum. Good Lord. When she saw me staring, she hollered, "Hey there, wish I could get *my granny* to come to this class." Then, she laughed through her nose. She led the way wiggling with every step, what my daddy called a ten-cent twist. I didn't think I would like her very much.

The side door led to the church gym that was also used as an auditorium. Dozens of folding chairs were set up but there were only a handful of people. The gym was dusty and poorly lit except for the areas spotlighted by the sun beaming in from high windows. I got a whiff of gun oil, but mostly the place smelled like dust and old sneakers.

I brightened up when I saw I was not the only one there with white hair. The other lady was older than me, though. I'd say she was eighty if she was a day. Her thin hair had been rinsed a little too much because it had an extra sheen of light blue. She held her shoulder purse under her arm the whole time. Before we got started, she asked the teacher in a shaky voice, "Excuse me, sir, is a permit good to carry more than one gun at the same time?" The sheriff that was getting ready to teach us assured her that it was and she grasped her hands in her lap again, squeezing that purse tight to her side with her elbow.

The three of us, Blue Hair, Bubble Gum, and I, sat at one folding table. I was on the end facing front with the other women on my right. A man operating an electric wheelchair joined us. He tilted his head to the side like he was straining to use his twisted hand to control the chair and his legs were strapped to the footrests. He rolled up to my left and I moved a chair so he could get closer to the table. He nodded his thanks. I tried to steal glances at his hand to see if he had enough fingers strong enough to fire a gun. I think he did, but I couldn't see a pinkie finger.

Under the table, I practiced with my hand and decided that you could grip a gun with two fingers and still pull the trigger and balance it all with your thumb and not even need a pinkie finger. I sure hoped he passed the test because he was absolutely defenseless. If he needed any answers that I knew, he could have them. I would leave my paper uncovered. Seems like there should be a waiver or something for handicapped people to carry a gun. No, maybe not, I guess that would be opening a can of political worms.

"You from around here?" I asked, trying to be friendly.

He nodded his head yes, but he didn't say anything.

"I live over at Pearisburg." Blue Hair had thought I was talking to her and missed the guy in the wheelchair nodding.

Bubble Gum chimed in, "I used to live with a guy in Pearisburg. His name was Johnny ... Johnny ... shoot, I can't remember his last name, but he was real nice. He lived over the old theater down there, 'The Pearis,' and we bought fun stuff at the indoor flea market they have downstairs."

"I buy my gun stuff at the pawn shop in Green Valley. Those young men there are so good to me and call me when they get in stuff that they think I'd like." Blue Hair pushed her teased blue hair up as if to impress the young men she liked.

Without any evidence that anyone else had spoken, BubbleGum continued, "I hated it when Johnny had to go back to his wife. We were having such a good time." Her mood improved when she seemed to suddenly remember her current boyfriend, "But it all worked out, I'm with Randy now and he is a guy who knows how to have f-u-n." The gum cracked loudly and she whooped a "Yee haa." Perhaps it was to sell us on Randy's ability to have fun.

Blue Hair leaned in to me and whispered, "That hussy can't even spell gun, she's going to have a hard time with this class."

Good Lord, I thought. I looked at Wheelchair Guy who rolled his eyes at me. That just blew me away – he might not be able to do much but he knew these women were crazy. I focused towards the opening door.

A woman not wearing enough to wad a shotgun came in adjusting tendrils of dyed blond hair. She pulled up a chair next to our table, her perfume overwhelming the gun oil and dust. I hoped it got warmer, she was noticeably cold, braless in the thin pink tank top, short shorts, and flip flops. Her hair was a mess but she had nice legs and had spent some time applying bright pink blush and red lipstick. When she took her seat, her yellow glass earrings dangled in and out of a sunbeam. They were eye-catching, almost hypnotizing. As she settled in and looked down at the forms to complete, she was as quiet as a mouse. When she raised her eyes and looked around, her attitude changed and she puckered those red lips into a circle as she boldly stared at one and all. I averted my eyes before she caught me staring back.

An elderly man dressed in a double-knit suit and a string tie like a riverboat gambler came in next. He walked old, with stiff legs and slouched shoulders. As he moved to a table, he rested brittle fingers on chair backs and steadied himself along the way.

Finally, four long-haired motorcycle buddies with IRON HORSEMEN lettered on the back of their greasy denim jackets strutted in and sat down together. I overheard them passionately promoting diet drinks, two liked Atkins and one preferred Big K and one told them about some Ideal Protein chocolate drink that was real tasty. The words seemed surprisingly civilized coming from pierced lips and bearded mouths. They ended their debate and sat up straight when class started, right on time.

The sheriff from Claypool Hill, Virginia, taught the class. I didn't even know where that was and I didn't know him or his people, so my imagination just ran wild. He had a tiny gun in his hip pocket, one in his sock, one in a shoulder holster and one in a holster on his belt. Wow. Was he a military man?

Was he bullied as a little boy? He wore a wedding band; how did his wife cope with all that heat? Did he have a temper? Had he shot anybody?

In spite of his slow-talking Southern manner, the sheriff covered a great deal of information in an hour. He first showed us all those guns that he liked to carry, then explained that there were places that you could not carry a gun even with a permit, like schools, post offices, courthouses, federal buildings, most churches, airport terminals, some state parks, and some restaurants that sell alcohol. He spoke so slowly that I was impatient to know more, and pronto.

"Excuse me, sir," Blue Hair asked, "I'd like to carry a gun in my purse and one in my bra. Is a permit good to carry more than one gun at the same time?"

He grabbed the fabric of his pants leg about thigh-high and pulled it up his leg to give himself some slack and put his big boot up on a chair in front of him and answered her gently, "Yes, ma'am." I was fascinated that he was comfortable like that and was proud of him for being so patient.

As he taught us about different kinds of guns and ammunition I made up reasons why each student in the class wanted to carry a gun. I figured that Blue Hair and the gambler were afraid. They were slowing down and knew they couldn't outrun or overpower anyone. That fit the guy in the wheelchair, too. I could relate to their fear; it was a good reason for a gun.

Bubble Gum from the loud truck might be mean. I could imagine her starting trouble waving her gun around and provoking her boyfriend. Wonder who had been mean to her to make her so ornery or was she born that way?

Miss Hooker wanted a gun to protect herself and collect what was due her, although she kept her true self hidden deep with her other secrets. She was bare on the outside and she seemed to invite attention, but part of her was missing from our view. Aren't we all like that, I thought, hiding pieces of our best self?

The soft-spoken motorcycle guys seemed like they had stretched the rebel part of themselves as far as they could. They obviously wanted to carry a gun and fit in with the big dogs but sure didn't want to commit any crime. Come to think of it, there was no roar of motorcycles before they entered. Maybe they had brought the family van so all of them could ride together.

Chapter 24

I was in the class partly because I wanted to be legal. Staying out of jail had been a lifelong priority and if going to this dumb class helped me do that, fine, I was here. Freedom was real important to me, but I knew I was going to use my gun if I needed her regardless of my legal status. First and foremost, I was in the class to make Jonas happy, but I was real interested in learning, about people **and** guns, so this wasn't so bad after all.

When the sheriff showed us a gun feature that would improve our aim, the idea was higher technology than my wildest imaginings. It was a laser grip sight. It could be installed on nearly any gun and the shooter activates it with their thumb even with their finger on the trigger. It points a red laser dot at the target and when you shoot, the bullet goes to the red dot. You can't miss. You just can't miss. I was excited. He proceeded to explain that most any gun shop could install these on most any gun. He estimated it would cost about $200, depending on the gun. Then, he demonstrated a Crimson Laser Grip that activated the laser beam by simply touching the rubber grip. It cost a little more, $300 or so, but, in my mind, worth every cent. A Crimson Laser Grip went to the top of my wish list.

I could use that technology in a few other areas of my life. Wouldn't it be great to aim a red dot at the ears of others and make people understand what I am trying to say? Or, aim that red dot at the good guys and reward them with a ray of good will. Point it like Cupid at those you want to love you and fire away. More accurate living. For now, I would have to settle for a bullet hitting the dot. Unbelievable. All I had to do was put the dot where I wanted a bullet and pull the trigger. I swanee, life was good.

Next, the sheriff talked about revolvers, rotating cylinders, safety mechanisms, calibers, and drew a picture of a bullet and labeled all the parts. I paid close attention and took notes because I didn't know hardly any of this stuff. He taught us about misfires and hangs fires and squid fires and ended with the five fundamentals of handgun shooting. I wrote them all down, word for word.

Then we took a break. I tried again to start a conversation with the guy in the wheelchair but he evidently had very limited speech. He seemed nice, though.

We sat back down and after a bunch of paperwork; he had each of us handle a gun. We slid the safety off and back on and aimed and squeezed the trigger. When it was my turn he let me use the laser sight. Wheelchair Guy used the hand in his lap to balance the gun and gripped it with his other hand, all four fingers. He did fine.

During her turn, I swear if Blue Hair didn't ask again, "If I decided to carry a third gun, maybe in my knee-highs," she pointed to her socks, "would this permit be good to carry more than one gun at the same time?" He took the gun from her and lowered his voice.

"Ma'am, what are you so afraid of?"

She looked at him right in the eyes, no tremor at all in her voice. "Not a damn thing when I get this permit." To his credit, he didn't laugh at her, but I could see his belly jiggling when he turned away.

Everyone had a turn handling the gun and we got ready for the test. I was excited. I nearly always did well on tests. What a letdown. He read each question and we discussed each one and then he told us the answer. Let me tell you, you could not have flunked that test if you could understand English and hold a pencil. Even Wheelchair Guy was keeping up until his hand got tired; then I reached over and helped him fill in his bubbles on the answer sheet.

We all passed the test and each got a certificate to take to our own county and pay more money and get our card. I still wasn't exactly legal, but it was just a technicality.

My first trip would be to Union, our county seat, to get that dratted card and then to a gun shop to get me a laser grip sight. I would be ready for whatever happened. It did not escape me that I was a little bit like all these characters and was glad to have a gun for all those reasons I had assigned them.

God bless the second amendment. God bless America.

Chapter 25
October: Charlene

Making my gun-toting legal had proved to be a lot harder than my usual way of carrying her around. Now I understood better why people didn't go through all this rigmarole and expense to get a permit.

As planned, I left the house early Tuesday morning to drive the twenty-four miles of winding two-lane road to the county seat. I had the paperwork I needed, my gun permit class certificate and Stella Boswell's birth certificate and I entered the old brick courthouse right at nine o'clock. The hours painted on the sheriff's office door said they didn't open until nine thirty. From my dealings with the deputies, I knew that the action part of the department was open all day and night, but

the secretaries were stingier with their time. It seemed funny to me that the building was open but the sheriff's office took another half hour to open up. I sat fidgeting on a bench in the hallway at the bottom of the stairs going up to the courtroom. I had been in a hurry, but I tried to keep my jaw loose and not grit my teeth, even forced a smile in hopes it would catch on and the rest of me would be happy.

"Good morning, Stella." The prosecuting attorney came in, the edge of his old-fashioned shirt collar a crisp white edge above his overcoat.

"Hey there, Lawyer Sanders. How's Alice and the kids?" He was another one of my Sunday school students from years ago.

"All fine as frog hair. You okay?" I nodded and smiled and he hustled on down the hallway to his office. The scene repeated with a half dozen courthouse employees coming in to work, each bringing a cool blast of air as the door opened. I didn't know all of them but I knew of them or I knew somebody in their families. The receptionist from the County Clerk's office came out with homemade sticky buns still warm and offered me one. I gobbled it down then licked the sugary cinnamon goo from my fingers. If I didn't have other things to do, I could've enjoyed people watching up there every morning.

Eventually, Sheriff Elmer Johnson's two office ladies showed up and unlocked the door. I followed them in while they unlocked filing cabinets and cupboards and put away their purses and coats.

"Can I help you?" the older woman asked me.

"I want to get a permit to carry a gun. I have the proof that I took the class, a birth certificate, and my driver's license." I spread out all my papers on the counter, feeling a little like a schoolgirl who had done her homework.

She looked them over, made a copy of the birth certificate and driver's license and handed them back to me. "Follow me, we need to get a photo." We walked single file back through narrow offices and she motioned a chair for me. I sat, looked at the camera, smiled, and it flashed and clicked. Evidently, my eyes closed when it flashed because she took three pictures before she was satisfied. "Thank you. You can check back in about a week for your card."

Chapter 25

Surprised at another delay, I could only nod without protest. I pushed the heavy office door open. The hallway bench looked familiar and inviting to me and I sat back down. My hairpins were slipping out, and I was sweating underneath my jacket. I had another week to wait. Dang. The bench felt colder than it had before, the sounds of office workers starting the day were clearer, squeaking file cabinet drawers, copiers and fax machines being turned on, a toilet flushing somewhere. Then voices from upstairs, not arguing but strong.

"I'm telling you to watch 'em and watch 'em close. There are two warrants from West Virginia and one from Virginia. We don't have any choice."

I perked up.

Then a muffled reply, I could make out the tone, but not the words. Something like "But ... still investigating ... need to wait ... harmless." Was it Sheriff Johnson whining?

"Doesn't matter," the first voice responded, "We have enough without waiting ... a murder suspect. I want to be able to put my hand on 'em at any time."

Who belonged to that voice? The sheriff's boss? Who was that?

I sat as quiet as a mouse, quivering with excitement waiting for the men to come down the steps, but they went into the courtroom and I was left craving more information and another cinnamon roll. I hurried to my car to watch the back door in case they were leaving immediately. No action there so I went down the street to the Calico Kitchen and got a homemade apple bear claw and ate it as I drove home.

All I could think about was that overheard conversation. Wonder who they were picking up? Who do they suspect of murder? Could it be about Anna or was it away from here? I would have given a pretty penny to know.

As soon as I got back into my cell phone service area, just south of Rock Camp, my phone started ringing. Union is between mountains, I think of it as the Bermuda triangle of Monroe County and phones and GPS gadgets only work in certain spots. I have a friend at Pickaway that can only make calls right in the middle of her flowerbed, but nowhere else on the farm.

It was Brooke. She had gotten a drunken phone call at 3 AM from Charlene who was crying and begging for money and a "way out of this mess." Brooke had waited to call me until daylight, but I couldn't get any calls until now.

Brooke was hesitant and she was hoarse, either with a morning frog in her throat or a scratchy voice from crying. "I'm pretty sure that she's okay, but …." Brooke swallowed several times and I was about to decide she might have strep, but she cleared it all up and spoke in a clear voice. "She only ever wanted money before. Her words are short and sweet, she always asks for money. This is the first time she has mentioned anything else. We used to be able to talk about stuff, well, before Jeremy got into cocaine. Lord knows her life has been a mess ever since she married that druggie husband of hers."

"Where is she?" I asked, balancing my phone between my shoulder and ear so I could use both hands on the wheel to steer around the worst curves.

"Didn't say, but I could hear cars and loud voices, maybe at a club in Welch?"

I was not sure there was enough life left in the town of Welch to have a nightclub, but Brooke knew her sister better than I did. "Why are you telling me this?"

"Stella, she admitting that she is in a mess. She never did that before. Jeremy didn't even stay with her for the funeral. You know that she stayed here by herself the night before and left from the cemetery. You saw her, didn't you? Skinny and banged up, bruised everywhere. I didn't know if she was hopped up on drugs or glad to be away from him."

"Happy, even though it meant being at her mother's funeral?"

Chapter 25

"She knows something, Stella. My sister is cold and she is probably mentally ill, but she is trying to tell me something."

I ran through about a half dozen reasons not to say what I was going to say next, shook my head, clenched the wheel with the hand not holding the phone and said it, "Then let's go get her and find out what she knows."

There was a sigh of relief and Brooke said, "I was hoping you would say that. Let me call her and have her meet us, then I'll find a sitter for the kids. Can you be here in an hour? I should be ready by then."

Then I lost cell phone service as I went through a valley about wide enough for the road. Shoot. Guess I was taking Brooke to McDowell County today.

Winter was not a friend to the rugged mountain landscape. Water that usually gushed off rock cliffs had frozen solid. There was not a smidgen of color along the road, no flowers, just dead grass and black stems and braches. An occasional raised red mailbox flag jumped out against the dull background. Thanksgiving was coming. I hoped I could sit at the dinner table that day and thank God that all this was over and my life could go back to normal.

Just then, my phone rang Jonas' ring. I fumbled to answer it. "Hey. Stella."

"Hey, Jonas."

"We need to talk. Where are you?"

"Heading to get Brooke and go get Charlene in McDowell County. Can it wait until this evening?"

Silence.

"Jonas? You there?"

"Yeah. Trying to decide if it can wait."

More silence. I sighed into the phone, making a bunch of noise.

"Yeah, it can."

"Okay, see you tonight."

"Yeah, oh, hey Stella."

Good grief. I pulled over in the high school entrance.

"What? I'm not driving now, let's talk."

"Well, I had a visitor this morning."

"You sharing breakfast with a new woman these days?" I was trying to joke but I didn't grin.

"No, nothing like that." His laugh was high pitched like he was nervous. Weird. Jonas didn't get nervous. "It was a man. I thought he was an antique dealer from Roanoke from the questions he asked."

"What did he want?" I had turned off the car. That was a mistake; my feet were getting cold. I'd probably freeze to death before Jonas spit out whatever was on his mind.

"I thought he had tracked me down from my computer hits on the Mountain Antiquities' website. He asked about the kind of memorabilia that Charles had and wondered if I could help him find similar items."

"Well, can you?" I wiggled my toes to get them warm again.

He paused again. "He wasn't really an antique dealer, Stella. He was an Special Agent for the FBI – Art Crime Team."

It took a moment for Jonas's revelation to sink in. I sucked in air and looked through the windows of my car all around as if someone was watching me. Didn't see a thing. I locked the doors anyway.

"Well, there it is. I've gotta get some sleep, Stella. Could you stop by my house after you get back from the great state of McDowell? Maybe we can figure this out together."

"You bet."

"Not sure I like having visitors." Then he laughed his normal warm rumble. "Except for you."

It was my turn to be quiet. I blushed, not that he could see, then, without a lick of sense responded, "Oh, Jonas, go on." He could turn me downright silly.

"See you later." His husky voice made me forget about going to get that odd duck Charlene. It didn't quite clear the creepiness of an FBI agent showing up at his door, but it was not as dark a shadow as the big one cast by Timmy Lee. I hoped the lawmen had him in custody by now.

Brooke called back before I turned at Wickline's Funeral Home to go up Back Valley Road on the mountain and I pulled over again so the call wouldn't be dropped. Charlene was going to meet us in front of the Flat Iron Drug Store in Welch at 1:00.

Two hours later, we found Charlene standing at the head of the blue lined parking space near the drug store beside a pile of something resembling a Salvation Army bin that had gotten dumped out. She leaned against the brick building blowing cigarette smoke in slow motion. When she saw us, she dropped the half smoked cigarette onto the asphalt and ground it out with the heel of her cowboy boot. A sooty cloud of smoke and filth surrounded her. She did not look up again, just studied the pile of blankets and clothes. After we parked and walked up to her, she scooped up armfuls of clothing and some broken down cardboard boxes to hand to us. Brooke and I reached out and took what she offered until all the clothes were in our arms. Brooke broke the silence, "Char, are you alright?"

"I am done with this mess. Really done."

Seemed to me we were still in the middle of a good-sized mess holding piles of stained, dirty clothes in downtown Welch, but I managed to keep my mouth shut and find the key and unlock the car's back door. The girls followed me. This was not what I had expected. After I placed my load in the car, I turned to her and asked, "Charlene, honey, where is Jeremy?"

"Dunno, Miss Stella, haven't seen him for a good while." After she stuffed her clothing in the back, she washed her hands in the air as if she were washing him away.

"Well, where do you want us to take you?" I thought a laundry-mat would be a good place, but I didn't want to get off on the wrong foot.

"Anywhere you want, Miss Stella, anywhere at all. I ain't got no money, I've sold all the furniture and all his electronics except my phone to buy groceries. We just loaded up everything I own." She pointed at the back of the car. "Jeremy ain't been home since Mama died and I owed two months back rent before that. If you can take me up on Welch Mountain, some people are living under a train trestle up there and I can stay with them." She didn't seem to care where she was going, but she was sure that couldn't stay there.

Brooke looked at me begging with wide eyes, and I directed Char with a strong voice, "Charlene, you get in the back seat. Your sister and I need to talk."

I leaned in toward Brooke and hissed loudly, "Brooke Ann, I cannot keep your sister at my house. She is about half crazy, probably messed up on drugs, and I can't have it in my house. Where is she going to go?"

Brooke did a double take. "No, no, Stella. I just need you to please give her a ride back home. I know she has a pile of junk and it stinks and so does she but if we can get her out of here, she can stay with me and get herself cleaned up. Maybe she can help me with the kids when she gets off whatever she is on."

Charlene stumbled out of the car and started screaming, her warm breath making puffs of white clouds as if she had stored up enough cigarette smoke to still be smoldering inside. She counted off on her fingers, "Y'all think I am stupid, I don't have a lousy husband, no friends, no place to live, no daddy, no money, and now I don't even have a mommy. I might as well be dead." She sniffed and changed her tone to be more positive, even laughed, "I wish I **was** dead and out of this mess. " She clenched her fists and looked at the sky like she expected to be beamed up just for asking. I tried to hug her but she stood stiffly, shaking in my arms.

I took her by the cold grimy fist and led her to the back seat and drug some of her clothing over the back seat for her to use as a pillow. We made one quick stop in Princeton at Dove's Gun Shop for me to replace my gun's grip with a Crimson Trace Grip. I now had my little red aiming dot. By the time we got back to Monroe County, Charlene was snoring and Brooke had talked my ear off about everything from drug addiction to single parenting to Xbox games. I unloaded everything at Anna's house and went straight to Jonas.

Chapter 26
November: Investigations

It was evening when I finally pulled up beside Jonas's truck in his driveway. The kitchen light was on as the early winter darkness was starting to edge out the days. I could see movement through the sheer window curtains as I drug my weary self up to his door. He opened the front door and greeted me with a "*Suvat*?" and a half smile. The delicious smell of cooked meat welcomed me and I put down my purse and patted him on the chest with both hands before he escorted me to the kitchen. I didn't bother to answer his Inupiat "What's up?" until I had found food.

The remains of a frozen dinner were spread on the kitchen table and a second one was awaiting the microwave. The meal was a bit disappointing based on the smell, but only for a moment. I dug in as soon as it was ready. Jonas brought a glass of sweet tea and sat it before me and I guzzled half of it in one swallow. Funny how wonderful any food can be when you don't have to fix it yourself.

Eventually, I pushed back my chair and breathed deeply. "It was quite a day, Jonas. I don't even know where to start. I was all over southern West Virginia, through three county seats, picked up Charlene who is one unhappy, possibly crazy woman, listened to Brooke's world for four hours, got a laser grip for the Pink Lady, overheard a courthouse conversation that might mean Timmy Lee is going to be arrested soon, and filed the paperwork for my gun permit. Whew."

Jonas nodded. "Sounds like a full day." He cleared the table.

"Your turn, tell me about the FBI guy. How in the world did he find you?"

Jonas sat down and laced his hands behind his head, big arms folded and elbows jutting out. He jumped into his story eagerly, talking fast and with his native accent stronger than usual. "I was still unwinding from work so I was up, all right. I heard him pull in and went outside to talk to him. He was driving a new Ford Escape, I think, black, clean and waxed." He chuckled a little and brought his hands down to open the refrigerator for dessert. "That was a wasted job coming up here on the dirt road."

"What did he say he wanted?"

"Any information I might have on Civil War artifacts. He said that there were a lot of facsimiles out there, copies of canteens and sabers, and even belt buckles, but that I had searched exclusively for original items, guns and other items, and had searched so often on Mountain Antiquities that my name had caught his eye and he looked up my computer number and somehow found me."

"Do you believe that?"

Jonas grinned from ear to ear as he put a pineapple-upside-down cake on the table. "Maybe. I've been around guys like him. He acted like a good investigator, like the honest feds who inspected the oil fields, like the younger quality control teams at the Celanese. His eyes were everywhere. I thought to ask him if he saw my lost nail clippers to let me know."

"But what is he looking for?" I took the knife Jonas handed me and started cutting us both a piece of cake.

Jonas shrugged. "Probably on the trail of thieves, but I couldn't say who or what. It must be big, though, to follow up on a lead as small as my searches over the past few weeks." Jonas's speech slowed down as he remembered something else. "He looked a long time at the shelves over my front window, must've been the baleen etched by my cousin or my other cousin, Jeroney's baleen basket or the little walrus ivory carvings. Maybe he didn't know what they were. Or maybe he did. He sure studied those shelves." Jonas took a bite of cake.

"What kind of questions did he ask?" I leaned forward, my forearms on the table, ignoring my cake. *Dang, I wish I had been there. It sounded like more fun than my day.*

"He wanted to know if I had any Civil War items so I showed him the bayonet Charles had given me when I helped him rake hay for Mr. Bradley. Charles got all the pay for two men for a week's work in the hayfield and he really needed the money so he offered me the bayonet instead." He shrugged again. "I was new here and the history of these mountains drew me in. I was happy to get the bayonet, complete with a tall tale from Charles about how his great-great-great-uncle camped near the field with the Yanks who were marching over Peters Mountain to defend Pearisburg."

"Yeah, yeah, and the bayonet belonged to his uncle, right?"

"Course it did, according to him. That Charles was a rascal." One side of his mouth lifted as his grin began. He kept on eating.

"Did the FBI want know about Charles? Seems like that would be logical."

"Yep, asked a lot of questions about Charles and his stuff. Asked me exactly where I got the bayonet, too." Jonas just lit up, his eyebrows going up high, forced up by his broad grin. "I told him my great-great-great uncle owned it, that he fought for the Union and camped up yonder." Jonas pointed to the fields above us. "He looked at me funny and I said, 'on my mother's side' before he handed the bayonet back. He asked where he could find more authentic Civil War objects and I told him he should try Mountain Antiquities, they seemed to have anymuch stuff, that is, they look well-stocked. He shook his head. Then, he thanked me and handed me his card in hopes I would call if I hear of anything authentic for sale."

"Jonas, were there really any Inupiat soldiers in the Civil War?" He chuckled and wiped his eyes.

"Who knows, darling? If we ever get all these things at hand figured out, we will take some time and look that up." He sobered up, his lips pressed tightly together. "Just know that somebody is watching even on the computer." His mouth loosened up again, "Sure glad that I don't have anything to hide, all right."

We finished our cake and visited an hour in front of the TV and Jonas got ready for work. I needed to go home and feed the animals, so I left before he did, the feel of his rough lips lingering on mine.

#

I was hard at work the next morning, finishing some accounting posts that I had let slide last week, had just about finished when I heard a pounding on the door. The dogs hadn't barked at all, so I wasn't concerned. That is, until I saw Preacher Booth's face. He was pale and drawn and sickly looking.

He began speaking formal, like he was reading from a cue card. It sounded like he had practiced his speech. "Miss Stella, I am here for two reasons. One, I need to tell you that we are relieving you of your church treasurer duties. Two, I need to ask you who had access to the deposit the night of the benefit dinner in September." His hands were busy fiddling with a legal sized note pad with a pen clipped to it.

I was stunned and began to function on autopilot. "Come on in Reverend Booth and have a seat. Would you care for a glass of ice water or sweet tea? Or some hot chocolate?" He also didn't know what to do but he followed me into the parlor.

"No, not a thing, Stella." He sat on the edge of the davenport and hung his head and I noticed some white hairs starting around his crown. Funny thing to notice at such a time. My southern raising, such as it was, kicked in, and I tried to ease his discomfort by matching his formality.

"I understand perfectly, Beau. I was responsible for that deposit and I left it unattended for over an hour in the dish-towel drawer in the church kitchen. Big mistake on my part. There were a number of people who could have removed the cash. Oh, and by the way, when I checked on the deposit later at the bank, it was all cash that had disappeared; the checks were all there as listed."

He nodded. "Yes, that is what Mr. Davis said, too. Can you remember who else was in the kitchen that afternoon."

I was burning mad. Mr. Davis was checking up on church business, huh? I plastered on a look that I hoped seemed thoughtful and not furious and began. "Hmm, well now, let's see. I was there cleaning up and Sally Spencer and Anna Bradford, and several other women." I brightened. "You could ask Sally, she has a good memory. Oh, and Mr. Davis was there late, also. Did he remember to tell you that?" How that came out of my mouth so sweetly was a miracle.

"No, no, I didn't know he was still there. It's all so ugly, Stella. I hate that this has happened." The formality was gone. He was the real Beau Booth now, confused and searching for answers. "What do you think happened to that money?"

"That is what I spend my late night hours wondering about, Reverend Booth. There is a chance that we made a mistake counting the money, but we have both been at this a long time, and I doubt that we made a mistake that big. The bank could've goofed, but it would've shown up after all this time as they resolved other deposits. It would've shown up. I should've noticed that the bag was thinner when I took it to my car, three thousand dollars in folding money is a pretty thick stack. I was probably tired after the dinner and not thinking clearly." *Oh, my, was I ever not thinking clearly, I had almost shot at a man in the church.* I looked upward as if in deep commune with God, but I was just trying to be logical. The preacher was nodding encouragement to go on. "Honestly, I don't know what happened to the money and I don't have it extra to replace it, even though I am ultimately responsible for it. I was entrusted with the church's money and I failed."

He had started taking notes but he looked up a new light in his eyes. "Stella, there were two bags. Remember, we didn't have room in one zippered bag, so we found another one. Did you take both bags?" He moved closer to me on the edge of his seat.

My mouth fell open. "No, there was just one in the drawer. One red bag. That's all I grabbed. That's all I took to the bank. I forgot that there was another one until this moment."

He exhaled. "Then, someone just picked up the other bag. It could have been any time before or since."

"No, sir, I checked the drawer and the ones beside it after I knew there was money missing, nothing but dishtowels and pot holders. I have cleaned out the cabinets underneath in case some cash had been dropped there." I thought for a second. "Preacher, I would have taken two bags if there had been two bags in the drawer. I believe that it was taken before I left the church that very day."

He was scribbling on his yellow legal pad, but I interrupted. "And preacher, don't worry about relieving me of my duties, I have been pretty stressed with Anna's death and have a lot on my plate. But, I want your promise that when this is over, when my name is cleared, you will give me my treasurer's job back?" He looked addled, probably still thinking about what he had been writing, so I added another level of pressure to get his attention and whispered it so he would have to listen. Beau didn't hear very well.

"I make my living keeping the books for people's money around here and this is going to affect my livelihood if folks have any notion that the church thinks am a thief. Please, please, tell me that when that money is found somewheres else that the church will see fit to reinstate me to the volunteer job I have had for the past 35 years?"

"Oh, yes, yes, Stella. I am so sorry that we are having to do this. I know there's never been a problem before. You gotta understand, there has been some internal church pressure on me to take action." His legal pad was twisted in his hands as he stood up to leave. I did not offer him my hand or reach to him for a hug even though the man was more torn up than I was.

As an afterthought, I called after him as he walked towards his car, "Hey, Preacher. Is Mr. Davis going to take care of the treasurer's job now? He looked at me stricken, and nodded.

I might have slammed the front door a little harder than I should've.

Chapter 27
November: I Will Survive

I alternated stomping and singing the rest of the week. Half of the time I was hurt and mad at the preacher and half the time I was glad to be rid of the church's financial responsibility. There was more time left for me to take care of my bookkeeping customers and I wanted to be extra sure that my work was perfect. I knew that Timmy Lee was going to lead the church to serious trouble, but I couldn't see what I could do about any of it so I sang along with Gloria Gaynor's version of "I Will Survive" which was my standard operating procedure for getting over about anything.

Timmy Lee was on my mind a lot, but I hadn't laid eyes on him since Anna's funeral. He was certainly up to no good, but all I knew for sure was that the church's money was going to end up being his money. I hadn't forgotten the threat he'd made with his eyes months before. While I was cooking, putting baking soda in hot applesauce for leavening for a cake, the smell reminded me of my mother's Thanksgiving kitchen and the beginnings of Timmy Lee's bullying. One year, when Timmy was small, so little that he hadn't started to school yet, he wanted a cookie while mom was stirring up a cake. He must've asked her 30 times and she said no 30 times. Finally, he threw the usual tantrum, kicking and slapping mom and throwing everything he could reach off the table and countertop, including the little pan of hot applesauce, which splattered down my arm and burned. He was sobbing and screaming when mom gave up and handed him a cookie and cleaned up the mess. I was dancing around trying to wipe the hot applesauce off my skin when he took advantage of mom's back being turned to grin at me with a mouthful of cookie. Not much had changed.

My phone had interrupted my thinking at least twice a day since I was let go as treasurer. Sally called to see if I would help with the pancake breakfast Saturday morning. The proceeds would go towards the kidney transplant for Mr. McKidney whose real name was Bobby Lewis. I declined. "Sally, there is just something about that man that puts me off. Is he even a member of the church?"

"Some say he lives up at Rock Camp, but honest to goodness, I had only ever seen him once before, in church a few weeks ago. He has made a big impression on a lot of people, though. Apparently, folks either love him or hate him, those I've called have been a pretty even split. Don't worry about it Stella, we'll have enough workers to get by in the kitchen."

My conscience bothered me a little. "I tell you what. I can send a few jars of cherry syrup down on Friday night if you can use it. My cherry jelly didn't congeal last summer and I have plenty of syrup instead. It is real good even if it was a mistake."

"That would be fine. It'll give people some variety. Thanks, Stella, you take care."

I hung up and wondered why she hadn't said anything about me losing the treasurer's job. Guess it would be a delicate subject to bring up.

Brooke called every morning. I was happy about that; it kept me connected to Anna somehow. With all this wireless phone service and Internet, I almost feel like I could get Anna's e-heaven address and contact her in the next world and boy, did I ever need to talk to her. According to Brooke, Charlene had slept most of two days, and then woke up less sullen and a little more ready to make herself useful. She settled upstairs in the room the girls had once shared, played with the kids and ate like a hog. She had been doing laundry all day today. Brooke asked me to come over sometime and visit and check out the "new, clean" Charlene. I told her I would, thinking all the time that Anna would have loved to been around to see her older daughter acting right. No word of Jeremy yet, though. He was a missing link.

The girls were going together to see Lawyer Dillon next week to contest the will found at Anna's house. It did my heart good to know they had enough gumption to challenge that perplexing piece of paper.

Tisha called to see if we were ready to start asking folks if they had loaned Charles any Civil War pieces. I told her to hold off, that probably Brooke needed to make the announcement and she was busier than a cow's tail in fly season. I know Tisha was disappointed but she hid it well. She was between projects and idle hands were not good for Miss Tisha; she needed to be busy.

Jonas, wonderful Jonas, had been working overtime, the Celanese had been losing power again and it was a mystery to be solved. He let me know that he had three more days on the

11-7 shift, then he went to the 7-3 shift until Thanksgiving week, which was also the week deer season started, so he was taking that week off from work to go hunting. I figured he'd spend lots of time with me, and goose bumps rose on my arms just thinking about it.

On Wednesday, target practice had confirmed that my aim had improved using my new laser grip. The Pink Lady had a new place of honor in a holster strapped to my headboard. Friday, I had caught up on all my accounting entries, backed them up on two different hard drives and felt better than I had all week. I had cracked black walnuts for a chocolate nut cake, one of Jonas's favorites, had the radio on, and the kitchen was warm and smelling good, I was pretty happy. I should've banked some of the goodness I felt, because nothing but wickedness was on the way. Fumbling Deputy Long didn't fit the bill for a harbinger of evil, but it turns out he was the messenger. He knocked on my back door in the late afternoon and stood sheepishly with his hat in his hand. Sugar was wriggling all over begging to be petted; she could be a fierce watchdog but not when she knew the intruder.

Anyway, the poor young'un had a folded paper in his hand hidden by his hat and when I invited him in, he gulped and handed me the paper, the screen door bouncing off his back in the wind.

"This here is a search warrant, Miss Stella."

I took it and stared at another folded paper in his hand. "What's that?" I pointed at it with my chin.

"Well, ma'am, it's a warrant for your arrest." I must've seemed surprised, even though I felt perfectly normal, because he touched me on the arm and tried to calm me, "It's not personal, Miss Stella, it's just business."

"Just business." I repeated stupidly. Then I raise my voice, "JUST BUSINESS, whose business? You would arrest me while real crooks are running the roads. What am I supposed to have done?"

Ivan Long unfolds the paper, crumbling it as he shakes it open. "Says here 61-3-24. Obtaining money, property and services by false pretenses and 61-2-12. Robbery." He looks up at me as if he expects questions. I extend both wrists. I was halfway expecting to be arrested for other crimes: I had shot a man in the cemetery and pulled a gun in the church fellowship hall and killed a deer by the side of the road among a few other little things. I hadn't ever stolen anything or been fraudulent, at least I didn't think so. If truth be told, these charges were better than I deserved, but I still wasn't real thrilled.

"Take me away, then, how often do you law men get to arrest their own Sunday school teacher? Ivan, you must feel real powerful." I motioned him on in the kitchen. "Come on in the house, no point in you getting pneumonia."

"Aww, Miss Stella, don't make this any worse. I don't like it any more than you do."

"That so? Are you wondering what will become of your animals, your home, and your life? I think not, this is just business for you, isn't it?" He finally had located both his handcuffs and the key. He stopped, cuffs in midair.

Chapter 27

"Miss Stella, reckon you ought to get a sweater?" I looked around the room, turned off the oven and covered my cake batter with saran wrap and put it in the refrigerator then headed to the front closet and got a jacket. It crossed my mind that I could've run out the front door, but didn't seem likely that I would get far, so I decided on just being a pain.

"Thank you Ivan, now can you feed my animals in the evenings and put up the chickens? I can get Jonas to let them out early every day. Oh, and I guess I'll need to drain the pipes so they don't freeze this winter."

His eyes bugged out, a dead ringer for Barney Fife. "Why, I don't expect you'll be gone but a few hours. The magistrate will arraign you and set bail. I wouldn't worry." I think I harrumphed him as he spoke "Could you please turn around, I'm supposed to handcuff you behind your back, ma'am. Since those troopers were killed in the northern part of the state by that perp who had a gun in the front of his pants, we have to handcuff behind your back." He added, "The sheriff says it is for our safety."

"Were you worried that I had a gun in my apron, Ivan? I giggled mentally because it wasn't as far from the truth as he thought, but I didn't let on. "Oh, wait, Ivan, don't I get a phone call?"

"Yes, ma'am, but I think it is supposed to be at the jail, not from home." He studied on this point of protocol a second and relented. "I guess it would be okay. Go ahead."

I called Jonas, hoping he would answer, but he must still be sleeping. I left a message that I was being arrested and no, it was not a joke, and to please put up the chickens tonight and check on me at the jail after a while. Oh, and I would need a ride home eventually. I hoped.

The young deputy's hangdog expression was getting longer and he kept apologizing as he put the handcuffs on. He left them so loose I think my hands would've slipped right through if had stretched my fingers out and made my hand skinny. But, I didn't. He led me through the back door but I made him get my purse and get my house key and lock the door as we left.

Then I remembered the search warrant. "When are you going to search my stuff?"

"Oh, shucks, Miss Stella, I forgot." He was supposed to have contacted another deputy, the one sitting in the cruiser in my yard to search before he arrested me, but he had gotten all shook up and didn't call him. I thought his partner should have at least checked on him, I could have had him gagged and tied him up in a closet in that length of time. I thought he would radio the other deputy, but he just went out on the deck and waved for him to come on in. He unlocked the door and we went back in.

The other deputy looked like a high school student but he had on a brown uniform like Ivan's, so I guess he was at least twenty-one. He was rubbing his hands together and acting like he was cold sitting in the car. Why didn't they leave it running? "Why didn't you come in with Ivan?" I asked. The answer was obvious in his hand wringing and deep breaths but he blurted it out.

"This is my first call." Then he realized what he had said and turned red. Maybe I should've run out the front door, after all. I suggested they reread the search warrant and offered to read it aloud, if they would hold it for me. He and Ivan bent their heads over it, and then looked through all my kitchen cabinets and bookshelves. I settled into the recliner, hands still pinned behind me.

"Y'all make a mess in my clean house and there will be a problem." I promised. "What are you looking for?"

"A red bank deposit bag and your computer records." What deputy number two lacked in experience he made up for in honesty.

"Look in the file cabinet in my office in the next room." I nodded my head at it and tried to point my foot. "There are about a dozen of them in the bottom drawer." I should return those to the preacher, I thought. "The computer is in that room, too." They had sense enough to unplug just the server and put it in a garbage bag and then we all left for the courthouse.

Deputy Ivan had also forgotten to read me my rights until we were several miles into our trip. He had the new officer do it – his name was Doug Comer and I think I knew his grandfather if it is the same Comer that has the hardware store in Union. Anyway, he had a little card with the Miranda warning on it and Doug turned around in the seat to read it to me, he had trouble with the word 'attorney' but Ivan helped him with the sound of each syllable, slowly and with lots of aggravated sounding sighs. All this was to no avail, because he mispronounced it again the second time. The road was curvy and while Deputy Doug was turning around to face me in the back seat, reading, and sounding out words, he got sick to his stomach. Probably had nerves working on him, too. Ivan had to find a little side road up at Wikel to pull over and poor Doug just barely got out of the car before he threw up. I was helpless, locked in the back seat handcuffed, so they just had to take care of it all themselves. I had always made my own decisions and enjoyed helping people and been able to do pretty much what I wanted to, but now I was at their mercy, so they had to clean up their own mess. I told him I hoped he felt better, which was true, because the vomit stunk to high heavens.

Not making decisions was a novelty. I couldn't put my arm on the door to brace myself going around the curves; I just swayed with the car's motion. I couldn't decide how fast or slow to drive, or control the music on the radio. This could be a new life theme, just going with the flow and never having another independent thought. When the deputies asked me if I needed anything, I told them I could use a cigarette. I don't smoke, but it seemed like the thing someone handcuffed in the back seat of a police car should say. Ivan kept glancing in the rear view mirror at me like he was worried that I had lost my mind. Doug offered to light it for me. He kept looking at Ivan for approval and then rolled my window down and inch or two, but I said, "No, just put it in my mouth," which is why I stumbled out of the car frozen, windblown and with a cigarette dangling from my lips into a scowling Jonas Akpik waiting on the sidewalk beside the courthouse.

"Get those handcuffs off her right now." Jonas, six and a half feet and 280 pounds of angry Eskimo, was blocking our path, hands on hips. His insulated coveralls made him look even bigger. When he slung his head back to toss the long hair out of his eyes and pushed back his sleeves, I could see that he wasn't playing.

I figured the sooner we got inside the sooner they would take the cuffs off, but he wasn't having it. I tried to show him that they weren't tight, I even squeezed one hand out and waved at him real quick and scratched my head to be sure he noticed and then fumbled around and stuck it back in the handcuff behind me. After an uncomfortable few seconds, he finally stepped aside and started making other demands. "Did they hurt you, Stella?" I shook my head no and spit that goofy cigarette out. "You boys help her on the steps, they might be icy." In the next breath, "Stella, you okay?"

"I'm just fine. How did you get here before we did?"

"Huh. You might say that I hurried."

"What are the charges?" I didn't know if he was talking to me or to them, so I was quiet. I was a lot more scared of Jonas than the police.

They talked while we walked up the steps to the side door of the courthouse and Jonas held the heavy door. Ivan removed the handcuffs when we got to the magistrate's office. After I signed some paperwork, we went into the courtroom. I was given a copy of the charges and it seemed like the magistrate had a copy, too, because he read it aloud. When he slowed down for a minute, I asked, "Who brought up these charges? It says Lindside United Methodist Church on my forms, but who actually signed the charges?"

He shuffled some papers and read silently for a bit, then looked up. "The church board president signed the claim, a Mr. Timothy Davis."

I thanked him. So, Timmy Lee rose from Church Treasurer to Board President in one week. He didn't lose any time. After a bunch of mumbo jumbo legal stuff, the magistrate released me on my own recognizance, whatever that meant. I had to be back on Monday afternoon for an official arraignment and would be asked how I would plead. That was the easiest part so far. I was innocent.

Jonas was so sweet to me that night. You'd have thought I had been tortured and beaten the way he coddled me. He was also very worried about the charges and wanted to discuss them on the way home. "This is serious, Stella Francis."

"But Jonas, I didn't steal anything, so I am sure not guilty. I can't see anything to worry about."

"Fraud is going to be about more than that. He is claiming that you were a financial officer under a false name. Stella, he knows that you are not who you say you are and he can probably prove it."

I was thinking fast, this was not something I'd ever worried about. "But I didn't change my name to hurt anybody, I did it to get away from him. The judge will understand that, surely."

"I don't know Stella, I just don't know." He had already called Darlene Dillon and was taking me straight to meet with her at her office in Peterstown. She talked to us for about an hour and agreed that the robbery charge was based on circumstantial evidence at best. If there were no records indicating my use of $3000 near the date of the deposit, she felt that charge shouldn't be too hard to beat. After she heard the story of my life, she was much more concerned about the fraud charge. I shrugged. It was what it was. I had survived.

Chapter 28
November: Night Terrors

We got to my house at twilight. The chickens were on the roost, so I closed the coop door and locked it. The goats were waiting in the barn for some sweet feed and baaed happily when I fed them. I looked at my house as I walked back, the soft yellow light spilling out the bay window, the wind rubbing maple branches together with soft squeaks and my dog at my side. The crisp night smelled of dry leaves and snow in the air. All was right again in this world and I wanted to keep it that way.

Jonas and I talked for a few hours, until he left about 10:30. Not about big stuff, but about a lot of little stuff, the details of life. The daily drama of seeing a redheaded woodpecker or

the burn on your tongue when you eat too many black walnut kernels. He told me another Inupiat legend, Tuttu-man, half man and half caribou, who roams the arctic tundra in search of those who need help. Everything and nothing. It was a magical night, as if it was all coming to an end and we had to savor the deliciousness of our time together. I thought he might decide to stay home from work, but he said that he'd be back before eight o'clock the next morning. I walked him to the truck and we kissed goodbye, ravenously, until he needed to leave.

I watched him walk to the truck in the moonlight, then floated back to the house and my bed. Sleep came quickly, but my cell phone ring tone jolted me awake with the lime-green numbers, 4:19, on my alarm clock lit up. Stupid with sleep, heart pounding, I answered it, "Hallo."

"You are my sunshine, my only sunshine, you make me happy when skies are grey." Someone was singing with a soft Atlanta accent. It took my breath away until the man's voice cackled. "Isn't that what Daddy always said when he woke up his little angel?"

"Timmy Lee?"

"You bet baby." Then the voice changed, almost singing. "His little angel is in trouble, isn't she? And it is just beginning. I can't wait to live in your house, or maybe in your little friend's house. Oh, unless they burn down."

"Timmy Lee, what did you do with the church's money?"

"Which money, doll? They have so much money." He laughed like a child, then his voice changed again and got harsh, "You listen to me, girl, you can never escape big brother. I have won this match and I'm gonna keep winning. You are going to jail, at least for a little while." While his speech was semi-sensible, I dared to interrupt.

"Why was your silk handkerchief at Anna's?"

"Well, Sis, I was cleaning up a little. No, I didn't kill her, but I sure was glad to see her dead." My heart pounded harder. "I had some business to transact with your friend, Mrs. Bradford, and she was not being helpful. After I knew she was dead, oh, and I stopped by your place to tell you but that damn dog wouldn't let me out of the car, I took her will and dropped it off, all signed and sealed. She was poor as a church mouse, wasn't she? Not one valuable thing in that house even with all the talk about antiques and Johnny Reb jackets."

"You didn't steal anything?"

"Hard to steal something that wasn't there."

"But how did you get her to sign the will? It was her writing."

"Why, thank you so much. Let's just say that she had signed the church register many times and I have a talent for, let's say, reproductions."

"The handkerchief, how did it get in the couch?" I figured that his focus was going to be short, but I wanted to get all the information I could.

"I was wiping off the pen and the door knob, can't be too careful, even with these country bumpkins, and the couch cushion was lying beside her bed. Whoever killed her wasn't very neat. I must've dropped the handkerchief when I put it back on the couch. I needed her death to be natural, straight-forward, so the house deal would go through quickly. What took you so long to find her?" He started whining. "I *need* a place to live. It's *not* fair. You have a big house and I have to work so hard for nothing." His voice got louder. "Why the hell didn't you call off that dog? You're nothing but a filthy slut, sleeping with a married man. Maybe that's against the law in this backwoods county. Maybe I should kill you both and end the abomination." Then he was quiet.

"Talk to me, Timmy Lee." I was yelling. As long as he was on the phone I was safe. "Tell me what to do. You are a man of God." I choked.

He spoke quietly. "I was thinking about your blood mixing with that man's. In a puddle in the middle of the bed. That might buy you salvation. God would like to see that." He laughed softly. "I would like to see that, myself."

Oh, good grief, he was crazy as a bedbug. "C'mon, Timmy Lee, talk sense now. Tell me about Mama. What did she die of ... did she suffer?"

"Did she suffer? Not enough, the bitch. She must've got smothered in her sleep 'cause she didn't wake up one morning. Lot of that going on, come to think of it. Must be contagious." Then he laughed and laughed.

"Timmy Lee, can you hear me?" My voice was still shaky. I tried to be calming and spoke slowly. "Timmy, what happened to Adam's mom?" Good grief, I could not remember his girl-friend's name. Great time to have a senior moment.

Chapter 28

Apparently this was not the best thing to say, because he went completely ape. I could tell he was throwing things and could hear him cursing and breathing hard. Maybe he was jumping, too, at least that's what it sounded like, almost like my bed was bouncing in time with the noises on the phone. My imagination had always been spectacular.

She must have left him without getting enough punishment to suit him. Good for her, whatever her name was. Melissa? His tantrum gave me a moment to catch my breath and think. The clock read 4:41. I could not keep this up for three more hours in hopes that Jonas would get here before Timmy did. But, I could move around and get ready while I was talking. First I locked my bedroom door in the dark. The clock dial gave me enough light to see a little. Then, I got the pistol. I counted five rounds as I loaded it, my phone pressed between chin and shoulder with Timmy's hard breathing wheezing through the phone. *Surely I wouldn't need any more even if it came to that.* I dug in the box of ammo hidden in my closet and stood more bullets on my windowsill. They shook a little as I lined them up, was it the windowsill or my fingers? Suddenly, I thought, *if I can move around and talk, so can he. With that realization, my heart stopped. I thought I heard floorboards on the steps creaking. Was he already in my house?*

Chapter 29
November: More Terror

I pressed the hang up button on my cell phone, tossed it on the bed and took aim at the closed door from across the room. Nothing. No sound at all. Why hadn't Sugar barked at him? Had he killed her? I tiptoed to the wall beside the door so he couldn't shoot me through me the door, but I kept the gun barrel pointed at it. The clock flashed to 4:55. Not even an hour had gone by and it felt like a lifetime. The phone rang and I jumped out of my skin but it was Timmy Lee according to the caller ID so I let it keep ringing. There was nothing more to say.

In a while, I grew tired of holding the gun and sunk to the carpet with it resting in my lap, still pointing at the door. Yawning, I struggled to pay attention; my life depended on it. I must've dozed for a minute, though, because a sound startled me awake. I tightened my grip on the gun. Something was different, darker. I checked the time. The clock was black. The bastard had turned off the power.

Time for me to act.

I nearly pulled the trigger at the closed door just to get this over with, but reconsidered. Raising the window a tiny bit, I pointed the .38 all around the yard, the red dot blurring as it moved. *Was there anything out there that I could hit and scare him away?* Then I remembered what the sheriff said in class, "The first time an intruder knows that you are armed should be when it is pointed at them. This gives them no time to plan." With these words driving me on, I eased the door open and aimed the laser all around. The moonlight near the windows helped me see, but the stairs were darker. It was weird. The dot stopped halfway down the steps where there was nothing, no wall, no railing – it just stopped in midair.

Chapter 29

In the same second that I realized there was a person on my stairs, there was a booming crash to the right, he had jumped the rail to the floor below. Enough mercy. I hadn't fired earlier when I could've but now I aimed at the noise and fired three times as quick as I could. My head ached with the ringing of the gun's roar. The only thing that kept the last two shots in the gun was the thought that he might shoot back.

I retreated to my bedroom and relocked the door. My head was spinning but I grabbed my cell phone to check the time. Could it really be 7:15? I had slept for a lot more than a minute. I crawled to the window and peeked out, the edge of the sky was barely light. Jonas would be leaving work soon. He can't come here and walk into danger. A normal person would call the police. I decided that I couldn't, this was my brother. But, I couldn't let Jonas get hurt, either. I texted him, "Woke with a sick headache, give me a few hours before you come."

He texted back, "On the way in a few." Damn. I needed to take care of this before he got here. *Was Timmy Lee lying in the hallway floor, bleeding or dying? Did I miss?* I kept sniffing for smoke, it was hard to tell what Timmy Lee could be thinking at any given time. I had the timeless conversation in my head about what I would grab as I ran out of a burning building and turns out, when faced with reality, *I would grab nothing,* I decided, *I would just run like hell to get out.* The ringing in my head was easing but it was still there.

It was a little lighter outside the next time I checked. I could see the outline of my car in the yard. I couldn't see any other vehicles, though. 7:45. As they say in the movies, I needed to clear the perimeter. That was my first goal, and the other was not to lose my house to flames. After removing the three used casings and reloading my warm gun, I unlocked the door and inched it open again. The hallway was empty. I moved so I could see the stairs. Nothing there.

Nothing in the other upstairs bedroom or the closet or the bathroom. Scared me to death to look behind the shower curtain, I just pushed it back with the pistol barrel. Light was seeping in the windows now so I eased down the steps, putting two feet together on each one before I went to the next one. It was colder downstairs, a lot colder. The back door was standing open. I searched the rest of the house and didn't find a thing out of order except the power switch was thrown and there were three bullet holes in the hallway floor. I needed to know about Sugar but I couldn't bring myself to go outside yet. I locked myself in the downstairs bathroom and after I used the toilet, wondrous that I had waited so long, I sat on the closed commode with my pistol where I could see the driveway and the back door from the window.

When Jonas's truck came into view, I wanted to yell at him to leave, but I couldn't have spoken a word. He whistled up the walk and bounded up the steps and across the deck. I was watching to see if I saw any movement in the yard and planned to shoot through the window to protect him. He made it all the way to the door and I ran to let him in. "*Ahthii*, you look like *anak* on a cracker, girl, what is going on?" His eyes rested on the gun. "What in the world?"

I sure was glad to see him. I told him a disjointed version of what had happened and he searched every inch of my house even the attic, without a word,. Then he went outside and found Sugar in the dairy. She was trying to wake up, stumbling around, he said, and he found a Styrofoam tray with plastic wrap on it showing that it held a pound of ground beef.

"Probably was poisoned," he reported as he showed me the label. ""Dunno what he used, but it was enough to shut her up."

I took her from him, carried her into the living room, and patted her while Jonas built a roaring fire. I was still cold, but I wasn't sure if it was the house or my horror chilling me. Sugar finally came around, licked my hand, and jumped out of my lap to sprawl out before the fire. Jonas went to wipe off his hands and came back drying them, "Where is Timmy Lee staying?" I really had no idea and said so. "Do you want to call the sheriff?" I doubted that it would do any good and told him so. The only physical evidence was an open door, a thrown power switch, three holes that I had made, and the record of a cell phone call that lasted nearly thirty-five minutes. I knew this kind of wrong couldn't be made right by any law. I shrugged. Jonas shrugged back and turned to feed the fire. "Okay, but I will be going to talk to him." I did not feel that his tone of voice invited a response. It hadn't occurred to me to object and I was a little ashamed to admit I would love for Jonas to punch Timmy in the nose. The first stirring of pity made a fruitless run through my mind. I hadn't known before how crazy Timmy Lee was. The line between mean and crazy was getting blurred.

Chapter 29

Jonas needed to sleep but he made a couple of phone calls first then he slept in my bed while I sat by the window with a shotgun across the arms of my chair. I guess I fell asleep and Jonas took the gun from me, very carefully, I imagine, and tucked me in the bed. That's where I woke up mid-afternoon. The night before was a bad dream now, out my window the sky was Carolina blue and pure white clouds were barely puffing by. I had a satisfying stretch of arms and legs and went downstairs. Jonas was on his laptop and looked up when I yawned into the office. I nodded to the space where my ancient desktop had been, "Guess my computer is out of commission for a while, wonder how long they'll keep old Methuselah?" My desktop model was ancient beside his slender laptop.

"*Atchu*, maybe not as long as you think. Lawyer Dillon wants to talk to you Monday before the arraignment. "

"Hmmm, wonder why? Does she know about Timmy Lee's escapade last night?"

"Nope, not from me, anyway. I think she has some new information on the fraud charge." He was focused on the screen, then abruptly folded the laptop lid out of my sight and asked, "You have any ink in your printer?"

"Sure do, help yourself." He moved over to the printer and plugged into it, I didn't know how to interact wirelessly with it yet. Page after page printed and Jonas studied them. I gave up and fixed myself some cocoa, sat by the fire and relived the last twenty-four hours. I went back to the arrest and out of the blue remembered the black walnut cake. The batter should still be good. I shot out of my chair to preheat the oven and greased and floured a cake pan. The batter poured slowly, it was cold from the refrigerator, but I spread it and popped it in the oven and set the timer. Finally, the cake was baking. Jonas came up behind me and hugged me hard, then spun me around and hugged my front side. "You silly man." I put both hands on his chest and pushed him away, laughing, then collapsed into his arms again. He bent down to kiss my hair and my neck, then straightened up.

"Stella, what are you going to do about Timmy Lee?" I could feel all the gears in his head turning and waiting for an answer so they would know which way to grind next.

"It's all I can think of, that and black walnut cake." I smiled, a real smile, not the fake ones I'd been flashing to seem braver than I was. "He says he didn't kill Anna, but I think he might have killed our mom. I'm sure he is stealing from the church, probably the missing money but other funds, too. I need to stop him before he does something bad again. We are in danger, but if I see him first, he won't hurt me or you." I gritted my teeth. I meant that.

"Are you telling me that when he says he didn't kill Anna, you believe him?"

"Yep. Always before, he has been as honest as he was mean. He would absolutely hurt you but he would admit it, even tell you he was going to before he did anything, and twist it all to seem like it was the right thing for him to do. Like it was all your fault. I don't know how much sanity he has left, though. He was real messed up last night, on the edge of terrible things."

"So you believe that you are in danger?"

I looked deep in those black eyes for a long time, until I could see Jonas's naked spirit, the kindness and compassion and anger and love and pain. "You are in danger and I am in danger. No one can save us but you and me. Not the law, not the church, just us." I was as serious as I had ever been.

Jonas cracked up. "Good God, Stella, you have been watching too many movies. If you are in danger, we are going to the law and the church and to that cuckoo bird Timmy Lee and we are going to pass this off at the head. Oh, by the way, that's what happens in cowboy movies."

"What? This is not funny. He's nuts and he wants to see a puddle of our blood in the middle of the bed."

"Did he say that?"

"Yep and he talked about burning down the house."

"Good grief, he is crazy." Jonas fidgeted, shifting his weight from one foot to the other. "You okay for an hour or so? I need to run to town before five."

"Sure, I just can't wait to sit here alone waiting to be burnt out or killed, but sure, run along." He didn't hear the sting intended by my words and grabbed his jacket and the papers he had printed and headed out the back door without another word.

I sighed and checked locks on all the doors and windows. While I was upstairs, I got my shotgun and laid it across the kitchen table. Eventually, Sugar woke up and joined me and we watched the cake rise through the window in the oven door. Good times.

Chapter 29

Jonas came home in a good mood. I hoped he had pounded Timmy Lee. But when I asked him if he had been visiting my relatives, he grinned and said that he couldn't find him, the family reunion would have to happen later. We had pieces of warm, crumbly cake before supper.

After supper, my phone rang and I squealed out loud. It was Tisha and I answered. I heard her chewing gun popping and cracking before I heard her voice. "Hey woman, whatcha doing?" Oh, she was up to something.

"Just another boring day on Peters Mountain. What do you have going on?"

"I been researching that Sugar Bowl character from over at Alderson. Turns out he used to live at Lindside. That's all I know, right now, but it's a good lead."

"I didn't know that you cared who he was. All I care about was that he didn't die and he quit stealing flowers off of graves."

"Dontcha wonder if his knee healed up or what he's doing now? I was thinking that if we find out who he is and where he lives now, we could take him some old faded plastic flowers and a get well soon card." She laughed.

"I know you needed something to do, Tisha, but are you really that hard up? Why don't you call Brooke to see if she is ready to make the announcement about the Civil War stuff? Or if you are into research, see if you can find Char's husband, that bad egg Jeremy Boyd, and talk her into divorcing him. Now, that would be useful."

"You are just not much fun, Stella Boswell." Undaunted she changed the subject, "Whatcha doing for Thanksgiving?"

"It's hard to tell, Tisha, I may be in jail by then." I said honestly, figuring Joey or one of the boys had talked to somebody who had seen me at the courthouse yesterday. She didn't bite.

"Oh, Stella, you are a card. Okay, happy, boring weekend. I'll talk at you later."

I hung my head and chuckled. She would kill me when she knew I had been arrested and didn't tell. What a relief to have a semi-normal telephone conversation. I could feel the knots in my stomach loosening although I hadn't realized they were even there.

Chapter 30
November: Official Arraigment

Jonas took the rest of the weekend off from work. The Celanese plant was running smoothly and he had so much overtime this week that his supervisor was glad for him to stay home. His vacation started on Monday for a week, but the hunting trip was off. I heard him tell Ben McDaniel that he had some family problems to work out, but he'd call him midweek. It tickled me that he called my court appearance a family problem.

We were supposed to meet Miss Dillon thirty minutes before I went into court, so we left the house in plenty of time to make the drive and catch our breath before the arraignment. My biggest decision was whether to wear a peach blouse or a pale turquoise one. I had bought four blouses at a time at Wal-Mart, all the same size, but four different colors. Saved me from trying all of them on and cut down on wardrobe panic. Khaki pants or jeans went with all of them and I had gold hoop earrings or silver hoop earrings and one pair of sparkly hoop earrings that all went with basically everything. It was peach and sparkly earrings today with khaki pants and dark brown fur-lined ankle boots. It mattered most that my feet were warm in that drafty courthouse.

There was a fancy conference room where we met with Darlene Dillon. She looked very lawyer-like at the head of a long shiny table sporting a pinstriped blazer and matching skirt. She looked up from stacking papers and sorting file folders and welcomed us. After we draped our coats over the backs of the other chairs, we sat down. I sat across the table from her and Jonas sat beside her.

When we were settled, she spoke, "Stella, I only have one question for you because there is not time to completely explain everything." She quit fiddling with the folders and folded her forearms on the table raising her index finger to point at me. "Do you trust me?" I looked across at Jonas, not because I didn't trust my lawyer, but because this seemed strange to me. He nodded at her, waiting for my answer.

"Why, sure I do."

Her face relaxed at my words and she started stacking up folders. "We have unearthed some documents that will probably get the fraud charges dropped. They may shock you, but it will help your case if you do not appear to be surprised during this arraignment." I was not very shocked so far. Jonas had been online a lot in the last two days and although he wasn't sharing, I knew he was up to something.

"Sounds good to me. I 'spect I can hide any surprise I might feel."

Miss Dillon reached and covered my hands with hers. "Stella, I promise that I will explain it all after the arraignment, in detail." I just nodded my head up and down, bewildered.

We left our coats there. Darlene stuffed her briefcase with papers and we all entered the courtroom together. I sat with Darlene on the judge's right. Jonas sat on the front row behind us. The lawyer for the church was seated at a table on the judge's left and rose to shake hands with Darlene. Preacher Booth was seated beside him and nodded at us. That worm, I thought, letting Timmy Lee by with this. Then I felt sorry for him because he truly didn't know what he was dealing with and he was going to be hurt, too; he could count on that as sure as shooting.

There were other people sitting on the spectator benches, but we must have been first after the lunch break because we went right up to the front and sat down. I didn't turn around and gawk but I felt their eyes on the back of my head.

Darlene grabbed some papers and left with the lawyer. They were gone less than three minutes and she came back in, beaming. The other lawyer whispered in Beau Booth's ear and Beau nodded eagerly, then looked and me and said something back. Just then the judge entered and a policeman said, "All rise."

We stood. The judge sat down and called the court to order. After we sat down, the bailiff read our names and stated the charges.

"What is your plea on the robbery charge, Miss Boswell?"

For a second I forgot the words, just blanked out completely. I was patient with my old brain and it came to me. "Not guilty."

"And on the charge of fraud?"

"Not guilty, your honor."

The other lawyer asked to speak and the judge allowed it.

"Your honor, new information has come to the attention of the Lindside United Methodist Church Board, the complainant, and they wish to withdraw both charges." He handed the policeman some papers and the policeman handed them to the judge.

The judge studied the papers. "Is the church board president present?"

The church lawyer conferred with the preacher and spoke. "There was a special board meeting last night and the former church board president has been replaced with the approval of the District Superintendent of the Methodist Church by an interim president, Reverend Beau Booth, who is present." He leaned towards Preacher Booth as if to introduce him. The preacher stood up.

"Does your presence confirm this decision, Reverend Booth?"

"Yes, sir." His voice was soft but firm.

"Case dismissed." He tapped his gavel. "Miss Boswell, the court apologizes for any inconvenience." He was handed another folder and he began to read the names for the next case.

I walked back to the conference room in a daze and about collapsed in my chair. Jonas was grinning and high fiving with Darlene. "What just happened in there?"

Chapter 30

Darlene couldn't wait to tell me. Her words were running together in the excitement until Jonas cautioned, "Whoa, Miss Dillon. Give her some air. She might need some time with this."

"Yes, you're right, you're right. First, Stella, here is the missing person report your mother filed on June 11, 1970, two days after your graduation. I glanced at the copy of that report and saw the tight loops of my mother's handwriting at the bottom. I wondered how she had felt when she signed, worried? Relieved to not referee any more fights between her children? Darlene's voice interrupted. "She had to wait twenty-four hours to do so." She added a paper on top of it. Here is your obituary, ten years later."

"How did I die?" My whisper was a lot more curious than upset.

"Death was by drowning. A body was found in Lake Lanier, floated into the marina and the police called families who were missing young women. Last night, I talked to a retired officer who remembered this case. They were so glad when you were identified." She pulled out two more papers and slid them in front of me. "Here is your death certificate and the body identification form." I was reeling now. Before me was a black and white picture of one of my high school classmates, Shirley Jean Jackson, swollen and bruised looking. It took up a big corner of my body identification form but all the statistics matched mine, age in 1980 when she was found, gender, race, height, weight, hair color, even eye color. Jonas and Darlene were watching me when I looked up.

"But who could have thought that she was me?" Jonas pointed to the signature. **Timothy Lee Davis.** Realization hit hard and I gasped. "He knew that it wasn't me and yet he signed off on it." I pondered that. *"How did he get by with it? Why did he fake my death?" I thought a moment and realized he probably had a motive. What, though? Inheritance – the farm, Grandpa's savings. Damn.*

"Others would have known. Wasn't the coffin open?" I wondered out loud, but I knew the answer as soon as I asked. "He had it closed, didn't he?" and my eyes sought Jonas's as Darlene handed me the funeral home report. I closed my eyes after I read, **Casket: <u>Closed (request of family)</u>**. *I imagined my grandparents grieving, standing in front of the coffin and maybe my mother was with it enough to be sad, too.*

"Were my grandparents dead by then?"

Darlene answered, "I don't know, we didn't check on them, but your mother lived a few more months after your 'death.'"

I spoke evenly. "We need to get Momma's death certificate. He might have killed her." I bowed my head said a little prayer for my mother and my grandparents and even asked for help for Timmy Lee. I felt them from wherever they were in the cosmos and felt comforted. They knew all this now and they were okay. Peace filled me and I added gratitude to my prayer. Before I raised my eyes, I said, "I guess I didn't know for sure how evil he was, but I knew I had to get away from him. Seems like it was the right choice, now, huh?" When I looked up, Jonas had a tear glistening in the corner of his eye and Darlene was wiping her nose.

I went back through all the papers and reread them. Long ago, in first grade, I read while running my finger along the line of words. Miss Ferguson would smack my finger and say "You don't have an eye in your finger," and scare me. To be sure that I didn't miss anything, I regressed back to my red bird reading group days. I even moved my lips while I read, another childhood habit. *Maybe I was reading out loud, wait, did I pray out loud a few minutes ago?* My head jerked up to look at Jonas and Darlene and see how they were reacting. She was drying her eyes and looking at her watch. Jonas was staring at me. I reread some more, until I was pretty sure that I had it all clear in my mind, and handed the copies back to Miss Dillon.

"Oh, those are yours, Stella. Jonas did a great job of figuring this out. I just knew who would know who to call on a weekend to get documents scanned and sent." She leaned back in the chair, pleased as punch. "I don't think a team of investigators could have found out more in this length of time." I was not ready to talk just yet, so I pushed back my chair and walked stiffly around the table to hug that woman. My legs and feet had been still so long that it took me a few steps to quit wobbling. Jonas stood when I stepped back from the hug, and our eyes locked. Darlene scrambled to get her coat and briefcase and mumbled something about an appointment. As she left the room, she called back over her shoulder, "I'll be seeing you" and smiled at the statues we had become, facing one another, oblivious to the world. I sighed and grinned and Jonas dropped to one knee.

"Stella Francis Boswell," he laughed, "or Penelope Ann Davis," he pulled a ring box out of his pants pocket. "You are the woman I want to spend the rest of my life with. I want to go to sleep with you every night and wake up with you every morning. Will you make me the happiest man in the world and marry me?"

I still couldn't speak so I just stared. He started to lean and balanced himself with one hand on the floor.

"What about Lena?" I narrowed my eyes at him.

"She's dead. Got another death certificate to show you." I waited. "C'mon Stella, my knee is about to give out, say something."

I squeaked out a tiny "yes," then tested it on my tongue a little louder, "Yes." Then yelled it so that it bounced around the room, "YES! YES! YES!" He wouldn't let me help him up, used the back of a chair to rise. He grabbed me and we did a slow dance around the table to mystical music only we could hear, the Beatles and Eskimo drums, holding each other tight and swaying to our heartbeats.

In a few minutes, we smoothed our clothing, helped each other put on our coats, gathered up papers, threw the unopened ring box in my purse, and proceeded with as much dignity as we could out the door.

The hallway was lined with courthouse employees and Darlene Dillon toasting us with tiny Dixie cups and water, hooting, and congratulating us. We scampered through the gauntlet like young newlyweds and ran for the truck. I did turn for a split second and blow a kiss to Lawyer Dillon who looked as if she were the cat's meow.

Chapter 31
November: Just Want You

I slid over in the middle of the truck seat on the way home from the proposal. It was warm and cozy when the heater finally started blowing warm air. I guess the arraignment had taken place, too, but I was thinking mostly about the proposal. We were the two-headed driver my mother had always *tsk-tsked* when she saw them on the back roads near the farm. When we rounded a curve too fast, the force threw me hard against Jonas and he grabbed the inside of my thigh and held me against him. He grinned and I realized that he had planned that slide perfectly.

"Just wait a minute, I better check out the ring before you go laying hands on me." I slid away from him and felt around in my purse and found the ring box. "It better be a good one to prove that the wait was worth it." I teased, then flipped open the lid. It was empty. I howled with laughter, tears flying as I shook my head. Jonas pulled over, concerned. He pried the box from my fingers and looked at the empty slot and tried to look amazed, opening his mouth wide but he couldn't keep up the pretense. His face finally softened and he apologized.

"Stella, I didn't know for sure until this morning and there wasn't anyplace open that I could go and get a ring and I needed to get your attention so you knew I was serious. I didn't figure you cared much about the actual ring. So, we can go anywhere you want and pick out any ring you want but I just don't have it this minute." I howled with laughter again and tried to explain.

"Don't want any ole ring, just want you." I tossed the ring box over my head to the back seat. I felt a little bit bad that I hadn't cared enough to even open it during the proposal.

Chapter 31

"Wait a minute, I need that box, I borrowed it from Ivan Long in the sheriff's office. He's going to ask his girl when he gets up his nerve and he carries it around with him all the time. Everybody knows that he has it, shoot, she probably even knows. He has the ring in his pocket now. Jonas chuckled. "Probably ought to slide it on his keychain." For some reason, that struck me as funny, too, and we laughed together. He stopped before he pulled back out on Rt. 219, sobered up, and took my hands. "I'm sorry for something else, too, Stella. I'm sorry that we didn't have kids. You wanted kids and so did I but we couldn't take that chance when we didn't know the future. I am sorry, it is the second biggest regret of my life."

"Oh, I had the chance, Jonas, it just didn't happen." My finger traced his cheekbones and I held his face in my palm.

"You mean, you didn't take precautions, back then when we were young? You told me you did."

"No, sir, if you remember my exact words, I told you not to worry." I smiled at him. "I wanted your child enough to take the chance, every time. It just didn't happen."

"And you would've been willing to raise a child by yourself if we hadn't worked out?"

"I was ... " I spoke shyly, like a schoolgirl, "... if it was your child." He sighed and rested his forehead on the steering wheel, then hugged me, a big twisted hug in the front seat of the truck. We sat a minute wrapped in each other's arms before we separated enough for him to drive.

Back at the house we walked hand in hand to the door. The grey sky was spitting snow. It was still daylight and Jonas talked about going for a walk but I was cold. Also, I needed a little space to consider all the news of the day. It was like weighing frogs, first one thing would jump into my mind and then another. I told him to go on and I would stir around and find something to eat. I thawed some frozen shrimp and heated some 'cream of' soup and put rice in the cooker. Jonas liked shrimp and rice.

I was still a little edgy, so when there came a knock on the door, I jumped. Reverend Booth was standing there, and I invited him in. He sat down right in the kitchen, wringing his hands, and started talking.

"Stella, I need to tell you that I, well, we, are so sorry about the charges the church filed against you. The church has pretty much split down the middle over it all. Mr. Davis ran off Chuck Paynter, the young board president at the last meeting, accusing him of all manner of improprieties. Then, a couple of board members quit and those charges against you were filed before we even knew it. Well, let's see, we met Wednesday night and papers were sworn out on Thursday. I had to call the Methodist conference to get a lawyer down here today. It was a mess."

I didn't know what to say, so I started making jello, put water on the stove to boil and sat down to empty the powered jello in a bowl.

"We know you didn't take that money. In fact, nobody took the money. Clark Adkins found it in a big pot underneath the dishtowel drawer this weekend. It must've fell out the back of the drawer. Either that or somebody hid it there. His mom was cleaning the kitchen and had him crawl back into the cupboard to drag out everything to wipe out the shelves. Smaller pans had been put on top of the deposit bag inside the bigger pot and it was hidden."

"That's good news, preacher." Yeah, right. The preacher didn't know that I had searched under the dishtowel drawer more than once on my hands and knees, not in prayer but cussing Timmy Lee the whole time I was looking for the other deposit bag. It was not there. Hiding stolen property was Timmy Lee's method of operation starting in second grade when he rifled the teacher's desk and hid her candy bar somewhere else to eat later.

"I've got some bad news, too. Our Mr. Davis has been arrested for conspiracy with intent to rob and for Anna Bradford's murder."

Both hands flew to my mouth and I knocked the mixing bowl of powdered jello to the floor. I could taste the strawberries in the air and would associate that taste and smell with Timmy Lee's arrest forever more.

"Yes," Preacher Booth went right on. "Mr. Lewis, that's the man who needed a kidney – you might have been in church when he made the request." I nodded and he went on. "He was given a check on Sunday for $5,000, an accumulation of the latest breakfast fund-raiser and offerings from several church groups, the ladies circle, the Bible study class, and even the church youth. He came to church yesterday morning to thank the congregation, then got a ride right from church to pick up a motor home he had purchased the day before. His mistake was in buying the motor home from JR Spencer's girl-friend's mother and telling her he was heading south for his health. You know JR is Sally's grandson. JR mentioned it to his grandmother who blew into my office like a house afire and told me before I left after church. We called the police early Sunday afternoon and they found him and the girl and guess who else?" He only stopped to take a breath. "Mr. Timmy Lee Davis." Preacher Booth hung his head but kept talking. "They were heading over the mountain on Route 77. State troopers pulled them over before they went through the tunnel. Evidently, they were on the way to sunny Florida." He shook his head like he was weary of it all. "The state troopers said that the men turned on each other immediately, each one pointing a finger at the other. Mr. Davis claimed that he was there to save Mr. Lewis' soul and Mr. Lewis said that Mr. Davis had set the whole thing up. They were carrying several thousand dollars in cash as well."

Jonas blew in the door then and the preacher caught him up on the arrest. He continued with the story, "They are all being held at the Southern Regional Jail. A murder charge was already pending on Timmy Lee. Elmer thought they had enough to go ahead and charge. They'd been watching him for weeks, I was told."

He had my attention. Now the water could boil, the rice cooker could beep, the soup could burn, I only had eyes and ears for the preacher.

"Why do they think he killed Anna?" In my lap, my fists gripped the wadded edges of my apron as I awaited his answer.

"Of course, I don't know all of the evidence, but there was the matter of his handkerchief being found at the scene, the will on her table listing the church as the only beneficiary, and out of his own mouth, how he wanted her house for himself, how incompetent the court system was in this county and how Anna was better off dead than alive. That slipped during a heated discussion with me about finding a place to live. Mr. Davis had been sleeping on a mat in a Sunday school classroom and I told him it had to stop. He lost his temper, called me names and started in on poor little Anna. He threatened me with a pillow, that's how crazy he was, and was just about foaming at the mouth by then. I fired him on the spot; I knew the board would back me up, at least those who hadn't already quit. I left him raving and ranting in the Fellowship Hall Saturday night and didn't expect to see him again. I shared that with the sheriff late Saturday, even before the motorhome escapade. The man needs help but he needs more than I can give him. All of it is circumstantial but it is a pretty strong case."

The preacher wrung his hands and rolled his eyes, "It's a pity. He had the gift of being charismatic and could have led many to the Lord."

"I hear the Lord works in mysterious ways," Jonas summed up the report unruffled, and starting getting three plates out of the cupboard for supper.

I let go of the apron, and grabbed Jonas's hand as he put a plate in front of me. "We have some news ourselves, Preacher, Jonas and me are engaged to be married." Reverend Booth jumped up and shook Jonas's hand.

"'Bout time. Hope you'll have the wedding at our church." He looked at me questioningly then at Jonas.

"Whatever Stella wants, Preacher. You wanna stay and eat a bite of supper?"

Beau chuckled. "Nah, I can't stay, but thanks for the hospitality. You have the makings of a good husband, Jonas. Whatever y'all decide." He made like he was ready to leave. "I have apologized to Stella for those charges, Jonas, maybe she can forgive us and help us straighten up the mess Mr. Davis left. He was board president for six days and just about wiped out the church treasury."

I was thinking so fast, my brain was doing flip-flops. "Preacher, I think it would be best if you hired someone from outside the church for a while, sixty days or so, to square up the accounts." Inside my head, I was dancing but I played it cool. "But I'll be more'n happy to take back the treasurer's job after all this settles down."

He nodded, shook my hand and apologized again.

Jonas walked him to his car and came back frisky and hungry. We made out all the way up the steps. I reheated the shrimp and rice an hour or so later.

Ben McDaniel called late and told Jonas that he had seen somebody stealing gas at my place early Saturday morning. He had been loading up cattle on the mountain pasture early to go to Narrows to the market and saw a guy running around the house with a gas can. He aimed the big spotlight on the top of his truck at the guy and watched him run on down the driveway with it. He said he wished he could've chased him or at least checked on me but he had a dozen steers in the trailer and he was heading out the other way. He had forgotten about until tonight. Jonas told him that he was moving in with me until the wedding, asked silently if it was okay by raising his eyebrows at me while he was on the phone. I nodded and grinned. There was laughter and several "Thank yous" before he told Ben that he would keep an eye on things, but he figured I could pretty much take care of myself.

As I lay awake in bed that night, I hoped that I could close the book on Timmy Lee forever and that the days ahead would be the happiest of my life. A good night's sleep cleared up more of the cobwebs of the past, but with morning, I realized that I had two nagging things to tend to before it was truly over. Shirley Jean's family had to be told. I would go back to Atlanta and show them the photo and explain that she had died years ago. Also, my mother's death had to be investigated. Timmy Lee had said too much to ignore. I would need to confront him one more time. No time like the present.

"Jonas, I need to go to Beckley to the jail and see Timmy Lee. Wanna come?" I yelled through the bathroom door.

He burst out the door, hair wet and shining, holding a towel at his side that didn't quite meet. We would have to get bigger bath towels, I thought. "I'll go anywhere with you, woman." He then dropped the towel and rolled it in two twirls of his wrist and started snapping it at my backside, naked as a jaybird, chasing me all around the bedroom. He stubbed his toe on a bedpost and collapsed into the unmade bed holding his toe and spewing all sorts of Inupiat words. While he was down, I flicked the rolled towel at him, and made a satisfying pop on his thigh. He pretended to grab that spot then grabbed me and threw me on the bed and tickle-kissed me all over like I was a baby. Oh, Lord, I was too old for these shenanigans, but I giggled until he stopped and rolled on his back. We just lay there breathing hard. Pure happiness.

"I gotta go ask Timmy Lee about Momma." That was sure a mood killer.

Chapter 32
November: Visiting Hours

When I called, the Southern Regional Jail official told me that Timmy Lee was on the way back to Union for his hearing. Jonas got dressed and we grabbed a cold ham biscuit and orange juice for a quick bite before we braved a skiff of snow to drive to Union where my brother was housed. Jonas had the ring box to give back to Deputy Long and he thanked him and patted him on the shoulder. I asked about visiting Timmy Lee.

Deputy Long was very official, "Only one at a time and we have to have an officer present." Then out of the clear blue sky, Ivan spoke softly into my ear, "Something's been bothering me, Miss Stella, can I ask you a question?" I steeled myself.

"Absolutely, Deputy Long." He blushed and nodded.

"Aww, Miss Stella, you can call me Ivan." He looked at me and then he looked at Jonas, seeming to screw up his nerve. "Doug and me been talking about it. We was wondering why you asked for a cigarette when we was bringing you in."

"Well, Ivan, it just seemed like the right thing to do at the moment. I 'spect I have watched too much television and was playing the role of a criminal. What did you and Doug think?"

He shuffled his feet a little, "Doug thought maybe you were a serial killer that everybody thought was a sweet little ole lady." It was as if the idea of a grey-haired Sunday school teacher smoking a cigarette was worse than any crime I could have committed. "But, I knew, Miss Stella, I knew you didn't smoke and didn't rob anybody and I told Doug so." He beamed.

Jonas lowered his voice, "So how much was the bet?"

Ivan grinned, "Ten dollars and I'm collecting today." He looked at me sheepishly and then told me to follow him downstairs.

Jonas waited in the hallway with my purse and coat and I was shown to an ugly little dungeon room, cool and bare except for a metal table bolted to the concrete floor and three chairs, two facing over the table and one more at the door. I took a seat at the table and studied the wooden rafters, the cracks in the block wall, the grid around the light bulb, and the peeling paint on the floor. In a few minutes,

Tommy Lee lumbered in wearing a wrinkled orange jumpsuit, handcuffed in front with a chain running down to his leg irons. For all that, he had a smile.

"Come to get me out, Sis? I always said blood was thicker than water." The jailer pulled out his chair and helped him sit down.

"I'll be right there, ma'am," the officer pointed to the chair by the door. We don't allow visitors to touch the prisoners or to give them anything except through us." I thanked him and took my place opposite of Timmy Lee who started right in.

"You know I didn't kill your friend. She was dead when I got there. I told you that on the phone. You gotta tell somebody that." I knew that the vision of this moment, his eyes staring at me, would appear in my memories for a long time.

"Timmy Lee, do you remember the other things that you said on the phone that night?"

He twisted in his chair, pretty much the motion of a spoiled child caught in mischief. "Yes, but you know I didn't mean half the stuff I said. I was frustrated, you know, having a hard time. And you ... you aimed your gun at me and that red light like to gave me a heart attack. I wrenched a knee and skinned up my back getting out of the way. Whadja do that for?"

I ignored his complaints but was grinning ear to ear on the inside at the news that my little red dot scared him. "You let on like you hated Momma." As that sunk in, the childishness left his eyes. "You said that she must have been smothered." He shrugged, eyes bright with hatred. "Timmy Lee, I need to know what happened. Are you going to tell me or do I have to start an investigation? They will review the death report, might exhume her body. Was there an autopsy?"

He was on me in an instant, swinging his fists from side to side, beating me in the head, knocking me out of the chair. The officer was on him in another second, yelling for help while he pinned him to the floor. I scooted away, pulling my legs out from under the men and farther until my back was against the wall. Timmy Lee continued to fight, to kick both legs together like a mermaid and writhe under the jailer. Ivan was at the door's barred window. "Don't have a key, where is the extra?"

The officer grunted a few words at a time, "Look in the key cabinet, the one marked 'interrogation room'." Then Timmy Lee bested him and rolled over on top.

"Hurry Ivan." I screamed and looked around the room for a weapon. My boots had soft soles; they'd barely hurt a bug. I stumbled to my feet and grabbed a chair and held it overhead. I wanted to at least get in one good lick, but the officer rolled back on top against the table using the space I had cleared and my target was hidden. There was a metallic jingle and the door opened with the shaking barrel of Deputy Long's Glock leading the way in. I had visions of a bullet ricocheting all around the room, hurting somebody besides Timmy Lee. "Oh, Ivan, go help him. Give me that." He didn't hesitate. He handed me the gun and jumped into the fray. I waited for an opening between bodies, stuck the barrel in Timmy Lee's belly, well maybe a little lower. Not much choice, his ribs and shoulders were pressed to the floor underneath the jailer and Ivan. I ground the barrel in. "I will blow your privates to kingdom come if you move another muscle. You know I will, too." My busted nose dripped blood on him and I didn't wipe it off. "I kinda want to, Timmy Lee. Go ahead, kick at me."

Timmy Lee's body was still, but he started talking to the jailer, "Get her off me, I have rights. Take that gun away from the crazy bitch."

"Shut up, Timmy Lee." He figured I meant it, which was brilliant on his part, because I did, and shut his mouth. The jailer lifted one arm, ready to put it back if needed, but Timmy Lee just lay there while the officers crawled off. I was on my knees poking a gun into him. By then there were four good-sized men there plus Jonas, but I waited until each of them had a hold of him before I pulled the gun out of his soft flesh and backed out to the door. That instant, Timmy started fighting again. He bit and spit and carried on until somebody punched him, then he went limp.

The jailer sent for a strait jacket and they uncuffed him and put him in it but not before he came to and made a circle with his finger and thumb and pointed it towards me. I gasped and screamed, "Don't trust him, he's playing possum. He's liable to jump up again and keep fighting," but by that time he was wrapped up real tight. The room reeked of panic and fear and exertion, like the fight had triggered all the past emotions that tiny space had ever experienced. Jonas would say later that I just smelled sweat.

Timmy Lee opened his eyes, looked around the room, looked down at the strait jacket, saw me, and smiled. Immediately, his eyes rolled back, his tongue lolled out and he started drooling.

They transported him back to the Southern Regional Jail where doctors ordered x-rays, MRIs, and blood samples and couldn't find a thing to explain the physical symptoms. They said it was "a challenging case" and used terms like "catatonic, conversion disorder, and malingering" in their report which I learned of from Elmer Johnson. They finally decided nothing was life threatening, so they brought him back the next week and marched him into the courtroom for his hearing.

I attended the hearing. Timmy Lee was wearing the strait jacket and looking like he was brain injured. His eyes were unfocused, his nose dripped and mucus and spit covered his chin. He was unresponsive to all questions and his arms and legs seemed stiff. He did not even flinch when the judge sent him up to the Mildred Mitchell-Bateman Hospital in Huntington, which houses patients when a court finds them unfit to stand trial or those who are criminally insane. Timmy Lee would be locked up until his condition improved. I wondered how long he could hold out. The judge ordered an assessment every month to see if he could assist in his own defense, at which time he would be transported back to the Monroe County Jail to stand trial. Otherwise, he was committed to the facility indefinitely. I hoped the staff was smart, the locks were strong and the walls were high.

Chapter 33
Thanksgiving Day: Graveyard Chat

Thanksgiving Day dawned cloudy and milder than the day before. The wind had died down during the night. Jonas was snoozing in our cozy bed when I threw my feet over the edge to meet the chilly floor. I grabbed my clothes and dressed on the landing so I wouldn't wake him then snuck out to drive the mile or so over to the Bradley Cemetery to visit Anna's grave. I left him a note on the table. I never wanted him to worry about me again. It was just getting light when I parked and walked up the frozen path to Anna's grave. Her artificial roses were bleached by the sun to a lighter shade but were still in the vase; Sugar Bowl must've found a safer way to get rich.

The girls hadn't had to buy a tombstone because Anna had begun payments on a "twofer" with both their names and birthdates when Charles died. Charles' side of the monument had his date of death and crossed swords engraved underneath, forever a cavalry soldier. Anna's side had a bouquet of daisies cut into the stone but the space for her date of death was still blank. I would have to remind Brooke to take care of that. There was a cross in the middle with engraved lines radiating to both names.

I looked around the graveyard in the rosy glow of sunrise. The maintenance shed had been rebuilt since disaster had struck back in the summer and even had a coat of white paint. It was clearly an improvement over the ramshackle shed it replaced, now a sturdy, cinder block, tractor-proof building.

I sighed and pulled my hood strings tight, smoothed the long fleece-lined coat around me and tucked it in as I sat down, the rising sun at my back, the Bradford tombstone just in front of me. The cemetery had all the gravestones facing the sunrise, so bodies were lying parallel to Peters Mountain. I gazed at the length of the Appalachian Mountains, with their rounded tops stretching in both directions as far as I could see. The mountain range could have been a giant plump woman stretched out asleep. Sunlight was filtering through the clouds and stripes of light decorated the grey mountains. Robert Bradley's cows were on the pasture up above and I could look to the corner of the road and see his barn below. I couldn't have if it were summer, but since the trees had lost their leaves the barn had come out of hiding in the seasonal hide and seek game.

I hated that Anna was in the cold ground, but the landscape would keep changing in this pretty place, there were evergreens now and peepers would fill the pond across the road in springtime and wildflowers would bloom come summer and the colors of fall on the mountains would surround her. I was just thinking a little bit of everything and it was cool enough to make me want to go inside and get warm, but I wasn't quite geared up to visit with Anna yet. Hound dogs were baying in the distance, and closer, there were crows cawing, yet not another living thing in sight.

Good. When I spoke, I wanted to speak out loud to Anna without interruption. I had a lot to be thankful for on this day, but I was not content. I had always been sure of right and wrong. Now I didn't trust myself and the only way I could justify my actions was by talking to Anna. Since she was dead, I didn't know what I expected but charged forward anyhow. I cleared my throat.

"Mornin'. I guess I've talked a good bit to you before now but it seems like you might hear me better up here on the hill. At least I feel closer to you." I sighed. "Just found out this week that my momma probably was surprised when she got there and didn't find me. If you can, tell her ... and Daddy, too, that I am fine and I don't want to leave this world anytime soon. I don't know how it works there, but if you are able, hug Grandpa and Grandma for me, too." The cold of the ground was seeping through my coat and I shifted my weight and tucked my coat tighter around my backside.

"Anna, I didn't tell a soul that you had sold all Charles' stuff so you could make ends meet and send a little money to Brooke. I think you did real good to make it almost a year without any outside help. You were able to pay the medical bills, the power bill, the house insurance, and feed yourself. I don't know how you did it. There has not been one bill show up unpaid. And the amount in your checking account will cover the funeral expenses and the balance on your tombstone with a little left over. Darlene Dillon is getting all that straightened out so the girls can take care of themselves for a little while, long enough to get jobs.

"Jonas has looked high and low on the computer for Charles' stuff and he found some of it, too! And the Feds have come around sniffing because of Jonas's computer searches. Remember how you expected they would show up a long time ago? You and me couldn't figure out for sure where Charles got all those artifacts and you knew it would catch up some day. Good thing he had a big family, all of 'em Civil War soldiers." I slapped my leg, like Anna would've done and forced a laugh before I focused on Anna's name engraved on the tombstone and got downright thoughtful. "Jonas has gotten so good at looking up stuff, he and Mr. Google, that he found my own death certificate, which got me out of a little trouble this week, AND, he found the death certificate of his wife, Lena, all the

way in the Philippines. I need to look at that one a little closer, but he said that she died in a car accident years ago. Ain't that something? Oh, Anna, he asked me to marry him and I said yes." I had to swallow hard. "Big surprise, huh? Wish you were here to be my matron of honor." I rattled on.

"Tisha is doing good, she is still as much fun as ever. Hey, do you know what Jeremy Boyd's mother's maiden name was? Tisha has it in her head that Sugar Bowl, you know the cemetery flower thief, once lived in Lindside. We think he was a Miller grandson, but Jeremy's mommy might be a Miller, which would make him a likely candidate. Maybe Charlene will know, I'll ask her.

"Speaking of your girls, they are both okay, both living in your house for now, helping each other out. They miss you, probably more than they expected. You know how kids are; they think we are all going to live forever. I bet there are divorces in both their futures, time will tell about that. Lawyer Dillon is helping Brooke figure it out, and oh, looks like the girls will inherit your house after all, but I'll tell you about that in a minute. Your grandkids are sweet, they mind their mommy and they are smart and happy, even if they don't have much."

I was swallowing hard, trying not to cry. "I just need to know if you are happy, Anna. Did I do the right thing? When I got there that morning, you were sitting there on the bed as if you were going to church and my heart lightened because you were smiling. But you were just glad to be leaving here. I tried to talk you out of it but you put up your little hand and told me there was no use to try, your mind was set. We said our good-byes and hugged and I prayed for traveling mercies. Then, I went ahead with what you had asked me to do. It was pretty awful, even though you were little and frail, your body fought and fought and thrashed around and I almost gave up but then I thought you might be brain dead or something so I couldn't let up.

"You were a lot stronger than I thought. Then you had spasms and then lay still. I just lay on top of that couch cushion what seemed like forever. If we ever do this again, we gotta find a better way." I rolled my eyes at myself; that was ridiculous thing to think much less say, and I knew it. "I know you didn't want to be a bother and you didn't have enough medical insurance and you were tired after being strong for so long. It was probably just a matter of days 'til the end anyway, maybe weeks, but I know that bone cancer was hurting you real bad. You were in pain every time you moved." I stopped because I didn't think I could go on but I had to.

"Anna Banana, I need to know, I need a sign, I need to be sure that you are happy." I sat absolutely still, hunched over, head in hands, feeling foolish for even asking. I was pretty sure, deep down I had done the right thing, that unspeakable act that my friend had begged me to do, but my spirits were sure dragging.

Within a few moments, the sun shone on my back and the dead grass beside me lit up and the tombstones cast long shadows across the ground. My shoulders warmed. I choked up. *What else could it mean? She was okay.* "Oh, honey, thanks for that." I sniffled and felt it all, her happiness and contentment, her pain all gone.

Then I relaxed and really started talking. I told her that I had forgotten to put the couch cushion back even though I had neatened her up and straightened her hair and placed her arms like she was sleeping, just like we talked about. "And I didn't notice your partial plate was on the cushion. How could I have overlooked that? Gee, whiz, I guess I needed an E-how video with some pointers on how to do this right. Did you just have your mouth open so wide, so willing, that your teeth got hooked?" I shook my head remembering the mistakes made in my anxiousness to get out of her house afterwards. I swallowed over and over before I could go on.

"Anna, oh, Anna, Timmy Lee is charged with your murder. Maybe you know that already. I have not told the truth. I haven't lied, but I have not been truthful. He shouldn't be charged with a murder I committed. You know, we didn't have any kind of plan for him getting involved. Who knew he would show up after you were dead? He even forged your name on a will that said you were leaving your house to the church and left it on the kitchen table. He wiped everything he had touched with his little blue handkerchief, but accidently dropped it into the couch when he put the cushion back. That's how we knew he had been there." I smiled. "What goes around comes around. He said he picked up the couch cushion so it looked more like you died naturally." I got a little angry remembering. "You were supposed to have died in bed and if you hadn't been so set on looking nice, you could've worn a nightgown and played the part a little bit better." *Was I really picking a fight with my dead best friend? ... that I killed?*

I hushed and sat perfectly still for a minute or two while I listened to my Timmy Lee memories, at least the highlights of the way he had abused so many people, then sighed so deeply that I shuddered. "Well, maybe it's best he sets in jail a while anyway, for all the evil he has done without getting caught. If he ever quits playing crazy and has a trial, I can speak up then to maybe keep him from being found guilty, not that I want to." *That was the best I could do but I was sure tore up about it. I didn't want Timmy Lee out and about hurting people but I had killed Anna with my own hands just as she had asked. He shouldn't be punished for it.*

I hid my face and begged, "Anna, help me, tell me what you think." I stretched out on the cold ground where Anna was buried and cried and moaned until I had no strength left. I knew that it was time to buck up and face what I had done but I felt as weak as a newborn baby. And this was important, I needed to think about it some more.

I lay there what seemed like a long time, finally gathering strength enough to sit up again. My spirits were lifting with the fog on the mountain. It **had** all worked out. Anna was not in pain. I was not in prison. Her girls were going to be okay. Jonas loved me. Timmy Lee was in prison faking insanity even though he wasn't guilty. He deserved to pay at least that much, didn't he?

The sun came out again and I stood. I turned my face into the blinding light, eyes open, before it clouded over again. I wanted Anna to see me smiling, to know that I was okay, too, well on my way to being tipsy with happiness.

#

Two deer hunters from the Virginia side, high on Peters Mountain, had watched a hooded figure trudge up the hill to the Bradley Cemetery. The men were sitting on a rock cliff without fear; it was too far into cold weather for snakes to be out. Their rocky seat offered a fine view of the valleys below. They each had a green metal thermos of hot coffee. One was pouring into the lid that doubled as a cup. He commented that it was a strange time to be visiting a grave. "They ain't carrying nothing, so they ain't putting flowers out."

Chapter 33

"Let's watch a minute," the other one answered, "Haven't seen a deer all morning anyway and it's fixing to rain."

"Looks like they are talking to the dead. Must be a husband and wife."

"Or maybe two brothers or a brother and sister. You gonna come and talk to me if I die first, little brother?" He laughed and slapped his brother on the back.

He swallowed a drink so hot it burned. "Shoot, I don't even want to talk to you now. Shut up, will ya?"

"Look how sad that one is, all hunched over."

"Maybe it's just the cold." He threw out the rest of the coffee in the cup and began screwing it on the thermos.

"Hey, look, the sun is shining right on that guy. Whoops, it's gone now. Did ya see it?"

"Anything in your thermos besides coffee? You're seeing things."

"I swear. I saw it." He sipped, never looking away from the scene in the cemetery. That person is lying down in the graveyard, maybe it's a suicide gonna happen right before our eyes." His brother grunted and began to gather up the thermos and his gun before his head jerked up at a shout.

"Look now! Just look!"

Both men watched the figure rise and turn to the narrow spotlight of the sun, arms outstretched. The brothers would describe it over and over at the Thanksgiving dinner table as a frozen bright white lightning bolt, lasting a 'goldarned' long time. The figure threw back the hood and stood silhouetted, a woman's figure who glowed a second after the light faded then blew a kiss to the grave and walked briskly down the hill.

Even though it was early in the day, they decided to pack it in and get on home where they knew their mama and them would be watching the parade and cooking Thanksgiving dinner.

If you enjoyed *Drunk on Peace and Quiet,*
you won't want to miss Becky Hatcher Crabtree's next novel
featuring Stella and Jonas and their life together.

Look for it at beckycrabtree.com.

Meanwhile, for a first taste of their future, turn the page
and slip inside the little country church,
somebody you know is gettin' hitched.

Stella's Wedding

"Shoo, y'all get on out of here." *Even if I am a 57 year-old bride, I need a moment of peace and quiet before the wedding,* I laughingly realized as the Sunday School classroom door was pushed shut by the last giggling bridesmaid. I could hear the songs from the iTunes mix that Jonas and I had chosen for the pre-wedding and knew it was nearing the end of music and time to start my walk down the aisle.

I needed just a minute more to talk to my best friend Anna, dead since last summer. Both her daughters were bridesmaids and I hoped her spirit was here, too. I bowed my head, closed my eyes, and spoke aloud, "Oh, Anna, I'm gettin' hitched! You know Jonas is THE one, the love of my life...I so wish you were here with me." I cleared my throat and changed my tone. "Dear Lord take care of her. And if it's not too much trouble, take care of my brother, Timmy Lee, too, and keep him locked up in the mental institution for as long as you can. And help me to be a good wife and friend to Jonas. Thank you, Lord, for this day, a weddin' day I never thought I'd have. Amen."

There was a soft tapping at the hollow door and one of Tisha's big eyes filled the crack of space as the door inched open. "Stella!" she hissed. "It is almost time. Jonas is getting antsy standing up front and the girls are ready to go."

I didn't say a word. My creamy velveteen dress fell into place as I stood. It was too fancy for an old country woman like me, but was plain compared to the frilly things that Tisha and Eliza pushed on me at the dress shop. It was fitted and beaded up top and hung straight down from my armpits and covered my knobby knees. Having friends with sense enough to dress me and put together a wedding on short notice during the holidays sure was a great thing. Plus, the church was already decorated with battery-powered candles and fresh cut evergreens and pinecones in every window and wreaths on all the doors with fresh new bows courtesy of Tisha. A Christmas tree twinkled on one side of the sanctuary and a nativity rested on the altar between two poinsettias.

It was quiet in the sanctuary now. I knew it was time. *Time to get this show on the road.* At the last minute, I unpinned the short veil. It felt silly to wear a veil. I wanted Jonas to see me, to know me, well, except for that one secret, until I got up my nerve. I stuck my head out the door trying not to tear up my new upswept hairdo and gave Tisha a thumbs up. She quit wringing her hands and scurried to the sanctuary entrance to signal to the piano player who started playing a wordless version of Jonas' favorite Beatles' song, "Hey, Jude," as the processional. I studied my little bouquet of baby's breath, mistletoe, and red roses as Tisha got everyone lined up and heading in the right direction. The bridesmaids and the ring bearer disappeared through the door of the sanctuary. Then it was just the flower girl and me. She was tossing poinsettia petals and trying to catch them in her mouth. *Weren't they poisonous*? If her mother had not been a bridesmaid and out of sight, she would have swatted that child. Tisha bent down to talk to her and the little girl nodded, refocused, and marched towards the center aisle, tossing petals by the handfuls as soon as she entered. A few seconds of oohs and ahhs and it was my turn. Tish was motioning wildly and mouthing, "Where's the veil?" silently. I stuck my tongue out at her.

No one was 'giving me away'. I thought of my father, dead since I was in 3rd grade, and my crazy brother, Timmy Lee. Even if Daddy had been there or Timmy Lee had been sane, I would have balked on being escorted. I was giving myself to Jonas, as much as I could anyway. The piano player came down hard on the opening chords of 'Here Comes the Bride" and I gulped my courage back down before it got away. Tish looked at me with questioning eyes and I grinned and nodded. She rolled her eyes and I thought I saw a tear. I filed that image away to enjoy later, my tough friend getting emotional, probably over that dang veil.

I stopped at the back of the church and the guests stood in a rustle of fabrics and a fragrant breeze of flowers and pinecones. For a second I had the urge to cover my heart as if the national anthem was coming next, but every eye was on me.

Can this be happening? This must be the way queens feel. Then again, I might not be queen material. My next urge was to wave. Fought that off, too, but I could feel my grin widening as I made eye contact with church friends and business friends and a whole crew of men that worked with Jonas at the Celanese plant. I took my time going down the aisle; little steps like Tisha and Eliza had coached me. When I finally sought out Jonas with my eyes, they locked with his. He was sweating, I could tell his collar and tie were tight and wished I could loosen them for him. His shiny dark hair was trimmed so it fell just over his collar in the back and across one eyebrow. He was clean-shaven for the wedding. I knew he was trying to hide the grey in his beard by shaving, but there was a little white in his sideburns. He was uncomfortable in that black tuxedo but he filled it out just fine. That little smile pulling up the corners of his lips looking as he looked at me was real. This was going to be okay.

All the hurried preparations had sucked the energy right out of me. I had rushed around like a deflating balloon whooshing this way and that to the floor. And it was for all the wrong reasons, like the length of my dress or the color of the flowers. But when I saw him, my mountain of a man, silhouetted against the pale blue of the church walls, the balloon spirit inside me just grew and grew until it was nigh on ready to bust. With his tux, he wore a grey sealskin vest and matching knee high mukluks decorated with fringe and beadwork. His sister had sent them from Alaska by priority mail to get these symbols of his Inupiaq heritage here in time for the wedding. I had never seen them before but he wore them proudly. He also wore that tight black bowtie. I figured he was wearing it so our wedding would fit in with what was expected by friends here and maybe me. It was clear that he was gracefully walking in two worlds.

Reverend Beau Booth was at ease, in his element in front of our little country church. He motioned Jonas and me to front and center. "Friends, we are gathered together to witness the marriage of this man and this woman." He stopped and looked at the audience. "I love weddings." He laughed a little. "I love baptisms. These are ceremonies of celebration with God." Then he grabbed Jonas by the arm and asked him out loud, "Would you like me to just get on with it?" Jonas nodded and there were chuckles from the guests. Loretta Cecil sang, "I'm a Believer," my song to Jonas. Then Clarence Price from church sang "Something" to me from Jonas and if I hadn't been old and strong I would've blubbered right there. Reverend Booth asked us to kneel before him and there were some more chuckles and I figured they were laughing at Jonas being so stiff at getting his knees on the altar cushions. The preacher prayed and I felt Jonas' shoulders shake and I peeked at his face. His eyes were squeezed shut and tears were dripping. *Weird.*

We struggled to our feet, helping each other. The ring bearer was a perfect doll handing us each a ring and we repeated our vows. The preacher was so comfortable that we were starting to feel at ease, too. He pronounced us husband and wife and Jonas kissed me so hard that he dipped me, his hand supporting my neck as he leaned me backwards. His buddies all cheered and we hurried back out the aisle to the Fellowship Hall. The photographer took some pictures as the ushers and bridesmaids joined us, then we lined up and greeted all our guests. Eliza and Tisha were always in the background, checking on cookie platters and refilling the punch bowl and checking on me.

Everyone was so kind, the men telling Jonas that it was about time he married me and the ladies telling him that they hoped they would see him more often. Even the Colonel hugged me and shook Jonas' arm half off.

The party was lively. A band had been thrown together just the week before and was playing in the far corner, finger sandwiches and cookies were disappearing and punch was flowing. By the time we hugged and shook hands with every guest, people had started dancing. Jonas loves the Beatles, so we slow-danced to "Let it Be." I was awkward, I guess I had never danced in front of people before, but after a few sips of punch and some divinity candy to sustain me, I warmed up and it became fun and I hardly noticed anyone else there while we danced.

The ladies of the church had brought the food and made the punch and it was awfully good. I heard my friend Sally corner Macie Amos, "I want that punch recipe, Macie, you've outdone yourself. It is really good. Macie stared in her cup and told her, "Same things as always, orange sherbet, orange juice, and ginger ale. But, this **is** good, we must've gotten a good 'do' on it today."

The preacher came through the refreshment line several times smacking his lips and pretending to dance by shuffling his feet and wiggling. I was resting in a folding chair under the braided rebar cross, hoping it wouldn't fall on my head, when I looked up to see Jonas, Ben McDaniel, his best man, and both ushers playing air guitars to the band's version of "Johnny Be Good." They were jumping around, shirttails out and bowties dangling. It was good to see them having a good time, but the average age on the dance floor was about fifty. Their muscles were going to be sore in the morning.

I watched the festivities from a folding chair near the refreshment table. Jonas had slipped out the back door to get a breath of fresh air I figured and I was startled when he reappeared waving an envelope. He flopped down in the chair beside me and threw an arm around me pressing his mouth to my ear. "Sorry about the punch," he choked and laughed. "The boys hit it pretty hard with booze." My eyes must have widened because he hugged me tight as if to pin my arms to my side and continued whispering, "... but it tasted good and the church ladies are drinking it and no one knows ..."

"What else have they done?" I sputtered, remembering the laughter when we knelt.

He pushed back from me and hung his head, shoulders shaking silently, laughing so hard he couldn't speak. I didn't know whether to laugh along or get aggravated. After I pondered my choices for a few seconds, he looked up, wiping tears from the corners of both eyes with the closed fist holding an envelope.

He stood, grinning from ear to ear, and faced the guests. "Listen up, I have an announcement to make." Then he turned to me and cleared his throat. "Stella, my family wants to meet you – they made us tickets." He waved the envelope overhead and did what may have been an Eskimo dance around me. "We're going to Alaska in the morning!"

I may have swooned.

CPSIA information can be obtained at www.ICGtesting.com
Printed in the USA
LVOW10s0856200915

454906LV00001B/1/P